'...
authen...
as the retired judge, now a widower, s...
youthful, arrogant behaviour ...'   ...terly, USA

'Based on a true and extraordinary love story — of a young British officer who fell in love with a German girl at the end of the war. They had an intense affair — but then he left her behind and it broke her heart. Today there is no bitterness in the heart of the woman who wept such bitter tears.'   *Daily Mail*

'A solidly constructed romance by Alfred Shaughnessy, this smoothly readable story cuts back and forth from the days when a young officer serving with the British Army of the Rhine had a love affair with a beautiful Lorelei — in defiance of the rule against fraternisation — to the present, when the same man returns to look for her. What happened to her during the long years of separation gives him and the reader a well-deserved surprise.'   *Daily Telegraph*

'A touching, erotic novel.'   *Daily Express*

'The story of the lovers' secret idyll is movingly told and the atmosphere of pre-war Germany is well captured; the characters live on the page. A mellow and humane book that leaves one feeling refreshed and optimistic.'

Plymouth Sunday Independent

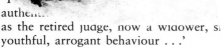

DEAREST ENEMY

DEAREST ENEMY

Alfred Shaughnessy

TABB HOUSE

First published 1991
Tabb House, 7 Church Street, Padstow, Cornwall, PL28 8BG
First paperback edition 1994

Copyright © Alfred Shaughnessy 1991

ISBN 1 873951 14 0

A catalogue record of this title is available from the British Library

Printed and bound by
The Guernsey Press Co. Ltd, Guernsey, Channel Islands

Among other writings by the author

Memoirs:	Both Ends of the Candle
Plays:	Release
	The Heat of the Moment
	Old Herbaceous
Film scenarios:	Brandy for the Parson
	Just my Luck
	The Impersonator
TV scripts:	Hadleigh
	Upstairs, Downstairs
	The Cedar Tree

For
Hildegard

Chapter 1

IT was very hot that June afternoon in 1945, when Karin Freidl came down the steps of the little school house in Mehlem-by-the-Rhine. She took her well-worn bicycle from its rack and cycled off along the leafy road by the river.

As she approached the flattened rubble of a recently shelled building that had spilled into the road, she bent low over the handlebars to pedal hard up its steep slope, beads of perspiration dripping from her forehead onto her black swimsuit and towel in the carrier basket in front of her. Reaching the top of the mound she sat back in the saddle, blowing the sweat from the corner of her mouth, then savoured the joy and relief of free-wheeling down the other side of the hump, to reach the normal road surface again.

The warm air rushed through her thin cotton dress, buffeting her bare legs, and while Karin was enjoying the sensation a British Army Jeep approached her at high speed. Suddenly it swerved to avoid a shell crater in the road. It veered towards her, missing her by inches, and she just had time to notice that it was driven by an officer in battle-dress before it roared on towards Bonn. The shock caught Karin by surprise. She wobbled violently and half fell, half dismounted from her bike, almost pitching headlong into a ditch. Then, hanging onto her cycle with one hand, she shook her disengaged fist in the air and yelled uselessly after the receding vehicle and the heedless driver: *"gottverdammter Engländer!"* Given a modicum of relief by the vehemence of her protest, she remounted, her heart still fluttering from fright, and pedalled slowly on along the road. Soon she reached the left turn where a small lane sloped down to a meadow beside the river.

She was still trembling a little from the shock of her encounter on the road while she changed among some thick bushes.

She stripped quickly, and moments later was immersed in the refreshing water of the Rhine, between the grassy bank and a little bit of island seventy yards out. Lying on her back, she gazed up at the clear blue sky. Outlined against it, through the sun's glare, she could see the Drachenfels mountain across the river. As she floated in the clear, pure water lapping gently over her, she reflected on the sharp contrast between her immediate surroundings and the acres of devastation ashore: the jagged remains of shattered buildings, the mountains of rubble, bomb-cratered roads and burnt-out vehicles everywhere. 'English and American bombs can wreck our cities,' she thought, 'but they can't destroy our river; they can never violate the Rhine.'

IF the driver of the Jeep had been honest with himself, he would have admitted that he had not been paying much attention to his driving, for the shell crater in the road had been clearly visible from fifty or sixty yards away and he'd had ample time to slow down, estimate the speed of the approaching cyclist and avoid swerving until she had passed him. But the fact was that his attention had been diverted by something on the other side of the river.

Captain John Hamilton was thinking, not of the Kraut girl on the bike pedalling slowly towards him, but of the Peterhof Hotel he'd spotted on top of the Petersberg and the old fortress on the nearby Drachenfels. He knew that it was at the Peterhof that Neville Chamberlain had stayed during one of his abortive trips to buy a temporary peace with Hitler, seven long years before.

Jack, as he was known to his friends, felt privileged to have survived the devastating war just ended, which Chamberlain had tried so hard to prevent. He had escaped with nothing worse than a jagged scar on his left arm, the result of a mortar bomb that had burst beside his scout car at Nijmegen in Holland – blowing his driver's head off.

In the heat of battle the shock of that moment, as of other incidents, was hastily buried, but the mark it made on him was lasting.

He had been with his battalion as it fought all the way from Gold Beach by St Aubin-sur-Mer on the Normandy coast to the small Hanoverian town of Stade, where on May 7th they heard of the cease-fire.

As Intelligence Officer of the battalion, it had been Jack's job, as soon as the good news of the end of the war came through on the radio, to get into his scout car and dash round the various companies, commanding them to stop shooting and stay where they were until further orders. When he finally returned to Battalion Headquarters an hour later he found that an entire German infantry division, which had been firing at them for the last few weeks, had surrendered to a man. He had spent the next four hours explaining the position to hordes of unshaven, grey-faced, defeated and disenchanted soldiers of the *Wehrmacht*. He had accomplished this in his best German, learnt at school and later with a family in Munich, before he went up to read Law at Oxford.

Just over a month after the official German surrender at Luneburg Heath, the Guards Division had been moved down to the Rhineland and Jack had received a summons to see his Commanding Officer.

"Come in, Jack."

"Sir."

"Got to say goodbye to you, old man."

"Sir?" Jack was puzzled.

"They want you at Divisional Headquarters. A staff job. I can't think why."

Jack couldn't, either. "What job would that be, Sir?"

"DADAWS."

"I beg your pardon?"

The Commanding Officer leant back in his chair and closed his eyes, as if reciting from memory. "Deputy Assistant Director, Army Welfare Services."

"My God!" Jack rocked slightly on his heels and and his CO sighed, with a suspicion of sympathy.

"All I know is that you've been posted to the Divisional Staff to organize welfare for the troops. ENSA parties, cricket, swimming – that kind of thing.

"I see, Sir."

"By the way, you can take your soldier servant with you. Must have *someone* to press your trousers for you.

"You'll be a member of the Div. HQ B Mess at Bad Godesberg."

After arriving at Bad Godesberg, Jack found that his job would be to arrange entertainment for all troops in the Divisional area, which was approximately the size of Wales.

A COUPLE of days after the start of his new job, Jack was easily able to brush out of his mind the near miss he'd just experienced on the road, and as he parked his Jeep outside the headquarters of a Royal Artillery Unit beyond Mehlem, he found himself reflecting on the size of his new empire. The RA commander had asked him to come over and discuss the requisitioning of a large field in his area to provide a cricket ground for his gunners.

That business over, Jack drove back to Godesberg, once again noticing the imposing Drachenfels, now catching the late afternoon sun. On an impulse he turned off the road and was soon bumping across a meadow to a spot where the Rhine was quite narrow and the sound of splashing and the shrill voices of children told him that German 'civvies' were swimming in the river. Jack glanced at his watch. It was just after four-thirty and still hot enough for a dip.

Presently he was in the river, floating luxuriantly on his back, enjoying the warmth of the sun on his face and chest, and the coolness of the water that supported him. Then, as he rolled over, he caught sight of a flaxen-haired girl in a black swimsuit, sitting on a rock on the strip of island opposite. A siren, a Rhinemaiden, he reflected; Lorelei herself, on her lone rock. His pulse quickened.

Failing to recognize this particular Rhinemaiden as the cyclist he had almost knocked down on the road, he recalled instead Heine's poem that he had learnt at school: *'Ich weiss nicht was soll es bedeuten, dass Ich so traurig bin . . .'* and the legend of the maiden who threw herself into the Rhine in despair over a faithless lover.

Just as the thought crossed his mind, Jack saw the girl slide off her rock into the stream and start to swim in his direction. The legend, Jack remembered, also told how any man seeing the Lorelei lost his sight and his reason; but this did not deter him from treading water to observe the girl, as she thrashed through the river towards the near bank.

She swam past Jack close enough for him to catch fleeting glimpses of deeply suntanned arms and legs, as her lithe body churned up the water. She was swimming the crawl, and as she raised her right arm to propel herself forward, Jack saw that she had a large, newly healed scar, just below her shoulder, as though something had been embedded there. The wound was ugly, having closed up awkwardly.

'She might have got caught in the open by one of our Hurricanes,' thought Jack, with a twinge of guilt. 'Women and children should not get wounded in wars.' But they did, in this one. '*Totalkrieg*', Hitler had called it, and so it had been – with old folk and babies, on both sides, blown to pieces.

He would like to have talked to the girl, then and there, in the water, to ask her in his best German what had happened to her arm. But there was a strict no fraternizing regulation in force, covering all Allied Service personnel.

'A pity,' thought Jack, knowing damn well that his real motive for starting a conversation would not be concern for her wounded arm or a desire to apologize for it on behalf of the Allies. The truth was, that after three consecutive months in action without leave, he was filled with desire by the sight of a lovely girl in a bathing suit.

For a while he watched her thrashing through the water in a wide circle, sorely tempted to make contact. As a captain, soon to be a temporary major, in His Majesty's Grenadier Guards, Jack knew he ought to obey regulations and leave her be. On the other hand, there was nobody about but a few German civilians, mostly mothers and children, swimming in the river. There was no sign of any Allied Service people, Military Police or other spoil-sports. His battle-dress jacket and trousers, socks, shirt and underwear were discreetly hidden in a small pile under a nearby tree, his Grenadier beret and the divisional signs on his sleeves face downwards on the grass. Surely one could speak to a German girl, in the anonymity of semi-nakedness in the middle of a river, without fear of detection?

Jack decided to risk it, and swam off vigorously in pursuit of his latter-day Rhinemaiden, planning to stage a near collision with her in mid-stream.

"*Entschuldigen Sie mich*," Jack gasped, as his feet finally struck her thighs under the water.

"*Macht nichts*," came the reply.

The girl had been forced to stop swimming now and tread water. Anxious to be taken for a fellow German, Jack's first impulse was to start singing the Liszt setting to the 'Lorelei',

'*Ich weiss nicht was soll es bedeuten*', but thought better of it and settled instead for a polite, conventional remark.

"*Ist schön im Wasser, nicht?*"

"*Jawohl.*" The girl nodded, still taken in.

Jack pushed his luck. "*Schwimmen Sie gern im Fluss?*"

His vowels must have sounded foreign enough to alert the girl, for she darted him a suspicious look.

Feeling a need to come clean, Jack said quickly "*Ich spreche nicht sehr viel Deutsch, bin ein englischer Offizier.*"

At this, the Rhinemaiden turned sharply in the water and thrashed out for the opposite bank. Jack gave chase and saw her, a few yards ahead of him, emerge from the water and hurry back dripping to sit in the sun on her rock.

In a matter of seconds Jack, too, clambered ashore and went over to sit brazenly beside her on the same rock, muttering "*Ich möchte mit Ihnen sprechen*".

"It is not allowed," said the girl, and Jack's heart leapt to hear her address him in his native tongue.

"You speak English very well."

The Rhinemaiden looked anxiously about her, realized there was nobody in sight and turned to glance at the darkly handsome young man beside her, noticing instantly the pallor of his dripping bare torso, the matted jet- black hair across his face and a strangely appealing Roman nose, that gave him a look of patrician distinction.

"Unfortunately, you must not speak with me, although we are not anymore enemies."

Jack nodded. "That's right. *Der Krieg ist beendet.*"

"*Gott sei Dank,*" said the girl, still a little on edge.

After a short silence Jack pointed to his own and then to his companion's scar. A quick dip into his mental German vocabulary came up with *Kugelloch* for bullet hole and *englisches Flugzeug* as a possible cause for it.

But the Rhinemaiden shook her wet head. "Not English aeroplanes. But American ones have wounded me."

"How?"

"I was on my way to Essen in the train last winter, when many hundreds of American bombing planes have attacked the Ruhr."

"Flying Fortresses," Jack muttered, "on a daylight mission."

Karin Freidl continued: "The train had stopped and the guard came running down the line to order the passengers out. Somebody opened our door and we all jumped down from the compartment to the embankment and crouched in a ditch. There was a terrible noise like thunder, and much smoke. People were screaming with fear."

"What happened to you?"

Karin's eyes betrayed the horror of the experience. "An old woman in the corner seat was too lame to get out, so she stayed in the train. A bomb fell very close to our carriage and she was blown out onto the line without her head."

The effect of this detail left Jack unmoved – he'd seen for himself all too much of that sort of thing lately. "I want to hear what happened to you; how you got that bullet hole in your arm."

"A small piece of the railway carriage flew into my arm and stayed there, until the surgeon in the hospital has taken it out. So you see," she said with a wry smile, as she touched her bare shoulder, "it is not a bullet hole. *Kein Kugelloch. Es ist überhaupt mein Eisenbahnwagenloch* – my railway-carriage hole!" Karin laughed almost apologetically, so Jack allowed himself a sympathetic smile.

Before the sun had dried them off properly Jack had discovered that Karin's parents lived at Coblenz, now in the French Zone of Occupation; her brother, Dieter, was a medical officer in the *Wehrmacht*, captured in Italy and now in an American POW camp; and that she was living nearby in one room in Mehlem, teaching the *Kindergarten* in the local school.

Her English was pretty good and it seemed to Jack that they

8

were in a halfway situation, each more or less able to converse in the other's language, and able to benefit from the practice.

"Do you come here to swim every day?" he asked.

"Only on my free afternoon, that is Thursday – and Saturday too."

Jack explained to Karin that his staff job with the British Army of Occupation was one which allowed him to work his own hours. "Maybe I'll see you again, next time I come here for a swim."

Karin shrugged her shoulders.

After he had gone, she stayed on in the evening sun for another half hour, reflecting on Jack, to whom she instinctively warmed, although she could not wholly trust him.

"YOU ought to get away for a while, have a change of scene."

"That's exactly what I'm planning to do," replied the older member.

"Good. Much the best thing."

The two resumed eating for a minute, in silence.

"Your claret, Sir John."

As the club's white-jacketed wine waiter put a carafe in front of him, the older member looked up. "Thank you, Sidney."

Sir John was tall and erect for his seventy years, with a good head of silky grey hair. But as he smiled at the waiter there was sadness in his eyes. The room was noisy and the centre table was crowded, for it was getting on for two p.m. and lunch in the Garrick Club's Coffee Room was in full swing.

"Anything for you, Sir?" the waiter asked Sir John Hamilton's neighbour and fellow-member Martin Travers, who was a somewhat corpulent, middle-aged barrister.

"A lager, please, Sidney."

By taking the only vacant chair at the long mahogany table, Travers had put himself next to His Honour Sir John Hamilton, the recently retired High Court Judge. Travers had appeared before Sir John in Court on several occasions and the two men were acquainted, but on finding himself obliged to sit next to a man whose wife had died only a fortnight earlier he had felt a moment of anxiety and embarrassment . He had heard the news from his clerk in chambers before it appeared in the *Daily Telegraph*, for Sir John was well known in the legal profession. He was respected by Bench and Bar alike, and Lady Hamilton had the reputation of a model wife.

But Sir John spoke freely and without emotion of his recent bereavement. "Christine and I often discussed what each of us would do when the other pegged out." He smiled gently, from a desire to put Travers at ease, rather than from any sense of mirth. "We both decided our first aim would be to get the funeral over and done with, then see our solicitor about the will and all that sort of thing, after which we'd probably want to go and spend a little time with Giles."

"Your son?"

"Yes. He's with the KDG's in Germany. Don't want to impose myself on him for too long but – " he took a sip of claret and wiped his mouth with his linen napkin – "we might find a bit of comfort in each other's company, I suppose. He was our only offspring."

"Quite." Travers consumed a morsel of Dover sole and put down his knife and fork, as the waiter brought his lager. "When do you plan to go?"

"End of the month."

"Where do you fly to?"

"Hanover, normally. But I'm going to make for the Rhineland first. I shall stay in Bonn and do a bit of sight-seeing around that area. Then go up to Giles for his August leave."

"You know that part, do you?"

"The Rhineland? God, yes! I was there just after the war."

The sharpness of Sir John's reply took Travers by surprise, until it occurred to him that it could be put down to his recent loss, and an underlying fear of loneliness. He was not to know that any mention of the area around Cologne and Bonn caused the learned judge a pang of guilt over a chapter in his early life that still haunted him.

AFTER Martin Travers had returned to his chambers, Sir John sat on for a while over his coffee, feeling not so much lonely as aware of his own solitary figure at the table, an object of pity perhaps. He suspected that any member of the legal profession who knew of his recent loss would avoid him in the smoking room or move two or three urinals away from him in the cloakroom, rather than come face to face with a recent widower and have to fumble for some inadequate expression of sympathy. – Sympathy? He wondered if he was entitled to much. Christine at sixty-eight had been fighting cancer for some time and had borne considerable pain for four years with a commendable display of English stoicism and guts. To be honest, he was relieved that the struggle was over and she was at peace now.

And what of his own life, the one that still had to be lived? Called to the Bar shortly after his demobilization from the Rhine Army in 1946, John Hamilton's career had never faltered. He had started 'eating dinners' while still on his Army pay, entered the chambers of the next Attorney-General in the same year, taken silk in 1964 and made the bench as a Circuit Judge in 1979. The chairmanship of a number of Royal Commissions and the publication of three notable books on the law of libel had made his knighthood a certainty. Finally, when he retired in 1984, glowing tributes to his distinguished services to the legal profession had appeared in the press and the Lord Chancellor himself had proposed a toast to him at a private dinner given for him in this very same Coffee Room at the Garrick.

All in all, Jack Hamilton had ample reason to congratulate himself on a successful and useful life.

But what of the future? He was now an elderly widower

with a grown-up son in the Regular Army, a large number of friends and nothing to do. He knew well enough that, as soon as it was decently possible, people would start bombarding him with invitations. Spare men were hard to come by and Christine had often said "If I go first, darling, you'll be in constant demand for dinner parties. You realize that, don't you?"

'Yes,' he thought, 'I must get away.' He would take the opportunity of doing something he had thought of occasionally for years. 'I must find out what happened to Karin.'

ALTHOUGH he had been in Munich and Berlin before the war and had taken Christine and Giles ski-ing in Bavaria during the school holidays, Sir John had not been back to the Rhineland since his demobilization in the spring of 1946.

Consequently, he'd never flown over Cologne in a German aeroplane. The Lufthansa Boeing 757 throttled back as it crossed the Rhine and started its descent into the Cologne-Bonn airport to the north of the city. Sir John looked down through his window and saw that the famous *Dom*, the great twin-towered Cathedral that had stood alone in a sea of wreckage the last time he saw it, was now competing for attention with a forest of black-glass and concrete office blocks and towering apartment buildings, reaching up ever higher into the sky.

'It's the same the world over – the western world anyway,' he thought with some regret. The developers had won and the face of Germany, more hideously scarred by bombing than that of any other country in the world – excepting certain Soviet and Japanese cities – had been rebuilt by a great miracle of plastic surgery.

Then all the old feelings of guilt flowed back. He thought of German guilt for the Holocaust and the collective responsibility heaped by the rest of the world on the German people for Hitler's crimes against humanity. There was, too, the guilt some Britons felt for the saturation bombing of German towns and the resulting mass slaughter of thousands of men, women and children by fire and high explosive; the merciless day and night raids that had reduced Berlin, Essen, Cologne, Dresden and many other German cities to deserts of rubble. That bombing was, of course, revenge for Warsaw, Rotterdam, Coventry and London. And then there was his own deep sense of guilt about Karin, who if she was still alive would now be about sixty-three . . .

He felt the wheels thump down, and the final call to the cabin crew to stand by for landing came over the speaker. He had arrived.

SIR JOHN took a taxi away from Cologne into Bonn, to the once-familiar Bergischerhof Hotel, still standing in the Münsterplatz, facing the Münster-Basilika, the Catholic Cathedral. As he climbed the well-remembered marble stair-case to his room on the first floor, he found creeping over him a strange feeling of unreality, which was caused by his reason for returning here.

He had a good night's sleep, however, and feeling refreshed, Sir John set out early the next morning on the first stage of his voyage of rediscovery.

He had decided it was essential, before anything else, to find the exact spot where it all began, so he now walked down the Poststrasse to the Bonn *Hauptbahnhof*.

Bonn's U-Bahn system proved every bit as clean, quiet and efficient as those he had experienced in Moscow and Prague. It was Japanese-designed and the trains ran smoothly and silently on rubber-capped wheels.

Fourteen minutes later he was at Bad Godesberg, no longer the quiet little riverside town he remembered but a sprawling appendage of the capital, Bonn. It was almost unrecognizable, with numerous new foreign embassies and government build-ings, mostly built along the river front. It was too far to walk to the place he was looking for on the river, opposite Bad Honnef and close to the little town of Mehlem, where a narrow strip of wooded island lay some hundred yards out in the mainstream. Sir John took a taxi towards Coblenz and instructed the driver to pull off the main road, go down a bumpy track and halt near the island in the river.

He knew for sure, when he saw the Petersberg immediately opposite and the Drachenfels mountain towering overhead to his left, that this was the exact spot. The Rhine was grey and dirty and flowing fast on either side of two little strips of island.

WITH a last, rather sad glance at the bleak, grey, muddy water Sir John walked with his driver back to the taxi and climbed in. "*Nach der Stadtmitte zurück, bitte,*" he said, not quite sure where to go next.

Back in Godesberg he paid off his taxi and went for a walk. He soon came across the road sign he'd been looking for, close to the railway station: Plittersdorferstrasse. Turning into the long residential road, which now started to look familiar, he began to search for No. 93, paused by the house, which had been entirely rebuilt, and went on round the corner to where he could have sworn the Officers' Mess had been. It was further down the road than he remembered; or at least, the building now on the site was: a hideous, modern stone monstrosity, four storeys high with balconies round each floor. On the front gate was a brass plate. Jack saw that the old Officers' Mess had become the Israeli Embassy to West Germany.

He stood outside, slightly dazed, wondering whether the place might be haunted by the ghosts of those Divisional staff officers with whom he had shared the amenities of B Mess, forty-three years ago. Many of them must be dead by now.

AT dinner in the Mess, the conversation usually ranged from experiences in battle to the problem of keeping seven thousand troops, stuck in a foreign country, from getting bored. There were some dozen officers dining in that night.

"My chaps won't get bored, I can assure you," commented Captain Philip Harper, the Education Officer. He was a lean, emaciated man of forty three, with untidy hair, horn-rimmed glasses and protruding ears, and his role was to run training courses in all kinds of crafts and skills to prepare the troops for employment in civilian life. "My instructors will have all their time cut out, trying to mug up their subjects and keep themselves a day ahead of their pupils. And the pupils are going to get plenty of home-work to keep them busy."

"Home-work?" Peter Franks, a young subaltern in the Coldstream Guards, sounded quite shocked. "You can't give grown-up soldiers, who've just fought in a war, home-work to do – like kids at school."

"Good point, Franks. We'll have to call it something more dignified, won't we? Extra-mural revision, or extemporary studies; how about that?"

Jack glanced at Peter Franks, who was sitting next to him, and caught his eye. Neither of them could be quite sure whether the Education Officer was being serious or sarcastic.

All the same, Jack felt the man needed support. Come to that, they all did, with their new responsibilities and the uncertainty of the coming months.

"I wouldn't mind going to classes and learning something useful," Jack said, "if I was a – an other rank. Better than endless guard duties and kit inspections."

"Quite right," murmured the Senior Chaplain. He was a short, rotund figure wearing a purple bib under his tunic, a dog collar, and a perpetual smile behind thick pebble-lens glasses. "If Philip can keep them out of mischief on weekdays, I shall see that their Sundays are well occupied with church services."

"Not too many, Padre," said Colonel Winter, the ADMS, who was a balding, sardonic man, "or they'll mutiny and have to be shot by firing squads, and that'll be your fault. God wouldn't like that. He might stop your promotion to Chaplain-General."

Nobody laughed, and Peter Franks continued on another subject: "Extraordinary thing how undamaged this area is. I mean Bonn and Godesberg are practically unscathed."

Philip Harper agreed they were all lucky to be stationed in an area that had been spared by both the RAF and the US Air Force.

"Not, I suspect," commented the ADMS, as he savoured his fourth glass of captured Mosel, "because Beethoven was born there. No vital industry; no arms factories. That's why Bonn and Godesberg escaped the bombing."

Jack spoke up again, spreading cheese on a biscuit. "There wasn't much industry in Cologne either," he ventured, "and look at it. Worse than a major earthquake. Have you been through the place? I have. It's a nightmare. Nothing standing for miles, except the Cathedral."

There was a brief silence. Then a short, stout, bespectacled captain in the uniform of the Royal Army Ordnance Corps looked up. He was David Levy, the ADOS responsible for all Divisional Ordnance supplies, whose father had started his career as a tailor in Stepney. Levy said quietly "They asked for it."

At that moment the German mess waiter came into the dining-room with a fresh decanter of port and the conversation abruptly ceased. In the ensuing silence, Jack wondered whether someone like David Levy could ever forgive the German race for what had happened to his fellow Jews at Belsen, which was now in the process of being evacuated, cleaned-up, fumigated – and photographed by the world's press.

The disturbing thought instantly brought Karin Freidl to mind. Mentally absolving her from any blame, he wondered if she would be on her rock across the Rhine on the following Saturday.

She was.

A SLIGHT breeze ruffled their hair while Jack and Karin sat together sunning themselves on the rock. Suddenly Jack spotted the red-topped caps of two British Military Policemen, strolling along the bank of the river. He stiffened. They were getting dangerously close to where he'd hidden his uniform. Karin saw them too, and noticed that Jack's expression betrayed something between anxiety and contempt.

"They're patrolling the river bank, hoping to catch some of our soldiers talking to German girls."

"Like us?"

"Exactly," Jack replied grimly, keeping his eye firmly fixed on the two MPs.

Karin said "You must not be punished for speaking to me. Shall I go away?"

"Certainly not," said Jack, indignantly. "You stay right here where you are. Nobody tells me who I may or may not talk to. It's all bloody nonsense. The war's over."

Karin touched Jack's shoulder and pointed across the river. "Look," she said. "See what they will do now."

Jack looked. The Redcaps were walking purposely towards a spot where two girls in swimsuits were lying on a towel, one reading, the other drying her hair.

"I'll tell you exactly what those bulls will do now."

"Bulls?" Karin looked baffled.

"That's what our soldiers call the Military Police."

"So what will the bulls do?"

"They'll stop and chat with those two fraüleins. Just you watch. Bloody impudence . . . " The Redcaps had reached the spot and were already squatting down to converse with the two sunbathers.

"There! What did I tell you?" Jack sounded almost triumphant, as one of the girls rose to her feet, picked up a bundle of clothing and vanished behind a nearby bush to change. "Those chaps are supposed to set an example to the troops, not go about in uniform, flouting the regulations in broad daylight."

"Maybe they are allowed to speak with German people, because they are the army's policemen and they must keep order."

"No excuse," Jack answered without taking his eye off the scandalous scene unfolding on the opposite bank. – "But who am I to talk?"

The second girl sunbather had now retired to dress behind cover and the two Military Policemen turned on their heels and moved away. Then, after a moment the first girl emerged from behind a bush, drying her hair with a towel. She was dressed in the khaki uniform of the ATS. Her friend followed, buttoning up the blue-grey tunic of the WAAF. Pushing their damp hair inside their caps, the pair of British service girls picked up their bags and towels and wandered off along the river bank in the opposite direction.

Jack turned to find Karin, her hand over her mouth, holding back a smile. As their eyes met, they both burst out laughing.

But laughter did not make the problem go away.

"How the hell do they expect us to ignore the German population, as though they don't exist?" Jack grumbled.

"Perhaps," said Karin quietly, "as time goes on they will allow us to speak with each other and become friends."

"They'll have to," said Jack. "We can't go on hating each other for ever."

Karin nodded and then slipped into the river to swim back to the bank.

As Jack followed her, his thoughts continued in the same train. When they were both lying on their towels on the grass, he said "As far as I can see the only way a German civilian can speak with a British soldier is by working for us. Our mess waiter, for example; Otto. We employ him in our officers' mess, therefore we are allowed to speak to him. We can say: 'Otto, bring me a gin and tonic, please,' and that's OK. But I'm not allowed to tell you how attractive I think you are. If I got caught doing that I'd be court-martialled and . . . "

"Shot?" Karin was smiling now.

"Lose my leave, more likely."

"*So*. If I worked for your army, I would be allowed to speak with you?" Karin asked thoughtfully.

"Certainly. Pity you can't." – A pause. – "Why can't you?"

Karin looked a bit thrown, caught off guard. "I do not think it would be . . ."

"What would it be?"

"I do not know how to be a mess waiter. And I have my work at the school."

"That's not your reason, Karin. You're afraid of what your family would say."

"They are not here."

"Is it the money? How much do they pay you at the school?"

"Enough. But it is very empty, many of the children are gone."

"I need an interpreter," said Jack on a sudden impulse.

"But you speak very well German."

"Not well enough," Jack replied. He had been visited that very morning by a certain Max Wendels, a local cabaret agent, who in rapid German had offered to put together a variety show for the British troops. Jack had understood the man's proposition in outline but had become hopelessly bogged down by technical terms about stage lighting, drapes, acrobatic equipment, props and the like. He could certainly do with an interpreter. Someone bright like Karin.

"Would you allow me to suggest it? I mean for you to come and work for us as an interpreter in our Entertainments Office? I'd have to ask the GSO1 – that's my boss – but I'm sure he'd agree. Can you type?"

Karin seemed a bit torn. "Yes, I do. I must always type letters for the school."

"There you are, then. I'm going to put your name forward as my interpreter- secretary. First thing tomorrow morning."

Karin managed a faint smile, as though half of her feared the consequences of working for the occupation forces; yet she knew it was a chance to get food and cigarettes, to live a better life. The British were not so hard or cruel – not like the Russians. And Jack seemed to be friendly, someone she could trust. It would be an adventure, a new experience.

"If you want me, I will agree," she said.

"That's wonderful." The prospect of seeing this beautiful, suntanned creature every day, openly and legally, in the office, excited him so much that he began to tremble.

"You are shivering," said Karin. "You must not catch cold. Let me dry your back."

"I'm all right," said Jack. "But thanks," he added, submitting happily to her ministrations.

THE little school in Mehlem had seemed to Sir John a natural starting point for what he believed would probably prove a long, tedious search that might well yield nothing beyond sad news. On the other hand, if Karin was still alive, she would be an elderly lady by now, perhaps infirm, living in squalor, short of money, embittered, even blind or deaf.

Over the forty-odd years since his demobilization, Jack had only occasionally found himself thinking about Karin. He had enjoyed a full, busy life, with little time for looking back. When he did remember her, the memories of those six months on the Rhine came to him as nostalgically happy ones, but tinged with a good deal of guilt and remorse, which caused him to dismiss them swiftly from his mind.

These remembrances occurred usually when somebody in the course of a casual conversation happened to mention the Rhine or Cologne, or when he heard on the radio or at a concert some piece of music that took him back to that summer and the following autumn. On those occasions, Jack would see a starkly clear picture of Karin and of himself as a brash young captain in the Grenadiers.

Now, the more he retraced his steps towards the places where he and Karin had met and fallen in love and savoured together the delights of that summer, the less the Judge liked what he saw of himself. He was, as it were, a judge sitting in judgement over a callous, perhaps arrogant young man in his late twenties, up before him in court. Was it too late now to apologize to Karin for his thoughtless, casual and off-hand behaviour? Somebody in Mehlem just might know her present whereabouts.

Although much of the landscape and the atmosphere of the Rhineland had changed beyond all recognition in the last forty-five years, the river still flowed on to Remagen from Mainz and Coblenz and the barges still plied their courses up and downstream, loaded to the gunwhales with their cargoes of timber, coal, steel and vast containers. The mountains and the castles were still there, with the proud skyline of the Siebengebirge range and its high peak of the Petersberg. And the ferry was still carrying cars and people across to Königswinter, as it always had.

Mehlem proved to be a dead end. The little *Volksschule* had long since been replaced by a large, modern academy and nobody in the building could remember much about the summer of 1945 – not even a septuagenarian cleaner who, it proved, had come to Mehlem only in 1974, as a widow in search of work after her husband had died in Mannheim.

Sir John found himself thinking that he was wasting his time here. If Karin was to be traced, the only possible way would be to get in touch with the authorities in Coblenz. Her home had been there and her parents had been citizens of the town for many years. There must be some record of them in the archives at the *Rathaus* or with the Coblenz police.

Armed with a German dictionary, the Judge went back to sit on his bed in the hotel and work out a few apt phrases on paper. Then he dialled the telephone number he'd found of the *Stadtverwaltung* in Coblenz. A man's voice answered, the

Judge asked for the town archives, and he was put through to a girl clerk.

His initial request, as a judge from London, for information as to the whereabouts of a certain woman who had once lived with her parents in the town, must have given the impression that he was some sort of lawyer with news of a legacy for the lady, for the girl clerk muttered something about "*ein Vermächtnis*".

But Sir John knew the only legacy he could possibly offer Karin, should he find her again, would be one of regrets and apologies. So he launched into the long, complicated but well-rehearsed story of his presence in Godesberg during the summer of 1945, "*kurz nach dem Kriege*," of his association with the lady he sought to trace and his anxiety to acquire news of her. The clerk now seemed to grasp the gist of Sir John's problem and told him that enquiries could be set in motion but that they would take a few days. Would he kindly give her the name and number of his hotel in Bonn, and be so good as to repeat once more the name of the lady he wished to trace?

"Certainly," said Sir John. "Freidl; Karin Freidl."

Chapter 2

"WHAT's her name?"

"Freidl," said Jack, "F-R-E-I-D-L."

Lieut-Colonel Geoffrey Wynn-Davies looked up, puzzled. He was a jovial, stoutish, balding officer who had been Adjutant to an armoured battalion of the Welsh Guards in battle before his appointment to Q branch at Divisional Headquarters.

As DAQMG he was responsible for all Admin. matters within the Division.

"D – L," said Jack, becoming impatient. "Freidl."

Colonel Wynn-Davies continued writing notes in a folder on his desk. Jack was perched on a window-seat, glancing out at the distant mountains.

"And what makes you think," the colonel asked without looking up from his notes, "that Fraülein Fried-Egg – "

"Freidl," Jack corrected him politely.

"Fraülein . . . Freidl . . . is a suitable person to be employed in the Entertainments Office?"

At the time when he decided to apply to the DAQMG for permission to employ a civilian girl as his interpreter secretary, Jack had carefully worked out his reply to this question. Now, in his anxiety not to sound too eager, he assumed an almost casual tone. "Well, first of all, the young woman in question speaks excellent English. Second, she can type; third, she's intelligent – wouldn't be a teacher at the school in Mehlem if she wasn't reasonably brainy. Also she's interested in the theatre, films, music, and so on."

"How do you know?" Wynn-Davies looked up from his folder and darted at Jack what the latter read as a look of deep suspicion. For in his guilty heart, Jack knew he wanted Karin working in his office for no better reason than a chance to see her every day. It was a plain case of carnal desire but he was damned if he'd admit it, least of all to the DAQMG, who had the authority to sanction or reject his request.

"How do I know? I've only spoken to her once or twice."

"How did you get to know her?"

"We met . . . swimming in the Rhine."

"Good Lord!"

"I asked her the time and she told me," Jack lied. "In perfect English. I was most impressed."

"I'll bet you were," said the Colonel with just the suspicion of a smile. "Wearing her wrist-watch in the water, was she?"

"No," said Jack quickly. "She guessed it . . . from the angle of the sun . . . and we got talking."

A pause, then Wynn-Davies looked Jack straight in the eye. "Good figure?" he asked. "In her bathing suit? Did you notice? Or was she swimming in the altogether? They go in for that sort of thing, the Jerries. *Nacktkultur*."

"She was properly clad in a one-piece bathing costume," said Jack, indignantly. He felt rather like the mother of a local beauty queen, trying to pacify her daughter's outraged granny.

Geoffrey Wynn-Davies kept his eye fixed on Jack. "Some of these fraüleins'll do anything for a packet of fags, you know," he said.

"I didn't know," Jack lied again. "Will they really?"

"Some of them. I'm not saying this one – "

By now Jack was flushed with anger. "Look, Sir, I need an interpreter for my office, someone who can type in German. I don't care what sex. Perhaps you can find me a guardsman, who can issue written instructions, legibly typed out in triplicate and comprehensible to a half-Polish, half-German variety agent in Cologne with details about stage lighting, sound equipment, scenery – otherwise – "

"Yes, all right, keep your shirt on, Hamilton. I'll tell the pay sergeant to put your bit of loot – "

"She is not loot, Sir, she is a respectable school teacher and her name, you may remember, is Fraülein Freidl . . . "

"Very well. I'll have Fraülein Freidl's name placed on the civilian staff payroll. With effect from next Monday."

"Thank you," said Jack, saluting his superior officer with a sarcastic sigh of relief. "Very good of you."

Wynn-Davies glanced at his watch and decided to pacify the enraged young officer, whom he rather liked. "Come and have a pink gin in the Mess."

Clearly, it would be as well to keep on the right side of the DAQMG, so Jack felt bound to accept. "Thank you, Sir," he murmured, as Wynn-Davies got up from his desk.

'A' Mess was the east wing of a large rococo *Schloss* on the side of a hill across the river from Godesberg. "Bit grander than our place," Jack commented, as they approached the entrance.

Wynn-Davies opened the heavy oak door into a vast, panelled banqueting hall, full of officers drinking and smoking. Among them Jack recognized the General and the GSO1.

"All the top brass," he commented.

"That's right."

Wynn-Davies ordered two pink gins from a German waiter and Jack looked about him. "Pretty good collection of odds and sods, your B Mess, I should think."

"It is," said Jack. "The education officer, coal officer, senior chaplain, me . . . " He was still smarting inwardly at the DAQMG's gibes about Karin.

Over their pink gins the DAQMG and the DADAWS discussed the recent 'Farewell To Armour' parade, at which the Guards Armoured Division had formally given up its tanks and armoured cars and reverted to the Infantry, and the Commander-in-Chief had flown to an aerodrome at Rotenberg to star in the show. Wynn-Davies commented "Old Monty obviously enjoyed his day. He always disapproved of putting guardsmen into tanks and armoured cars."

To Jack, the temptation to outrage the stuffier officers he came across was always strong, and after hearing this chap's gibes about Karin, the opening he had now been given was irresistible. "Absolutely," he said. "He said as much when he inspected us before D-Day. 'We need you in the Infantry,' the little shit said, but what he really meant was that a platoon of guardsmen will go without question into the attack against anything and anyone, once they've been ordered to, usually by some eighteen year-old viscount, whose great- grandfather did the same sort of thing at Waterloo. They've been conditioned into imagining that, if they don't advance, they'll get an hour's pack drill on the barrack square at Caterham under a drill-sergeant. Some call it discipline, others call it rule by fear. Take your choice."

"You're a bloody cynic, Hamilton," was all Wynn-Davies could think of to reply, apparently shocked by his colleague's lack of respect for the Brigade of Guards.

Jack hoped he hadn't gone too far, and attempted to retrieve the situation by changing the subject to racing, which was Wynn-Davies' lifelong passion. But as the Colonel remained cool, Jack judged it prudent to swallow his pink gin smartly and leave quickly.

A WEEK later, on June 14th, Karin Freidl reported for work at the Entertainments Office, No. 93, Plittersdorferstrasse, several houses up the street from the Officers' Mess. The house had been requisitioned by the army, and its rooms emptied of the owner's furniture, pictures and carpets. Jack's section was a spacious ground-floor suite with sliding glass double doors dividing the front sitting-room from a back section, down a step at a lower level. This had presumably once been the dining-room.

He had claimed the back room for his own office. There was precious little in it but a plain wooden desk and swivel chair. In the front room, the general office, Jack's assistant, Corporal Bridges, seated on a collapsible chair, worked at an army trestle-table. Marks on the bare walls showed where the pictures had once hung and in place of a large painting on the main wall there was now a green baize notice board, displaying posters and army information. The uncarpeted floor was of green linoleum and from each ceiling there hung, incongruously, a large, ornate chandelier.

Corporal Bridges was a thirty-one year old Cockney from Deptford, married with two children. Some pre-war experience as a backstage electrician at the Lewisham Hippodrome had enabled him to qualify as a wireless operator in Jack's battalion and Jack knew, from censoring Corporal Bridges' letters, that he was a happily married man with an enthusiasm for all matters theatrical. For this reason he had applied for Bridges to be posted to the welfare branch as his right-hand man.

At the appointed time, Karin arrived at the house. Noticing the wooden sign painted in Brigade of Guards red and blue nailed to the white fence outside, she walked in through the open front door. She was feeling nervous, especially as Jack had explained to her that, owing to some meeting he had to attend, he would not be there when she arrived. His assistant, Corporal Bridges, would receive her and show her what her duties were to be, and he would join her at the office around midday.

Karin had expressed mild concern at this arrangement but was soon reassured that she would find the corporal helpful and sympathetic and that there was nothing to fear. Privately, Jack wished to avoid arriving at the office at the same time as his German secretary, since this might suggest that a relationship between them already existed. To drop in later and casually ask Bridges how the new member of staff was getting on would look better.

"Good morning, Fräulein. The Major told me you was coming in today." Corporal Bridges, a burly figure wearing battle-dress and ammunition boots, had risen from his desk to greet Karin, as she peered anxiously in from the narrow front hall.

"Come along and I'll show you what you'll be required to do . . . "

A moment later he had launched into an explanation of her work, and Karin found it impossible to get a word in edgeways as he talked about forthcoming visits by ENSA parties, sports fixtures and application forms for tickets to an all-ranks dance to be given by the Second Household Cavalry Regiment at a school in their area. There was nothing she could do except nod and try to look intelligent.

This enforced lack of response from the fräulein threw a sudden doubt into Bridges' mind about the girl's actual comprehension of the English language. Jack had told him she spoke it quite well, but the corporal decided not to risk any misunderstandings, and now began speaking as to a backward child. "I want you," he said with painful over-emphasis, accompanied by extravagant hand gestures, "to make – lists – write – down – so – here, here – write – down – with – typewriter. – This is a – type – writer." The corporal pointed to the large Olivetti on the trestle-table and started to mime typing gestures with his fingers.

"If there's anything – you not – *compree* – not understand – *savvy* – ask me." He pointed his finger at his own chest with a friendly grin. "Ask – yours truly. *Is gut?*"

Karin's nervousness was successfully banished by amusement.

When Jack arrived at midday, he found Karin hard at work at the Olivetti and asked politely how she was getting on.

"I learn . . . slowly," she smiled.

Bridges turned round in his chair and endorsed this. "Doing fine, Sir, is Fraülein Freidl. Answering the 'phone and all."

At this point the office telephone rang and Karin picked it up. "Entertainments Office? *Ja, gut. Ich will Ihn fragen. Moment, bitte.*" Karin put her hand over the receiver and turned to Jack, as he paused by the step down into his own inner sanctum. "Max Wendels on the line, Major. He can provide an evening cabaret entertainment for Brigadier Cooper's farewell party on the 8th. Is it OK?"

"OK," said Jack.

"He will come tomorrow morning with photographs of the acts he has booked. What time will you see him?"

Jack shrugged. "Ten, ten-thirty."

Karin turned back to the 'phone. "*So, ungefähr um zehn . . . sagen wir zwischen zehn und zehn Uhr dreissig.*"

Jack glanced across at Corporal Bridges, who was listening, pen poised. "Ten to ten-thirty, tomorrow," he said. "Max Wendels, OK?"

Bridges said "Sir," made a note of the appointment and then got up. "I'm wanted over at the 2nd Coldstream by dinner time, Sir. About the cricket match."

Jack nodded. "Right you are, Corporal Bridges. You be off."

At the door the corporal turned to Karin. "Not much wrong with your English, Fraülein, is there?"

Jack went into his own room, leaving the dividing door half open. In the ensuing silence, he suddenly felt a strange sense of desire, panic and excitement. Karin was sitting through there, just beyond the door, looking fresh and delicious in a cotton dress with her marvellous long, bronzed legs protruding from under it, her feet encased in white sandals. He was alone with her. This was what he had planned, to be close to her all day, working side by side, able to converse with her legally during the day and with luck to get better acquainted in the evenings. But he would need to be careful. All kinds of people dropped in during the course of the day, such as officers from outlying units, enquiring about sports facilities and checking the dates of ENSA shows. There must be no hint of anything improper about Karin's presence.

To every visitor that first day, including the senior chaplain who came in to see the DADAWS with the times of church services to be distributed to all units, Jack introduced Karin as "Fräulein Freidl, who is kindly helping me out."

Around four in the afternoon, a brash young captain from the Royal Artillery arrived at the office. He'd come some way from Iserlohn in a staff car to borrow a couple of footballs for his Battery. In Corporal Bridges' absence the Gunner captain started to chat with Karin, and asked her if she was free that evening.

Jack was amused and relieved to hear her through the half-open sliding door, pretending she could not understand. "I am sorry. I – not – speak – so very well – English – please tell the Major – what it is – that you wish – yes?"

Thwarted, the Royal Artillery officer collected his footballs and departed. When he had gone Jack laughed, calling out to Karin "I'm afraid you'll get quite a bit of that from now on. Do you mind?"

"Not if you are here, Jack, or Corporal Bridges. If I am alone in the room and an English soldier comes in and will order me to kiss him or so, I will have to obey him. We Germans must be polite to our conquerors."

"Not that polite, Karin," came the voice from behind the door.

THE next morning, after a leisurely breakfast in the Mess, Jack strolled along to the office to find Corporal Bridges in a state of mild agitation. Karin had failed to turn up for work and there was plenty for her to do.

"I could take the Jeep down to her lodgings and sort her out, Sir, if you want, Sir."

"No. I'll go," said Jack quickly, his heart missing a beat. "You stay here and get those notices out. It's possible the 'bus from Mehlem isn't running today."

THE journey along the tree-lined road into Mehlem, which ran parallel to the Rhine, took about twelve minutes. Jack passed several houses and hotels that had been destroyed by shell-fire, and on the roadside midway between Bad Godesberg and Mehlem a German anti-aircraft gun, its barrel twisted like a corkscrew, still pointed horizontally down the road. Plainly, it had been used as an anti-tank defence weapon against the recent American onslaught, in the closing stages of the Rhine crossing at Remagen.

As Jack sat at the wheel of his Jeep, following the line of the river in an easterly direction, he could not help wondering whether he might have made a grave mistake in recruiting, as his assistant, a girl of whom he knew so little.

Karin had told him she lodged in the house of Frau Pauels at No. 42, Nibelungen Allee. He found the place easily enough, a medium-sized, white stucco house with green shutters and a small garden at the back, dominated by a monkey puzzle tree. The moment he stopped and switched off his engine, he became aware in the silence of loud banging and angry shouting coming from inside the house. Jack got out and rather apprehensively rang the bell. Nobody came. The angry voices paused. Jack rang again. After a while a middle-aged woman wearing an apron and carpet slippers unbolted and opened the door.

"I've come to fetch Fraülein Freidl. Is she in?"

At that moment a window overhead slid up and Karin's voice called down "Please ask Frau Pauels to give me my clothes and unlock my door. I cannot get out, so I cannot come to work."

As she spoke, Jack looked up, to see Karin hanging out of the window in her nightdress. She was in tears.

The woman, who had said nothing, started to close the door, but quickly Jack thrust forward his foot to prevent it from being shut. "You'll have to unlock her door," he said, with as much authority as he could command. "The young lady works for the British Occupation Forces."

Frau Pauels darted a look of smouldering hatred at Jack, glanced down at his suede shoe that was firmly wedged in the door, and said "Please remove from my door your large boot."

Jack, believing the woman was about to allow him in, promptly complied, whereupon the door was sharply slammed in his face. Recovering partially from the shock, Jack attempted to reassert his authority by banging on the door and shouting "*Machen Sie auf, bitte*," adding that his request was in the name of the British Army.

But all was quiet inside the house. Not even the sound of Karin weeping could be heard – there was nothing but a deadly, sinister silence. Jack climbed into his Jeep and drove away back to Godesberg, not quite sure what to do next.

AS he sped back along the road, angry and frustrated, he could not but reflect bitterly that Frau Pauels was bloody lucky to be living in the British Zone. Had she been in the Russian-occupied part of her Fatherland, she would have received a hail of machine-gun bullets through her front door and Karin would have been removed from her care at gunpoint. 'Bloody arrogance,' Jack thought; 'they're all the same!'

But his resentment soon mellowed to something close to pity, as he saw, all along the road to Godesberg, living examples of what Hitler's monstrous war had done to his own people, and the scale of human suffering and misery he had brought upon the *Herrenvolk*, not to mention the rest of the world. Besides, one could hardly blame them for being bitter after all they had suffered from Allied air raids.

A few miles out of town Jack passed a war-weary, ageing German woman pushing a heavy handcart towards Bonn. She was dressed in black and wore a shawl, and her face was lined with grief and hunger. She must have been homeless, for her cart was piled high with personal belongings: an old gramophone, a birdcage, a small trunk and a quantity of men's clothing. Jack guessed that these objects were all she'd managed to salvage from her wrecked home, objects to be swapped in the street markets for food.

Moments later, approaching Godesberg he saw a farm wagon, drawn by an emaciated horse, laden with vegetables, swedes, turnips and beetroot. The driver and his wife were on their way to the wrecked streets of what was left of Cologne, there to exchange farm produce for cigarettes, jewellery, articles of clothing; anything that was currency.

THAT night Colonel Wynn-Davies happened to be dining in B Mess, so before dinner Jack was able to corner him by the bar and discuss his delicate problem over Karin's lodgings.

"Nothing delicate about it, old boy," said the DAQMG, lighting up a cheap, captured German cheroot. "You must order the woman to let your Kraut girl come to work. Stand no nonsense!"

Jack agreed that firm action was called for, but what?

"Talk to the Provost-Marshal about it. Those chaps are responsible for disciplining the civvy population."

"I'm not sure it's a matter of discipline," said Jack.

"Not on your girl's part. It's her landlady, from what you tell me."

"So what could the Provost people do?"

"Borrow a Redcap from them and put the fear of God up the woman."

After dinner Jack went over to the *Schloss* to find the Provost-Marshal, and tracked him down in the billiard-room.

He was a tall man, grey before his time, called Geoffrey Sallis, and he was in the middle of a break. When he failed to bring off an easy cannon, his opponent, an ADC whom Jack knew, introduced them.

The P-M's reaction to Jack's request was rather surprising. "Why not?" he said with a broad grin. "Have a bit of fun." He excused himself from the game for a moment and put through a call to Military Police Headquarters in Honnef.

The following morning Jack set out for Mehlem with a small task force consisting of himself in his Jeep, driven by Corporal Bridges, and a 15-cwt truck of the Divisional Military Police, with a Redcap at the wheel and a sergeant armed with a Sten gun.

As Jack led his convoy of two vehicles towards Mehlem he encountered more refugee traffic on the road, which was still pitted with craters. Along the verges many telegraph poles and lines had been brought down in the recent shelling, for the Americans had fought a sharp action along that road a month or so earlier, after crossing the Rhine at Remagen. At one place, the burnt-out wreck of a French Citröen car, marked with the Maltese Cross of the *Wehrmacht*, lay in a ditch. In it three German officers had been attempting to escape from the Allied advance when a rocket from a low-flying Typhoon of the RAF had put an end to their war and their lives. Now it lay, so much charred scrap-metal, a grim reminder of the recent fighting. Jack had passed it often, when he had wondered whether the charred bodies of its occupants had ever been removed. He certainly wasn't prepared to stop and look.

After they'd driven for some minutes in a brooding silence, Corporal Bridges at the wheel asked suddenly "How'll we go on, Sir, if the lady won't open the door this time?"

"We'll have to see," was all Jack dared to say. 'The truth is,' he was thinking inwardly with a mild sense of shame, 'this is the kind of thing the SS have been doing all over Occupied Europe for the past five years. Arriving in vehicles, armed, banging on people's doors and shouting *"Machen Sie auf."* Then he thought 'No, dammit, we're not dragging Frau Pauels off to Ravensbruck. All I'm doing is trying to recover my secretary from her landlady. Not quite the same thing.'

At this point the task force drew up outside the house in Nibelungen Allee. Jack jumped out and, signalling to the others to stand by, rang the bell. Nobody came. Next he bent down and put his mouth to the letter-box, took a deep breath and was about to bellow into it, 'Machen Sie auf', when the front door flew open, causing him to lose his balance. Instinctively, he steadied himself by clutching the nearest object to hand, which happened to be Frau Pauels' skirt, as she stood there, looking down at him. Jack swiftly let go of the woman, straightened up to his full height and glared at her, hoping to resume a dignified, official manner.

"I have come to fetch Fraülein Freidl. May I see her, please?"

"She is not here," came the icy reply.

"Oh? Where is she?"

Frau Pauels hesitated. She looked across at the Military Police truck and its occupants with their Sten guns at the ready. Then she looked at Jack. "I see that your soldiers are armed, Herr Hauptmann. Does this mean that you intend to shoot me if I refuse to answer your question?"

Jack seized the chance to win a quick trick. "The British don't go in for that sort of thing. Fraülein Freidl has an agreement to work for us. I am here to see that you allow her to fulfil that agreement. By persuasion, not with bullets."

After a second's pause Frau Pauels said "She has gone out early – to the Rathaus to register her new employment."

Jack wondered if that was true. Karin might well have spent another night up in her room under lock and key or, worse still, been sent back to her family in Coblenz.

"When do you expect her back?"

Frau Pauels shrugged her shoulders. "I have allowed her out for this purpose only. Not to go to work for your people."

"Very well. I'll make a deal with you," Jack said, "and I think you can rely on me as a Major of the First Regiment of Foot Guards to keep my side of the bargain."

For the first time Ingrid Pauels showed a flicker of interest in Jack, if not exactly of respect then of a new willingness to listen to what he had to say. "What is your deal, Major?"

Jack glanced across at the Task Force and said "I'll agree to send my troops away if you'll agree to discuss the matter with me in a civilized manner."

Still a glassy stare of bitter loathing from Frau Pauels.

"Well?" Jack asked, standing his ground.

At last the woman inclined her head, just a fraction, in assent. "But I cannot discuss my private affairs in the street."

"I agree," said Jack.

Another slight pause, then Frau Pauels said, with minimal courtesy, "You will please come in."

"Thank you," said Jack. He turned towards his Jeep, parked opposite. "Corporal Bridges!"

"Sir."

"Tell the *MP*s I shan't want them any more."

"Sir."

"Get a lift back with them and leave the Jeep for me. I'm going to be here for a bit longer."

"Sir."

Frau Pauels held the door open for Jack. "Come, please," she said.

JACK followed the tight-lipped woman into a small, spotlessly clean sitting-room on the ground floor, where a large Blüthner grand piano stood in one corner. It was covered with a piece of heavy velvet material, embroidered in gold like an altar cloth, and on it were a large onyx lamp with a silk shade and tassels and several signed photographs in silver and gold frames.

"Sit down, please, Herr Major."

Jack perched on the front of a velvet, button-backed armchair, anxious not to appear too relaxed. Frau Pauels sat on the sofa and waited for Jack to speak.

"What I have to say to you, Frau Pauels, is that you have no right to prevent Fraülein Freidl from doing her job with us in Bad Godesberg. If it occurs again, there will be trouble."

Frau Pauels ignored the threat. "It is not right," she said evenly, "that a German girl will work for the British."

"Fraülein Freidl volunteered to interpret for us and to act as my secretary," Jack snapped back. "There was no compulsion."

Frau Pauels rose and walked over to the window. Although her carpet slippers diminished her height and the apron suggested an ordinary *Hausfrau* interrupted in her morning chores, there was something imposing about her. She had authority, style, breeding. She gave the impression that she was someone used to having servants.

With her back to Jack, she said "You cannot expect us to welcome your soldiers with open arms. Our cities and our towns are all destroyed – "

"Ours too, Frau Pauels," Jack interposed, "and those of our allies: Warsaw, Rotterdam, Coventry, Stalingrad – " Frau Pauels said nothing, so Jack went on "The war is over now and we have to rebuild our countries and restore trust between us."

"The war may be over for some," she said quietly. "For others, it will never be the same again."

Frau Pauels remained at the window, her back to Jack. From his chair, he noticed that she was dabbing her eyes with a handkerchief.

After a short silence, she turned from the window to face Jack, well under control now, her voice quite steady. "May I offer you a cup of coffee?"

Jack thanked her.

"I have only ersatz but there are some biscuits. Please excuse me."

As the dignified woman left the room, Jack rose, then wandered over to the grand piano, where his glance fell on one of the photographs on display. It was a full-length portrait of a tall, handsome man, proud and erect in the uniform of a Colonel of the Waffen SS.

As an Intelligence Officer, Jack had interrogated several Waffen ss Officers. They had ranged from the charming and polite to the arrogant and loathsome. He wondered which category this man fell into and whether he was alive or dead. Jack suspected, since Frau Pauels had just been weeping, that he was her husband.

Next to it there was a photograph of Lotte Lehmann in the costume of the *Feldmarschallin* in *Der Rosenkavalier*, signed '*Liebste Ingrid, deine Freundin, Lotte. Maerz, 1937*'. Similarly inscribed photographs of Felix Weingärtner, Richard Strauss and Otto Klemperer also adorned the piano, together with a number of small jade ornaments, piles of music and a metronome.

Jack was amazed, thrilled and impressed all at the same time. Frau Pauels' grand manner and bearing were now explained and he suspected that he was in the house of an eminent opera star.

She came back from the kitchen rather suddenly, causing Jack to spin round somewhat guiltily, while she put down a tray of coffee and biscuits.

"I was admiring your photograph of Lotte Lehmann. 1937 was the year I saw her as the *Feldmarschallin* in *Rosenkavalier* at Salzburg. I shall never forget that experience." Jack had, indeed, been invited to the Salzkammergut in Austria that summer by a girl friend, whose mother had rented a chalet for the opera. But Jack also recalled that 1937 was the year of the last Salzburg Festival before the *Anschluss*, when people like Colonel Pauels marched into Austria and made it an extension of the Third Reich.

Ingrid Pauels, however, was not a party to Jack's inner thoughts. As she poured her English guest a cup of revolting ersatz coffee, she launched, as Jack had intended she should, into the story of her long and distinguished career as an operatic soprano. "I have sung all the great Wagner roles, you know; Sieglinde, Isolde, Brünnhilde, Eva in *Meistersinger* and in so many places: Berlin, Vienna, Bayreuth, Stockholm – not so far London . . . "

"You must . . . miss it."

"I cannot sing now. There is no opera. It is finished. *Kaputt*."

At this point the front door banged and Karin came tentatively into the room. At the sight of Jack and Ingrid, happily chatting over coffee, her face lit up with pleasure and relief. There was an outburst of voluble, high-speed German between the two ladies, relating to matters of irritating red tape encountered at the town hall. Then good manners prevailed and Ingrid told Karin in English to get herself a cup from the kitchen and to join her and the Herr Major in the salon. "We were speaking of music together."

Karin's eyes shone. Music was the greatest thing in her life, her passion and her fulfilment. The very thought that her English boss, her officer employer, might know about, appreciate and possibly love good music, caused her heart to race. Here was something they could really share, a common bond between them.

"The Herr Major was in Salzburg in 1937, when Lehmann and Schumann were singing. He has heard them."

"You have?" Karin tingled all over with joy to see the expression of enthusiasm and excitement on his face, as Jack confirmed this. "When I heard Schumann, Lehmann and Novotna sing the trio '*Hab mir's gelobt ihr Lieb zu haben*' from *Rosenkavalier*, I experienced a feeling of total ecstasy; it was like being lifted up out of my seat."

Karin stared at Jack, her eyes shining, for a few seconds. Then she turned quickly and went off to the kitchen to fetch a cup and saucer. On her return, she poured herself some coffee and perched on the arm of a chair.

"I long to hear *Der Rosenkavalier* again," Jack said.

"Then I shall sing it for you." With that Ingrid Pauels rose to her feet and without more ado poured out a few bars of the parting scene between *Feldmarschallin*, Baron Ochs and Octavian at the opening of Act l. Karin clapped her hands with delight.

"You must do it again – you must put it on – " Jack said.

But Ingrid sat down, suddenly deflated. "How can we put anything on, Herr Major, when there are no opera houses left in Germany, no singers, no musicians? They are all dead or wounded or – *Kriegsgefangene* – what do you say – prisoner of war? *Alles ist kaputt*."

Karin said calmly "It's true. Every theatre in Bonn and Cologne and Aachen has been burnt down. Only Düsseldorf stands, but there is no roof left."

Jack got up and paced the room, suddenly excited. "Then *we* must do it together . . . "

"How so?" Karin looked puzzled.

"We shall get together an orchestra; a German orchestra; and a company of singers capable of performing opera and concerts for the British troops. It's my job to provide entertainment for them. That's what I'm here for." Some good music would provide a very welcome balance to the light entertainment that was the troops' usual fare, Jack told himself. The momentary silence was broken when Ingrid said quietly to Karin *"Aber nicht für die Zivilbevlökerung, verstehen Sie?"*

Karin must have forgotten momentarily that Jack spoke German, for she flushed with embarrassment when he added "And the civilian population too. Certainly. If the authorities will permit it."

Ingrid now exploded with enthusiasm and excitement. *"Gut. So,* we shall do all my best roles, and we shall find singers and musicians to support me and we will build a new opera house and start with *Der Rosenkavalier*. I have still my costume – "

"Just a moment," Jack interrupted, wondering what he had started. "I'm not saying our people will allow it. After all – we have our own forms of entertainment. And don't forget there is still a rule about non-fraternization, as Karin knows. But I promise I will suggest it. I'm afraid there's not much chance of building a new opera house in Bonn or anywhere else, certainly not until everyone has a roof over their heads and food and clothing and all the Displaced Persons are repatriated and – "

Ingrid chose to ignore this line of argument and went plunging on, with unabated zeal, chattering to Karin. "I have heard nothing for two years of Dr Heuss," she said and turned to explain to Jack. "He was *Intendant* of the opera here in Bonn before the war; but he may be dead. And nobody knows what has happened to our conductor, Emmerich Karl. He joined the *Kriegsmarine*, you know, our German Navy."

Karin thought she'd heard that Herr Karl had gone down in the *Bismarck*, but it was only a rumour. The mother of one of her school-children had been at university with the Karls' daughter, Liesl.

"Erich Weyers, the leading bassoon player has gone mad, I hear, but there is a good 'cellist in Gummersbach, Franz Kessler," said Frau Pauels. "He is back, I know, from the *Ostfront*. But I heard his fingers were so badly frostbitten he may not be able to play any more."

"Then we must go to see Herr Kessler," said Karin excitely. "It is possible his hands are better now and he will play for us. I shall make a list of all the old *Stadtoper* musicians who are registered in the *Rathaus*, make enquiries and see if they have still their instruments. Many will have been lost or damaged in the war."

As the two women talked, Jack had the feeling that something very important was happening in that little salon near Bonn, so auspiciously near Bonn, the birthplace of Ludwig van Beethoven. He could see the first glimmerings of a great resurgence of music amid the devastation of Hitler's Germany. He could imagine the German people finding hope and some sort of life again through their singers and orchestral players; and by performing concerts and opera for themselves and their victors somehow, through the glorious international language of crochets and quavers and semitones, creating a bridge between two ex-enemy nations, a common bond to help accelerate peace and reconciliation. Frau Pauels already appeared a different woman, no longer a sour, defensive *Hausfrau* in apron and slippers but a formidable, proud *prima donna*, ambitious and hopeful for the future.

Nothing more was said of her attempt to imprison Karin in her house rather than allow her to work for an English officer. On the contrary, the three characters in that little drama: Karin, the teacher from Mehlem; Jack, the British Guards officer; and the landlady, Ingrid Pauels started then and there to plan a musical alliance. They would track down each and every former player of the Cologne and the smaller Bonn Symphony Orchestra, together with any conductors, singers, dancers or designers they could find. Depending on their success, they were determined to get an opera performance of some sort onto a stage somewhere in the area, before the month was out.

Jack decided to carry on with the plan on his own and not involve the General, until they had a production lined up. At that point, he would need to requisition a hall of some sort and seek official permission to sell tickets to German civilians.

Rosenkavalier was ruled out, owing to its large cast and the difficulties of a piece requiring three different, elaborate settings.

"*Zauberflöte!*" Karin exclaimed so suddenly out of the blue that Jack momentarily took it for a German oath, until he realized she was suggesting Mozart's opera *The Magic Flute*.

"Not Mozart, my dear," said Ingrid. "They are very difficult to do with bad singers. And we may not find enough good singers. We will be safer with Wagner. Maybe *Fliegende Holländer* or *Lohengrin*."

Jack had seen *The Flying Dutchman* once at Covent Garden and knew it entailed the building of an enormous mock-up ship on stage, complete with deck, wheel-house, masts and rigging, all of which must go up and down on the waves. Much too elaborate, he thought. Besides, he had a vague idea that he'd read somewhere – probably in a British newspaper – that the Allies had banned Wagner, decreeing that it was not to be performed anywhere under the Allied Occupation. "I'm not at all sure we'll be allowed to do a Wagner opera," he said tentatively.

"Why not?" Ingrid was glaring at him, almost defiant.

"The Allies tend to associate his work with your late-lamented – or dare I say, unlamented – Fuehrer," said Jack boldly. "I believe our people fear Wagner's music might generate an upsurge of Nazi fervour and passion – and . . . sort of . . . "

"Sort of what?" Ingrid Pauel's eyes were still on Jack, daring him to finish his sentence.

" – cause trouble."

There was an ugly silence.

Jack had received no direct orders from anyone in authority forbidding it, but he could imagine what some of those officers in B Mess would have to say. Especially the ADMS, Colonel Winter. 'Wagner? Good Lord, that stuff whips the Krauts up into a frenzy of hysteria; all that dark, brooding twilight music, and the crashing brass passages; Wotan, Alberich and Siegfried's sword and so on – all good Germanic war music – dangerous stuff.'

"I know what we shall do," said Ingrid, suddenly resolved.

"What?" Jack asked, hoping to hear her suggest a nice, safe piece of Viennese operetta, such as Lehar's *Merry Widow* or *The Land of Smiles*.

Instead, she said "*Die Walküre*, Act l, will be perfect."

"Wagner," said Jack.

"Wagner," Ingrid agreed.

Her arguments for presenting it were very sound. They were also personal. Its length would provide a whole evening of opera. Ingrid herself counted Sieglinde among her most successful roles; the cast was minimal – only three characters; Siegmund the tenor, Sieglinde, and the bass part, Hunding; and the setting, Hunding's forest dwelling, would be simple to construct with some foliage and a few pieces of wood. "I will speak with Joachim Grün and his brother, Heinrich, if they are still alive."

"Who are they?" Jack asked.

"Scenery builders in Bonn. For many years they made the *décor* for the Opera."

"I'd better go and see them. Just give me their address."

Karin wrote down the Grün brothers' last-known address on a piece of paper and handed it to Jack. It would be up to the British to acquire a theatre or hall and organize the building of sets.

For a venue, Ingrid suggested the open-air theatre in the park at Bad Godesberg, since no other halls were standing for miles around. The *Parktheater* was undamaged and the area round the stage could take three hundred people, seated on bandstand-type iron chairs.

"But where shall we find an orchestra and singers?" asked Ingrid.

"It will be a challenge," Jack said, with a tinge of doubt in his voice.

WHEN Karin came down the stairs of Frau Pauel's house the following morning before cycling off to work in Plittersdorfer-strasse, alarming sounds were to be heard coming from the drawing-room. She knew that Ingrid Pauels had already begun to brush up on her Sieglinde, accompanying herself at the piano. But this morning the piano was accompanying a deep voice, somewhere between a contralto and a tenor, pouring out *"Kühlende Labung gab mir der Quell, des Mueden Last machte er leicht . . . "* which Karin recognized at once as one of Siegmund's arias.

Anxious to see what kind of a singer Ingrid had managed to find for the part, Karin stopped by the drawing-room door, her hand poised to knock. But something made her hesitate. She was afraid of incurring her landlady's wrath by interrupting the rehearsal. But after a moment's indecision her curiosity won. Knocking gently and turning the handle at the same time, she eased the door open and peered in. As Siegmund's aria continued, Karin could just see Ingrid's head behind the lamp on the piano, bent over the keyboard. But there was no sign of a tenor in the room. Karin realized that Siegmund's words were coming from behind the piano score on the music stand, for Frau Pauels was singing the role herself.

Seeing Karin by the door, she stopped, only minimally embarrassed. "I must learn again the whole work, you see," she said with a faint smile.

"If we cannot find a Siegmund, will you sing both roles yourself?" Karin asked.

"It may be necessary," said Ingrid and crashed into the next passage with renewed vigour.

As Karin mounted her bicycle and set out for the office, she was still laughing happily to herself at the thought of it.

When she returned to her billet that evening, Ingrid was still rehearsing. Karin recognized a passage she could remember hearing for the first time in 1935, when as a child she visited Bayreuth with her parents. This time it was from the role of Sieglinde herself, and Ingrid's glorious soprano voice was filling the whole house with vibrant sound.

The *diva* rehearsed regularly over the next three weeks, working in the mornings only, for her afternoons were spent sometimes with Karin, sometimes alone, at the Bonn railway station, a scene of ever-increasing chaos and confusion.

Under its badly damaged roof, which left most of the platforms open to the sky, trains loaded with discharged German prisoners-of-war and repatriated troops were arriving every day from Hamburg, Lübeck and Kiel. Against a cacophony of whistles, escaping steam and shouting, the battered locomotives pulled in their shell-scarred rolling-stock, the carriage windows shattered and the glass replaced with sacking to keep out the draught. Every coach was jammed with members of the defeated *Wehrmacht*, some with bandaged arms or legs in splints, all red-eyed and exhausted. Some of those who had failed to get a seat had made the journey on the steps of the coaches, clinging onto the door-handles. Others were perched precariously on the roof.

One afternoon both Karin and Jack accompanied Ingrid to the station. For some hours, the three stood at one of the barriers. Ingrid's sharp, steely blue eyes searched the faces of every new arrival, for she was looking for any former musician or singer who might get off a train. Ingrid and Karin had already made some enquiries at the *Rathaus* and managed to compile a short list of four or five former players of the pre-war Bonn *Stadtorchester*, who were known to be alive and living in the vicinity. But the most urgent need was for competent singers.

Jack was expressing some pessimism on this subject when a particularly crowded train came in from the Baltic coast and Ingrid suddenly cried out in a spasm of excitement: "*Sieh mal, Unser Siegmund!*" Through the smoke and confusion Frau Pauels had spotted a face that seemed, at some distance, to be familiar. Sliding down off the roof of one of the coaches was a tall, handsome *Oberleutnant*, pale and unshaven, his uniform torn, his feet wrapped in sacking.

As the officer landed painfully on the platform and limped his way towards the exit, Ingrid's recognition was confirmed. It was Otto Maier, a promising young singer from Siegburg, whose *début* she had witnessed five years earlier in Cologne.

"*Der* Maier will have matured enough at the war to sing Siegmund," she announced, and set off to intercept the singer. Karin and Jack stood where they were, speechless, as Frau Pauels hurried off down the platform. But *Oberleutnant* Maier was anxious to get out of the crowded station and make his way on foot, rather than queueing for transport, to his mother's small house across the Rhine in Siegburg. As he made his painful way along the platform as best he could, Ingrid chased him, running at full speed and calling his name: "Herr Maier! *Oberleutnant!*"

Almost at once she came to a barrier, manned by the British Railway Transport Officer and his staff, who were directing the prisoners by loud-hailer to some army trucks and coaches waiting outside the station. Out of breath, but with her natural authority commanding instant attention, Frau Pauels shouted at the Transport officer "I want that man stopped," pointing to the rapidly receding figure of Otto Maier. Then she added, the better to convince the RTO, "He must be told that someone wishes to speak with him, urgently."

Assuming the lady to be his mother, the RTO, a man of some kindness, agreed to help.

Sooner than Frau Pauels had dared to hope, a German-speaking British sergeant of the Intelligence Corps, who was working alongside the RTO, was speaking into the Tannoy, his voice echoing through the noisy station, loud and clear. "A message for *Oberleutnant* Maier. *Oberleutnant* Maier, just come in on the train from Lübeck. The *Oberleutnant* is requested to report to the RTO on Platform 2. *Oberleutnant* Maier, please."

Ingrid could see Maier in the distance, as he pulled up sharply when he heard his name called out. Then he appeared to panic and, despite his bandaged feet, he broke into a run, dragging his kitbag along the platform beside him. She decided not to wait for any further assistance from the authorities but hurried off in hot pursuit, pounding along the platform in her high-heeled shoes.

From where they stood at the barrier, helplessly watching, Jack and Karin felt that Ingrid had the edge on Otto Maier. They were right, for the man's feet were sore and badly blistered after a march of some 120 miles from his POW cage near Rostock to Lübeck. Here he and his fellow prisoners had been released by the Red Army and later put on the train by the British authorities and repatriated to the Rhine area.

Otto Maier was moving fast now, for he had heard the summons over the loud hailer and, as a recent guest of the

Russians, feared he was wanted for some trumped-up crime, for which he would be arrested and shot.

Jack decided he owed it to Ingrid to join in the chase, so he raced off, leaving Karin to follow.

Ingrid finally caught up with Maier in the street outside the station and seconds later Jack and Karin arrived on the scene, in time to hear Maier protesting "I am innocent, I have done nothing; I have been freed."

"I am Ingrid Pauels of the Cologne Opera House, Herr *Oberleutnant*," came the reply.

Maier's look of relief was immense. "You must understand, *gnädige Frau*," he said, "that I have been a prisoner of the Soviet Army for seven months. I ran because I believed you to be a female police agent, who would have me arrested and shot for some imagined crime. With the Russians, you can never be sure."

"I'm so sorry we frightened you," said Ingrid. "But if you are Otto Maier, the tenor, as I suspect you are, I have to tell you that we hope you will sing Siegmund to my Sieglinde in two weeks' time in Bad Godesberg."

"Shall I?" Maier looked stunned.

"The British Military will allow this. Here is Major Hamilton of the Grenadier Guards. Now, before you go home, you will come with me to my house in Mehlem, where you will get a bath and some clean clothes and we shall discuss rehearsals. *Gut*?"

"*Grossartig*," said Maier, with an engaging grin.

48

Chapter 3

OVER the next three weeks the Entertainments Office buzzed with activity. Jack, Karin, Corporal Bridges and Frau Pauels, who had moved herself in as an unofficial member of the Welfare Staff, all worked round the clock, sometimes staying until nine or ten in the evening when Jack would send Corporal Bridges over to the Mess for coffee and rolls.

One morning Ingrid Pauels arrived at the office in a state of excitement. "I have news of Dr Heuss," she proclaimed. "He is alive but very old. He is in the mountains. Like Hunding."

"What mountains?" Jack asked.

"Across the river, beyond Königswinter, together with his sister. They are living in a small villa near Karlsdorf. I shall take my bicycle over on the ferry and ride up there and beg him to sing Hunding for us."

Jack offered to accompany Ingrid but she declined. "It will be a slow journey, a man must pull the ferry across by an old rusty chain."

"Couldn't it take my Jeep?"

"A motor car would send it straight to the bottom of the

river, my dear. Besides, I will better approach Julius alone. He would be nervous and suspicious of you."

"Me?" Jack was quite offended, seeing himself as a friendly ex-enemy, if ever there was one.

But Ingrid was adamant. "If I cannot persuade the old fellow to come out of retirement and sing for us, nobody can."

The next morning she pedalled, or rather wobbled, off to the Königswinter ferry, and carried her cycle aboard. A strong young woman in knee-breeches took the money, and soon Ingrid was on her way slowly and steadily across the Rhine while the same young woman hauled on the steel hawser, which was attached to a capstan on the opposite bank.

"I AM by many years too old to sing," protested Dr Julius Heuss. "I am sixty eight."

But Frau Pauels wouldn't have it. "*Schofel*, Julius," she retorted. "You have sung the role dozens of times and you will sing it again."

"I could never learn it again."

"Of course you could, foolish man. You told me yourself, when I first joined the Cologne Opera, that once you have sung a role, you never forget it."

Ingrid was standing, slightly out of breath and holding the handlebars of her bicycle, close to the chicken-run outside the former *Intendant*'s shabby little chalet on the side of a hill. She was facing the ageing Doctor of Music and his sister, Margharete, who looked very frail and coughed a good deal, as she clutched her shawl around her emaciated shoulders. Heuss, on the contrary, looked relatively healthy. Apart from an occasional air raid on Cologne, the war had hardly touched his life in the peace and quiet of his widowed sister's mountain retreat. The thick, flowing grey hair, which Ingrid remembered so well, had turned to silvery white and he was much thinner and a little more bent, but his eyes still had the old sparkle and, for a man of sixty-eight, his voice was strong.

"If I agree to sing with you and Otto Maier," said Heuss, "who will conduct?"

A silence ensued, during which the poultry clucked and scratched about in the run and a scrap broke out between two cocks. Margharete sloshed at the warring birds with her shawl. Then Dr Heuss repeated his question.

"So far," Ingrid admitted hesitantly, "we have no conductor. I must be honest."

"No conductor?"

"Not yet."

"*So.* Are we to give the musicians the beat ourselves from the stage?"

Julius was almost sneering now. Ingrid feared that he would jump at any excuse not to sing Hunding, in case a poor performance destroyed his reputation.

"It is not amusing, Julius."

"Well?"

"This afternoon goes my dear English major – "

Heuss wagged a finger of mock disapproval at her, accompanied by a naughty smirk. "Ingrid, my dear . . . "

She was irritated by this, but could not afford to lose her only possible bass. "There is a certain *Gefreiter* Kommer, we have heard of in Düsseldorf," she said. "The man has just been repatriated from an English prisoner-of-war camp. Nobody knows him, but he claims to have been a reserve conductor for the Düsseldorf Opera before the war."

"How can you be sure?"

"Major Hamilton will question him closely and examine old opera house programmes, which have been found in the city records."

'*So,*' was all Heuss would say, and with that Ingrid had to be content, knowing she would have to confirm the appointment of a suitable conductor before Heuss would commit himself to singing.

ABOUT the time that Ingrid was free-wheeling back towards the ferry, Jack was driving up to the entrance of the *Rathaus* in Düsseldorf to check on *Gefreiter* Kommer.

There, to his disappointment, he found that *Gefreiter* Kommer had conducted nothing more than a string quartet at his daughter's school, and also that he was on a list of people wanted for questioning about atrocities committed by his unit in Poland.

"*Aber das is wunderschön,*" Ingrid declared with bitter sarcasm, after Jack had delivered the bad news. "We have a lame tenor and a not so young soprano, who is out of practice, but no bass and no conductor."

"Then we must either cancel or postpone," said Jack, who was beginning to tire of the whole business.

But Karin looked up at him with tears of disappointment in her eyes, and he put his arm consolingly round her shoulder. "It's OK, Karin; we'll solve it, somehow."

Privately, Jack could not see a solution to the problem. Perhaps it hadn't been such a good idea after all. The German community was far too disorganized and punch-drunk from the bombing and fighting around Cologne to think about opera performances. It was enough of a struggle for them to get food and cigarettes and repair the damaged walls and roofs of their dwellings.

But Ingrid was not to be thwarted. "Julius was a fine conductor, in his time," she said. "He could handle an orchestra now, if we can collect one together in time."

After a short discussion, it was decided to go ahead on the assumption that Dr Heuss would conduct and a good bass would one day step off one of those crowded trains steaming into Bonn.

Meanwhile, there was much to be done.

Tickets and posters were produced at a resuscitated printing works, recently requisitioned by the Military at Gummersbach. The posters were circulated to all units for display in their areas. Posters were also stuck up in German shops and cafés, on walls and telegraph poles and on the wreckage of bombed buildings.

The small squad of four volunteer bill-stickers detailed by Corporal Bridges for this task reported mixed reactions from the troops and civilians. Some of the military personnel saw the whole thing as a highbrow attempt by the top brass to force culture on them, when they'd have preferred a visit from Max Miller or Tommy Handley. Others asked eagerly where they could book tickets. The German civilians, for the most part, stared vacantly at the posters, suspecting some form of English propaganda. The occupying forces, they decided, were trying to ensure the final humiliation of the German people by indicating that their ex-enemies would exercise complete control over their opera as well as their daily lives.

All the same, a number of Germans called at the Entertainments Office in Plittersdorferstrasse to buy tickets.

One poster, announcing the great event, was stuck onto the burnt-out Citröen on the road to Mehlem. Jack reflected that an advertisement for a British production of a German opera on a wrecked French car in which three Germans died from a British rocket-attack while escaping from the Americans symbolized the crying need of mankind for an end to war and for lasting peace.

THE morning of July 16th came, leaving only seven days before the advertised performance; and still no bass. Jack realized they now faced a serious crisis. Ingrid and Maier were rehearsing, and posters had gone out far and wide, announcing Act 1 of Wagner's *The Valkyries*, but there was nobody to sing Hunding.

"I suppose I could try and find an operatic bass among our own troops; maybe the Welsh Guards," Jack said gloomily, "but it's not very likely. Besides, it would spoil the whole thing to have some hefty Welshman bawling out the stuff in English with you and Otto Maier singing in German."

"It would be better than no opera," said Ingrid sharply.

"I agree," said Karin.

But Jack stood firm, insisting on a wholly German cast or no performance. So the following day they decided, with heavy hearts, to scrap the opera and announce in its place a recital of arias from Wagner's operas to be given by the soprano Ingrid Pauels and, provided he was willing, the tenor Otto Maier.

The plan was to complete the morning's rehearsal before breaking the sad news to Maier, the orchestra and the stage crew.

On the stroke of twelve, midday, during a short break for notes, a pale, middle-aged man in dark glasses limped into the back of the hall. Ingrid was about to make her announcement to the assembled company when the newcomer hobbled onto the stage with the aid of a stick, and asked who was in charge.

"I am," said Ingrid, and then quickly added "and Major Hamilton from the British Military Headquarters."

Jack looked coldly at the stranger, resenting the interruption. But something in the man's manner and bearing merited attention. "Anything we can do for you, Sir?" he asked.

"My name is Emmerich Karl," said the new arrival, firmly. There was a low murmur from some members of the orchestra, as they recognized the newcomer. "I have been discharged from the German *Kriegsmarine* with a wound to my left leg, sustained in a sea battle off Crete." Then, almost casually, he continued, "As the former conductor of the Bonn Symphony Orchestra, I am ready to conduct your performance of *Die Walküre*, Act I on the 23rd of this month."

After staring at the newcomer with breathless incredulity for almost half a minute, Ingrid Pauels fell on Karl's neck and wept.

"*Gott sei Dank*!" she cried, "I did not recognize you. We are saved!"

Jack looked at Karin, who was beaming all over her lovely face with joy and relief.

The problem appeared to be solved.

A WEEK later, shortly after eight o'clock in the evening, the orchestra reached the crashing climax of *The Valkyries'* noisy overture. While it depicted a great storm with thunder and flashes of lightning, Jack's hand stole out to grasp Karin's clenched knuckles. Her hand was shaking, but not with cold, for it was a warm night. As they sat together on their hard iron seats under the night sky, Jack and Karin both felt sick with nerves. A lot was at stake that night.

Feeling for a fleeting moment the warmth of Karin's thigh through her thin summer dress, Jack prized open her hand, finger by finger, until their palms touched and their hands locked passionately together.

Above them strong arc lamps, lashed to the trees, boosted the lighting on the stage, their beams catching and illuminating leafy branches that hung in their way.

Around them on the park seats, some lit by pools of light, others fading into shadowy darkness, sat rows of troops in battledress and members of the shabby, emaciated civilian population. The German people were listening attentively but with mixed feelings, as the first notes of Wagner to be played publicly in Germany since the Fuehrer's death, echoed round Bad Godesberg's amphitheatre in the warm night air.

The great orchestral storm finally died down and the curtain of the *Parktheater* rose, to reveal Hunding's dwelling. Siegmund staggered onto the stage, leant exhausted against the door of Hunding's hut in the forest, then entered and sank onto a bearskin rug on the rough floor. The tenor, Otto Maier, looked magnificent in spite of his makeshift costume, which was an Army blanket from the Quartermaster's stores with holes cut in it for his head and arms and a piece of cord round his waist.

For a while the orchestra played the Siegmund 'motif', a melancholy tune on the basses and 'cellos with an accompanying figure on the horns, which seemed to emphasize Siegmund's weariness. As Otto Maier began to sing his first aria, 'Whose hearth this may be, here I must rest me', Karin and Jack squeezed hands even harder and held their breath with tension. Otto was in fine voice and his high notes soared into the starlit sky above the *Parktheater*.

The fact that his Sieglinde, when she entered to find him in the hut, looked old enough to be his mother, mattered not at all to the spectators: for those who were unversed in the ways of Grand Opera the identity of the three characters on stage was uncertain, and did not interfere with their enjoyment of the spectacle and the singing; and for the connoisseurs, Ingrid Pauels was still a big name in the Rhineland, while such an age differential between lovers on the opera stage was common-place. Ingrid Pauels sang the lovely Sympathy motif with firm, warm notes, so gloriously and sensuously expressive that Jack found himself wishing he'd heard her sing in her prime.

With a menacing staccato little march figure on the tubas came the entrance of Hunding. What was, perhaps, most remarkable was his extreme age, but old Heuss looked imposing enough, and sang the role with remarkable attack and gusto, to the delight of the people of Bad Godesberg and their conquerors.

After two hours came the great climax when Siegmund finally grasped the sword and drew it from the ash-tree, brandishing it in the air; and seizing Sieglinde with an ecstatic reprise of the glorious love motif 'Oh, wondrous vision, rapturous woman', carried her off, as the threadbare, dusty curtain of the *Parktheater* fell on Act I.

There was a second of stunned silence, then a great storm of applause, and hearty cheering that emanated mostly from the healthy lungs of British soldiers, while the hands of the frail, elderly Germans in the audience were busy brushing tears of emotion from their eyes.

As Jack and Karin hurried backstage to congratulate the cast, the orchestra and stage crew, Jack heard a guardsman say to his companion, "Smashing singing. My Mum and Dad would have enjoyed that lot", and that remark alone made him feel that as an exercise in providing culture for the Allied Forces the evening had been worthwhile.

Backstage, Jack had arranged for soup, bread rolls and half a dozen cigarettes to be handed out to each musician. Satisfied that Corporal Bridges had enough to go round, he and Karin then went ahead in the Jeep to Ingrid's house to put on ice the bottle of champagne that Jack had provided from the Officers' Mess and to prepare some food from the same source.

Half an hour later Ingrid arrived, flushed with triumph, accompanied by Otto Maier, Dr Heuss and Emmerich Karl. Jack noticed how Karin's eyes shone with excitement that evening, and he watched her while she laid a clean lace cloth on Ingrid's sitting-room table and served the cold collation of bread and cheese, cold ham and salami, garlic sausage and fruit. This was washed down with four bottles of Möet et Chandon '37, which had originally been looted from France by the German army but later recaptured from a large cellar in Brussels by the Grenadier Guards.

It was, Jack felt, a memorable evening: an act of Wagner opera had been performed once more in Wagner's homeland, as a joint production by the defeated Germans and the conquering British, in an atmosphere of friendly reconciliation.

As the wine flowed, Ingrid became sentimental and tearful, at one point gazing lingeringly at her husband's photograph on the piano. Jack saw her take Karin's hand, murmuring under her breath, "If only Werner could be here . . . "

Karin gave her a little hug. "You must keep hoping and praying, then perhaps he will come back safe to you."

Jack felt that such a warm gesture of concern on Karin's part further demonstrated the reconciling power of music, considering how harshly Frau Pauels had treated Karin a few weeks earlier.

Ingrid, realizing that Jack had overheard Karin's comforting words, explained, "My husband is missing since three months and there is no news. His regiment was fighting in the Netherlands."

It was on the tip of Jack's tongue to say 'So was mine', but thought this might be tactless. Instead, he said "I'm sorry. The uncertainty must be very hard to bear."

Presently there were speeches, one made by Emmerich Karl, who thanked Jack and the British "*militärische Herrschaften*" for making the evening possible. Old Heuss thanked Ingrid, Karin and Jack for persuading him to sing Hunding, "with one foot," as he put it, "in my tomb already."

Later, while Heuss, Karin, Ingrid and Emmerich Karl became involved in a deep and passionate discussion about the symphonies of Gustav Mahler, Jack found himself asking Otto Maier, soldier to soldier, what it had been like to serve on the Russian front.

Otto described the icy winter of 1944, when his unit was heavily shelled by Soviet artillery around Kursk for five days on end. He spoke quite casually about the whole incident. When Jack asked him if the Soviet gunners were any good, Otto smiled and said "Not very accurate. They send their shells all over the place and hope they will hit something. Their soldiers are dirty and do not respect their officers."

Jack said "So I've heard. And some of them are orientals, are they not?"

"They come from many parts of the Soviet Empire," said Otto, "and they speak many different languages. Also, they are very brutal, you know. If a man shows fear in the battle, they shoot him through the head and leave his body to the wolves."

"Really!" said Jack, while the thought came to him that he ought not to be snaking the Russkis to a German. 'If the Jerries hadn't siphoned off hundreds of Divisions to smash Stalin,' he told himself, 'I wouldn't bloody well be here, sipping champagne at a Kraut party in Bonn as a victorious Briton.' Now Otto was saying "When they capture me and my troop with a patrol in the forest, the soldiers tell us at first that they will execute us. But the Russian officer say we must be questioned for information, so we were allowed to live."

Jack's moment of curiosity had passed. He wasn't keen to go on talking about the war, having had his fill of fighting and being shot at and shelled; enough to last him a lifetime. It was more agreeable to think of Karin, who was looking adorable tonight. At that moment, she was sitting curled up on the floor, her hair shining in the lamplight, and as she reached out for the plate of cold meat to pass it round, one ribbon-thin shoulder strap slid temptingly off a shoulder. Jack excused himself from Otto and moved over to join the others, helping himself to another glass of champagne on the way.

Somewhere around midnight, after Karin had been persuaded by Ingrid to sing '*Erlkönig*' for the guests in a charming, soft voice, accompanied at the piano by Emmerich Karl, the party broke up.

An old taxi-driver friend of Herr Karl, who had brought them all to Godesberg for the concert and out to Ingrid's house in Mehlem for supper, came to collect the three men and deliver them to their respective homes. Dr Heuss was anxious not to be too late, as his old sister who kept house for him was not well, suffering from a bad chest. Maier had a mother waiting up for him in Siegburg and Emmerich Karl was quite ready for his bed, after a strenuous and tense evening.

After the taxi had driven away into the night, Ingrid went upstairs to her room, also exhausted after the performance. Before she went, she invited Jack to stay on in the sitting-room downstairs with Karin for a while longer. Jack had the impression that Frau Pauels now approved of his friendship with Karin and might even be cherishing hopes of seeing a romance blossom under her roof between her girl lodger and the English officer.

Jack made sure the door was firmly closed and turned off the lamp on the piano.

"I feel so happy tonight," Karin said quietly.

He took her hand, pulling her down to sit beside him on the sofa. "Me too," he said.

Karin's head fell against his shoulder. "People are singing again and music is coming back to shut out the sound of guns and bombing."

"I know," said Jack, his voice shaking a little. He had started to stroke the back of her neck and meeting no resistance, he now began slowly to unzip the back of her wine-coloured satin dress so that his trembling hand could move down her warm, bare back until it reached the strap of her brassière, releasing the clip with ease and proceeding slowly down her spine. This caused her to breathe more deeply and stiffen a little, clutching Jack's free hand and squeezing it, until her nails began to dig into his flesh.

Karin murmured in German "*Oh, mein Schatz, mein Lieb . . . . küss mich . . .*"

Jack turned her slowly to him, pressing his lips to her moist, open mouth and lowering her gently onto the cushions of the sofa, sliding her dress off her shoulders, until she was naked to the waist. The nipples of her firm, young breasts betrayed her excitement, as Jack kissed them too.

It was then that Jack lost control, became a victim of the long weeks in battle when there had been no time to think about girls, or anything except the need to keep his head down and survive. Now the sudden release of his warm, moist, pent-up desire flooded over him, and with it, a realization that perhaps what had happened was for the best. Karin should not know that her young British officer had reached the climax of his yearning for her already, so that a safety valve had forestalled any further physical exchange between them.

Karin felt him relax.

"I ought to get back to my billet," he said. "It's getting on for one."

"Don't go yet. Stay with me a little longer, please."

"I mustn't. We'll see each other tomorrow, in the office."

Jack rose carefully from the sofa, turning away from Karin, so that she would not notice the damp patch on his uniform close to his loins. "Stay where you are, Karin. I'll let myself out."

"Please kiss me once more before you go," Karin murmured, still on her back in a state of semi-naked abandon. Jack bent down and kissed her once more on her soft lips, sliding his tongue into her eager mouth. Hungrily she grabbed him by the neck and held firm for a while.

"I let you go now," she said finally, and a moment later Jack slipped away. As he closed the front door soundlessly behind him and went out into the night, he noticed that a light was still on in Frau Pauels' room upstairs.

He jumped into his Jeep and drove off back to his billet, feeling just a bit ashamed of himself, but far more excited by the thought of a continuing romance with his Rhinemaiden.

"I MUST say, considering the buggers had to be given a bowl of soup and a packet of fags to get them going, I thought those Kraut singers and the orchestra produced a splendid sound last night."

Jack winced, as Colonel Winter thus pronounced judgement on the First Act of *The Valkyries*, which he and a handful of officers from B Mess had been persuaded to attend for the good, as Jack put it, of their souls.

"Never cared much for old Wagner," said young Peter Franks. A subaltern in the Coldstream with an MC recently won in the Reichswald, he had now become the Coal Officer to the Division, responsible for allocating fairly what fuel there was, between the Allied Forces and the vanquished German population.

"But I agree with the ADMS. Last night was pretty good stuff. And didn't go on too long."

"Wagner's OK in small doses, eh?" said Jack, helping himself to scrambled eggs from the sideboard.

"Absolutely," said Franks, grabbing a piece of toast before sitting down. "Girl I used to take out in London before the war, gorgeous creature called Penelope, was potty about the opera. Been at a finishing school in Florence, where they took the girls every other week to the Scala in Milan. She got a taste for it there. So I bought tickets for some Wagner thing at Covent Garden one summer evening – *Götterdammerung* – only to find the damned thing started at five-thirty in the afternoon and didn't finish until half-past ten at night."

"Did you see it through?" asked Jack with a faint smile.

"Had to, old boy. Couldn't waste the tickets. We had high tea at Lyons Corner House in the Strand before it and supper at the Savoy Grill afterwards. Bloody expensive evening, but it cooled Penelope's ardour for the opera. Next time I took her to a show we saw *Careless Rapture*, Ivor Novello's thing. That was an improvement. At least you could hum the tunes."

"Wagner wrote good tunes," Jack remarked, spreading the marmalade thick on his toast.

"Well," said Peter, "sort of."

"Are you coming to the Rhineland Symphony Orchestra's concert on the 15th?"

"Might. Where is it?"

"We've managed to get a big lecture hall in the Bonn University precincts," Jack told him.

"What are they playing?" It was David Levy of the Ordnance Corps who now intervened from the far end of the table.

Jack had the information at his finger tips, for he had spent most of the previous day with Karin, getting out the leaflets for distribution. The programme was to begin with the *Meistersinger* overture, followed by the ever-popular Grieg Piano Concerto, with a soloist called Willy Pohl. "He's an anti-Nazi Luftwaffe pilot, who's been on the run from the Gestapo. We found him working as a waiter in the Bergischerhof Hotel."

"Did you really?"

Jack nodded. "We did. The concert will finish with the Tchaikovsky No. 5."

"I thought it was the Cologne Orchestra we had last night."

"No," Jack corrected him. "Before the war there were two orchestras in this area, the Bonn and the Cologne, but they're now both so decimated and scattered that Dr Heuss, Ingrid Pauels and I have decided to merge them for the time being into what we've christened the Rhineland Symphony – that is until enough players can be found to re-establish both."

"Ingrid Pauels? Is that your Kraut girl in the Entertainments Office?"

"No," Jack replied, bristling at Colonel Winter's condescending tone. "Ingrid Pauels is the very distinguished, international soprano, who sang Sieglinde last night. Her name was quite prominent in the programme."

"Oh. Didn't notice."

"Frau Pauels is helping me to collect together the orchestras and singers and arrange the programmes."

"I see."

A pause and then Jack added, "The Kraut girl in my office, as you call her, is Fraülein Karin Freidl, daughter of a *Landrat* in Coblenz, who lodges with Frau Pauels and acts as my secretary and interpreter."

"Ah," said Colonel Winter.

"She is officially on the strength and payroll of the Divisional Welfare Services and extremely useful to me in my job."

"Good show," was all Winter could think of to say, as he returned to his coffee and the latest issue of the *Lancet*, sent out to him by his wife.

THROUGHOUT August the musical evenings continued unabated. A large modern building on the banks of the Rhine between Bonn and Godesberg, formerly an institute of some sort, had now been taken over by the Education Department and rechristened the Divisional College. Here, the retraining of army personnel in civilian skills took place by day in the many big rooms and smaller lecture rooms. At night the large assembly hall, which had a fine stage at one end of it, became the official theatre for the Division. In it Jack and his staff could mount and stage variety shows, plays, operas and concerts for the Divisional Headquarters personnel, using the annexe as a rehearsal room and as a base whence the productions could go out on tour around the various outlying units. Most of the scattered battalions by now had their own local theatres. Some were properly equipped small town playhouses and some were village assembly halls and schools. All were eager to play host to the opera productions and the symphony concerts. Their own unit transport, 3-ton and 15-cwt lorries, would be sent over to Bonn or Godesberg to collect the singers and musicians, who would get bumped about over the rough roads, as they sprawled in the back of the trucks, clutching their precious instruments. Over the last weeks quite a number of newly demobilized musicians had reported to Jack's office, as rumour spread round the Cologne area of orchestras reforming and concerts and opera productions being mounted.

The success of Act 1 of *The Valkyries* in Bad Godesberg had, as Jack told Ingrid, made their point, and established a taste for German music among many of the bored British troops who had no previous knowledge of such matters; the genuine music-lovers from all ranks of the Division and its ancillary services were now booking their tickets regularly for every musical event that was announced in the *News Guardian*.

In late September the Cologne Symphony included in one of its concerts Beethoven's Piano Concerto No. 1, with Willy Pohl as the soloist. The weather was colder than usual that night; winter was approaching. Before the concert started the long queue of musicians, clutching their instruments in one hand and a bowl of soup in the other, found themselves once again able to minimize the mild indignity of their situation with a sense of gratitude, for their chosen profession was entitling them to warming sustenance, free cigarettes and a chance to make music. And this was at a time when much of their country was still flattened and ravaged by war, food was scarce and the entire population was still smarting under its humiliating defeat. What faint hopes of a future there might be for the German people seemed to that emaciated, downcast company of players to lie in the revival of music, the international language that knows no frontiers. Karin had reminded Jack earlier in the day that, with the No. 1 Piano Concerto, for the first time since the war ended musicians of the Rhine area would be actually playing Beethoven in the composer's own birthplace. This was pointed out to the audience by Willy Pohl when he came on for his solo performance, and the announcement raised a warm round of applause.

It was on the Sunday following the concert that Jack and Karin embarked for the first time on a serious conversation about their relationship. Jack had begun to realize that his feelings for the German girl were slowly changing from superficial bodily desire to a deep fondness for her, for her way of talking, her humour, her love of music and for the warm glow of happiness he felt in her company, which was something he had never experienced before.

They walked hand-in-hand that Sunday afternoon, strolling along a path high in the mountains and looking down on the broad curves of the Rhine below. Already a few barges, so familiar in pre-war days, were beginning to reappear on the river, loaded with timber, coal, cattle and scrap iron, as day by day the drained life-blood of Germany began slowly to flow again through the veins of the shattered nation.

Presently Karin sat down on a grassy slope to look across the river towards the thick woods beyond. The wind caught her golden hair and blew it away from her lovely high forehead, enhancing the sparkle of her clear pale blue eyes, and as Jack looked at her, he thought she was the most beautiful girl he'd ever known. He remembered the *débutantes* he used to dance with at smart balls in London during the thirties; all those sweet, pale, rather frightened nineteen-year-olds of titled families and limited conversation; and thought they could not compare to her. 'Is it because Karin's foreign?' he wondered. Foreign girls always had it over English ones: there was the charm of a foreign accent, the unfamiliar way of speech, the unexpected reactions and opinions, the belief of most Englishmen in the superior capacity for passion of foreign women. 'Perhaps it's because she's German. A *Boche*, a Hun, a Kraut. Is there, perhaps, some deep, masochistic fascination with "the enemy", in coming close to and achieving intimate terms with, the people against whom you've been waging war, trying to exterminate?' Jack remembered Montgomery addressing the officers and men of 30 Corps in an aerodrome hangar near Driffield on the Yorkshire Wolds in early 1944, not long before D-Day. They'd all been 'bussed over from far and wide to hear the Commander-in-Chief, centre-stage on a rostrum wearing his badge-covered beret like a popular music-hall star, telling them to go out there and kill Germans. "That's what we're all training for, to go over there and kill Germans," he'd proclaimed in his high-pitched staccato voice with his mis-pronounced R's. It had somehow made him sound like a prefect giving the chaps in the Upper Fifth a pep talk. "Kill Germans."

'Well, it's over now. And I have no wish to kill this German, nor to stick a bayonet in this gorgeous girl sitting by me on a grassy bank, this Rhinemaiden, Karin . . . I want to undress her and make love to her, that's what I want.'

Karin must have been reading his mind, for suddenly, out of the blue, she said "Soon I will leave Frau Pauels and find a room somewhere else."

"Do you mean she's throwing you out?"

Jack looked shocked but Karin laughed. "No," she said, "it was only arranged for a short while. She does not wish always to be a landlady. And I will enjoy to have a place by myself."

"Yes." Jack could now anticipate uninterrupted evenings

with Karin away from the chaperone that Ingrid Pauels had become, and the thought stirred him.

"If I can find a room somewhere in Godesberg," Karin added, and Jack was immediately trying hard to remember the name of the billeting officer at Div.HQ, who had requisitioned whole streets of Bad Godesberg and Bonn to house the Divisional Headquarters. He would surely find a billet somewhere for the DADAWS's German secretary.

On the way down the mountain path Karin suddenly stopped, took Jack's hand and squeezed it hard, pressing it to her soft cheeks. Then she kissed his knuckles and, as she did so, he experienced a strange tingling excitement that almost knocked the breath out of him, like an electric shock.

"Oh, *mein lieber Freund*, I am so happy," was all she said, but with such a wealth of feeling that Jack experienced a strange elation, so strong that it almost choked him. Soon their mouths were locked together and his hands encircled her warm, bare neck. He knew she must be able to feel the extent of his excitement, for she was wearing only a thin cotton dress and precious little underneath.

When they finally drew apart, Jack could see down the slope to the river bank where they had first met, dripping wet, in the June sunshine. And there was the midstream island, where he had caught his first glimpse of the willowy blonde and her bare, wounded arm, as she swam across from the opposite bank, pursued by himself, a lecherous young captain in the Grenadier Guards.

His thoughts turned into words, as he murmured to Karin "It's been more than three months".

"Almost four, *Liebchen*," she whispered, as they walked on down the path.

AS they made their way hand-in-hand towards the river below, Jack found himself wondering if he might be falling in love, for the first time in his life. He thought again of those pale *débutantes*, and of an earlier shipboard romance, born of warm, starry nights on the boat-deck, that had been ultimately destroyed by the down-to-earth-with-a-bump return home to port. He had experienced that one summer when he was sixteen, and had been sent across to Canada alone during the school holidays to spend three weeks with an aunt in Montreal. On the voyage home in *The Empress of Britain* Jack had met a girl called Sheila Wapshott, also returning from a visit to relatives, in Vancouver. They'd danced together, had their meals together, and swum in the ship's pool. They'd played games and walked on deck and, on the last night at sea, attended the Fancy Dress Ball together. Convinced they were deeply in love, Jack and Sheila, whose family lived in Walthamstow, had parted tearfully at the gang-plank, but arranged to meet for tea in London a fortnight later. At first Jack couldn't think of a rendezvous. All sorts of places came to mind: the Swan and Edgar corner of Piccadilly Circus, outside the Knightsbridge tube station; the Peter Pan statue in Kensington Gardens. Finally he decided an indoor spot would be safer, in case of rain, and plumped for the Palm Lounge at the Piccadilly Hotel at 4 p.m. Then had come the disillusion, beyond the gang- plank, of that damp, misty morning in Southampton, all grey sky and cranes and wet, slate roofs; and a fortnight later, the meeting in London.

When he arrived at the hotel he found Sheila waiting for him at a corner table, got up in a hideous beige coat and a ridiculous little hat with a piece of tulle on it. Immediately she struck him as desperately plain and dull, and he wondered what on earth he had seen in her. Conversation was painfully forced as they both tried to get through the set tea that Jack ordered. Long silences were punctuated by inane remarks such as "Do you remember those people called Spooner on board, with that ghastly child?" "Yes." Pause. "I enjoyed the deck quoits, didn't you?" "Yes, I did." "The Purser was quite a decent sort of chap, wasn't he?" "Yes." Then Jack nodded towards the chocolate éclair Miss Wapshott was eating, as he attacked his own. "Is yours nice?"

"Yes, mine's very nice. Is yours?"

"Yes, thank you."

The string orchestra, which had been playing Chopin, began to play excerpts from *The Maid of the Mountains*. Sheila wiped some cream from her mouth and said "That's my Dad's favourite tune."

Soon after Jack had paid the bill for tea they parted in the street outside, where Jack, with ill-concealed relief, saw Sheila Wapshott onto a no.19 'bus.

They had never met or communicated again.

KARIN interrupted his thoughts by squeezing his hand again and saying accusingly "You are so quiet, *Liebling*."

Jack snapped out of his reverie.

"Sorry, just thinking my own thoughts. A bit far away."

But he knew that his own thoughts were simply that this was no shipboard romance, no Sheila Wapshott from Walthamstow.

It had happened to him at last, what he had read about in books and seen in films. He had fallen in love.

Chapter 4

AT eleven o'clock on the following morning Jack held his routine Monday meeting in the Entertainments Office, at which he, Ingrid, Karin, Dr Heuss and the four orchestral conductors in the Guards Divisional area met to discuss policy, dates for concerts and opera performances, and above all, to solve the vexed question of scores and orchestral parts.

Jack had by now four orchestras under his control: the Cologne – now reinstated in its own right – the Bonn, the Düsseldorf, and the Aachen. There was no longer a Rhineland Symphony Orchestra, for enough players had been found and instruments for them to play to enable four separate orchestras to operate in the zone. The music libraries of these orchestras had been virtually wiped out in the recent bombing and as scores and band parts were hard to come by, Jack had suggested a sharing scheme.

Emmerich Karl had a number of scores in a cupboard at his house near Gummersbach and Hans Wand of the Aachen had also been able to lay his hands on most of the Beethoven symphonies and piano concertos plus some Brahms, Bruckner, two of the Tchaikovsky symphonies, among other bits and pieces. The new conductor for the Cologne, Bruno Eichmann, could offer absolutely nothing, for the Cologne Opera library had been totally destroyed by RAF incendiaries.

Thus Eichmann would borrow the *Fidelio* score from Aachen for a performance in the new Divisional College Theatre on October 7th; Bonn would give a concert on the 9th using its own Beethoven No. 5 plus Max Bruch's Concerto in G Minor for Violin and Orchestra, borrowed with a recently-repatriated U-Boat crewman as violin soloist from Düsseldorf; and, to open with, the ever popular *Freischütz* overture of Weber, of which the leader of the Düsseldorf happened to have discovered a copy, hidden with a quantity of hoarded food in his cellar.

Many of the scores had been rescued, half charred, from burning buildings, and put together again in haste. Jack was told that a performance of Mahler's 3rd, for the Household Cavalry over at Brühl, had to be stopped in mid-phrase, because when the woodwind players turned over their pages halfway through the second movement they found themselves playing the closing bars of *Lohengrin*.

The following day Jack and Corporal Bridges dashed about the area in the Jeep, bouncing and bumping through the wreckage and rubble of Cologne and Aachen, to collect and re-distribute the vital orchestral parts in time for various rehearsals. A good week's music seemed to be promised for that second week in October, and it was with a feeling of some satisfaction and pride that Jack Hamilton returned on Tuesday evening from his travels, to enjoy a pink gin in the Mess.

On his way into the ante-room he noticed a buff envelope bearing his name on the message board inside the door. It was a memo. from the new GSO1 at Divisional HQ. Lieut-Colonel Andrew Marriott, a Scots Guardsman, had recently taken over from Michael Brand, the officer to whom Jack, on his arrival at Godesberg from his Battalion in June, had first reported. That affable, gentle Grenadier, who had been G1 from the

Normandy landings to the Cease Fire had departed a week or two back, to take up a post at HQ London District.

Jack had never met Andrew Marriott but, having heard no ill of him from the few officers he knew in A Mess, Divisional HQ, he hoped his sterling work as DADAWS would be appreciated.

'Keep up the good work,' Jack could hear the G1 say. 'The General believes the morale of the troops out here is paramount and we need as many good shows as possible to keep them amused and out of mischief, what?'

It was with a confident swagger that Jack Hamilton presented himself the following morning to the GSO1's office.

ANDREW MARRIOTT turned from the window of his vast, ornate office, complete with period gilt furniture and an enormous chandelier, as Jack entered and saluted. To his surprise Marriott did not say 'Sit down, Hamilton. I just wanted to congratulate you on the splendid job you're doing.' That line did not come. Instead, the Colonel sat down himself at his huge French Empire desk. 'Well,' Jack thought, 'I don't mind receiving my congratulations standing up, if that's the way the chap wants it. Rather bad manners though.'

"I expect you can guess why I've sent for you?" Marriott was speaking to him without looking up from his blotter.

"No, I'm afraid I can't."

After a short silence, while he signed a memo., Marriott went on "I think you've got to be very careful with this German girl working in your office."

"Careful? What does that mean?"

"For one thing, there's a certain amount of talk around the Division. I know you employ her as an interpreter; there's nothing wrong with that. But there is a rule, as you well know, about fraternization. We just don't want the troops being set a bad example by the officers."

Jack choked back his anger, his face flushed, his voice

shaking. "How in God's name can I employ a girl in my office and never speak to her?"

"Don't be a bloody fool, Hamilton, you know damn well what I mean! It's none of my business what you do with your spare time out here, but I have to say it might be more in keeping with your appointment as Major in charge of Welfare to this Division, if you spent a little less of it in the company of your Teuton secretary outside office hours."

"What makes you think . . . " Jack faltered, knowing that he must have been shopped by someone, probably one of the officers in B Mess, and that he hadn't a leg to stand on.

"If you encourage these Krauts, they'll only take advantage, get arrogant and truculent like the German POWs; start asking favours; you know what I'm trying to say."

Jack paused, forced by a half-truth into a defensive position. "Fraülein Freidl is an excellent interpreter and enormously useful," he said, trying to control his wavering voice. "She speaks good English, types out all sorts of lists and programmes for me and announcements of shows for the troops and, quite frankly, Corporal Bridges and I couldn't do the job without her."

"I've no doubt of that, Hamilton. Just watch out, that's all. Don't get too close to the girl. Don't get too close to any of them, come to that."

Jack said nothing. A vein in his forehead throbbed.

"And there's another thing," Marriott went on. "I'd be inclined to cut down on these German opera shows and highbrow concerts you're organising. It's all right for the civilians, but the troops didn't fight their way into Germany and topple Hitler to have Wagner and Mozart rammed down their throats. I had the Second Army Welfare people here yesterday from Hamburg. They tell me there are plenty of first-class shows about, concert parties . . . that sort of thing."

"Yes," said Jack, "and we have them, too. Gallant, worthy little troupes with one end-of-the-pier comic, an ageing blonde with an accordion and two dancing girls in silver tinsel."

"Bloody good people too," said Marriott, "performing in barns and aerodrome hangars, getting shelled and bombed for their trouble. They've got guts, those ENSA people; what's more they speak and sing in English and *they* ought to be out here doing shows for our troops, not a lot of dead-beat Jerry opera singers, Nazis most of them anyway."

There was a pause. Then Jack said "I try to maintain a balance between the available ENSA shows and the local German talent, which is not all opera and concerts, anyway. We've had two or three German Variety Shows, and very popular they were, and we take great care to weed out the Nazis."

The GSO1 grunted, so Jack went on: "It seems to me important to resuscitate German music for two reasons. First, because there's nothing better for restoring some sense of order and hope to these shattered people than to see their conquerors showing respect for Beethoven, Mozart and Brahms; second, a lot of our troops, for the first time in their lives, have experienced and are experiencing the beauty and excitement of a fine orchestra playing a classic symphony – What were we fighting the war for, if not to preserve the best things in our civilisation? – And thirdly, it's a way of bringing people together, troops and civilians, victors and vanquished if you like, to sit side by side in a hall or theatre, sharing something constructive, something that can encourage reconciliation – the common language of music . . . " Jack allowed himself to get carried off by his rhetoric, away from the sensitive issue of his friendship with Karin Freidl. It worked.

"Yes, all right, Hamilton," Marriott said testily. He got up to indicate that the interview was over, showing Jack to the door. "Just take my tip and don't get too familiar with your staff. That's all."

Jack saluted and marched out, relieved that the interview was over, ruefully aware that it was far from the seal of approval he had expected, and anxious about his future with Karin.

WHEN Jack got back to his office, he was told by Corporal Bridges and Karin of a visit by Dr Heuss during his absence.

Julius Heuss had come to the Entertainments Office around eleven, in a very downcast state. He had asked to see Jack, but when pressed by Corporal Bridges to state his business, he had become emotional. At that point Karin had come in from delivering some announcement slips round the town and taken Heuss into Jack's office, where the old man had broken down and wept. Karin told Jack how she had put her arms round him, as he related how his widowed sister Margharete, with whom he lived, had suddenly been taken ill in the night and had died early that morning, in the *Krankenhaus* on Eibstrasse. The old man was shattered, dazed and unable to contemplate a future without Margharete, who had loved him and looked after him ever since his wife died in a car crash in 1937.

By the time Jack had had lunch in the Mess and blown off steam to some of the more understanding of his brother officers about the rocket he'd received from Colonel Marriott, and then returned to his office, Karin had already acted on behalf of old Heuss.

First, she had taken the 'bus to Mehlem to convey the sad news to Ingrid.

Ingrid had instantly agreed to Karin's suggestion that Dr Heuss should move house, as soon as his sister had been buried and the chalet in Königswinter could be sold.

"Julius cannot live alone up there in a mountain shack – like Hunding – surrounded by chickens."

Karin agreed. "I shall soon have a room of my own, so perhaps Dr Heuss could take mine here," said Karin, diffidently.

"*Bestimmt,*" was Ingrid's resolute reply. Minutes later, she jumped onto her bicycle and pedalled off to Godesberg to find Dr Heuss, who was still with Corporal Bridges in the office, and tell him about his new lodgings. Meanwhile, Karin walked round from Ingrid's house to the undertakers in Mehlem, to make the preliminary arrangements for Margharete's funeral.

By the time Jack returned from lunch, Corporal Bridges had sent Ingrid, Heuss and Ingrid's bike back to Mehlem in an Army truck that happened to be going into the town.

Soon after, Karin arrived back from Ingrid's by 'bus to report that she'd fixed a date for the funeral, and then dashed off again to order flowers in Godesberg.

When he returned, Jack commended Bridges on his helpful action and marvelled at the speed with which the arrangements had been made. True German efficiency. There was a splendid German word for it that he'd learned in Munich before the war: *Gründlichkeit*. That's what they had, these Germans, the gift for seeing things through; practicality.

And so it was that, even as Dr Heuss stood in the cold wind at his sister's graveside in Königswinter three days later, his grief was tempered a little by the knowledge that he had a new home to go to at Ingrid Pauels', a woman to look after him, and lodgings at the centre of the musical revival that was taking place.

For Jack, it was not so much the urgency of re-housing old Julius Heuss, but the prospect of having Karin installed in a place of her own, that prompted him to put pressure on the billeting officer to find, over the next few weeks, somewhere for his interpreter/secretary to live. And it wasn't long before he received a memo. that a large room with a kitchenette had been requisitioned in a dentist's house in Frankengraben in Godesberg for Fraülein Freidl, and that the young lady could move in as soon as convenient.

Jack drove Karin round that afternoon to fetch the keys and transport her and her few possessions; a small trunk and a suitcase, a tennis racquet and a couple of boxes filled with books; from Ingrid's house to the top floor flat of No.2 Frankengraben.

On its front door was a brass plate: 'Albrecht Inner, Zahnarzt'.

"If you get toothache in the night, you only have to creep down and wake up your landlord," Jack whispered and Karin laughed happily, as they carted her stuff out of the Jeep and up the steep narrow stairs, to a light and airy room at the top of the house, with a fine view of the Drachenfels.

The dentist, Dr Inner, was elderly, grey and a trifle vague; his wife was very deaf. Other than them, there was nobody else in the house, which was another factor in favour of it. But from Karin's window Jack observed that a small row of houses across the street had been appropriated as billets for Battery headquarters, 12th Battery, RA, which meant that his comings and goings of an evening must be accomplished with great care and discretion. Even now, his Jeep with its ostentatious identification was shouting his presence to the world . . .

Dismissing this from his mind, he sat on Karin's trunk and smoked a cigarette, enjoying the feeling of intimacy that came from watching her unpack her belongings and hang up her clothes.

Now that Karin had more living space than she'd had at Ingrid's, she seemed anxious to bring a few more things from her home at Coblenz, including winter clothes that she would be needing soon. But a journey down there was fraught with problems. The railway line was still damaged and no trains were running, and the only hope was to hitch a ride in a civilian lorry or a farm wagon. Also, Coblenz was in the French zone of Occupation, which meant that special papers and permits would be required to enter the area.

Karin showed Jack a photograph of her parents' house just outside Coblenz; her father was a *Landrat*, the chairman of the district council, and her elder sister, Lotte, had lived there with her three-year-old child, since her husband was killed in Italy in 1942.

Jack mulled all this over while he sat watching and admiring Karin's long, bronzed, bare legs, as she moved between her suitcase that was open on the big double bed to the hanging cupboard, with her modest collection of skirts and dresses.

"I'll take you down there," he said finally.

Karin stopped half way across the room and stared at him. "Oh, no," she cried out, "you cannot; it will be not allowed, you are too busy . . . "

"Nonsense," Jack interrupted. "If you want to go down the Rhine to Coblenz and see your parents and sister and collect clothes for the winter, I shall drive you down in my Jeep."

"Then you can meet my mother and father!" Karin cried excitedly, her objections rapidly dissolving, "And I shall show them my English captain."

"Major," said Jack with a smile. "Temporary Major."

"Herr Temporary Major," Karin saluted him, and then went on with her unpacking, cheerfully humming an aria from *Forza del Destino*, which they happened to have put on the week before.

It was Friday and there was to be a new form of entertainment at the Divisional College on the coming Saturday night. A former choreographer and dancer of the Cologne Opera Ballet, Klaus Spiegel, had returned to the area from Frankfurt, where he and his wife had been living for a year, and had suggested presenting a *Tanzabend*, an evening of dance – all kinds of dance; classical ballet, Spanish Flamenco, Hungarian Czardas, American Jazz – to be performed by a troupe of girl dancers with himself and his wife and partner Lili. Tickets for the event had sold like hot cakes.

Jack and Karin decided they would go down to Coblenz on the Sunday following the *Tanzabend*, just for the day. If they started early enough in the morning they could get there in time for lunch and be back by ten in the evening.

FRANKENGRABEN! That was it. No. 2, Frankengraben. He had supposed it meant 'French graves'. Graves of the French.

That macabre supposition suddenly came back to Sir John, as he stood under the dripping trees in the park, in the middle of Bad Godesberg, staring with unseeing eyes at the ugly, modern *Stadthalle* and hearing distantly the sounds of

Wagner's *The Valkyries*, Act 1, echoing in the mists of time, from forty-three years ago . . .

He turned on his heel and walked resolutely back to the station, to enquire where Frankengraben might be. Although he must have driven to and from that address dozens of times in the past, he had no recollection of where it was in relation to the Park Theatre, the Entertainments Office in Plittersdorferstrasse, or the Officers' Mess. He could recall only the name of the street, not the inside of the house itself. He must ask.

"*Frankengraben? Leider nicht.*"

Several German heads were shaken under wet umbrellas, mostly those of middle-aged folk. Then the Judge spotted a small, elderly lady coming his way, led by a little dachshund on a lead. She looked well over sixty, so Sir John accosted her.

"*Frankengraben? Ach, so heisst die Strasse nicht mehr. Sie heisst jetz Kennedy Allee.*" And she explained the best way to get there, pointing the tall, grey and distinguished-looking stranger on his way.

How symptomatic of the passing of time, Sir John thought, as he set off towards the Kennedy Allee. How indicative of the march of recent history! Apart from the Heuss Allee, Adenauer Allee and the Friedrich-Ebert Allee, all honouring the architects of the new Federal Republic of West Germany, he had already noticed on his map a Martin Luther King Strasse. How shocked Hitler would have been to know that a street in the Third Reich would one day be named after an American negro!

The Judge found No. 2, Kennedy Allee without difficulty. A brass plate on the door that said *Zahnarzt* made his heart jump for a moment, until he remembered that the dentist he was looking for was not likely to be still alive and practising after all this time. He rang the bell.

A woman wearing a white surgical coat and horn-rimmed glasses, and carrying a clipboard, came to the door. Sir John explained his mission.

"Come in, please," she said, and ushered him into the

waiting-room. The room, which smelt strongly of disinfectant, was dark and full of carved wood furniture and ornaments. There were heavy brocade curtains, some views of the Black Forest on the walls and in the centre a table covered in back numbers of the *Der Stern* and *Spiegel* magazines.

Due to her excellent English, the woman was quickly in possession of the nature of the elderly English tourist's enquiry and able to answer all but the vital question. Yes, the practice was bought by her husband from Dr Inner in the summer of 1946, when Dr Inner retired. Soon afterwards they heard from Frau Inner that the Doctor had died from a heart attack in Freiburg.

"Yes, there was a young woman lodging here when we took over the practice, a Fraülein – Forster – Froebel – I cannot remember the name . . ."

"Was it Freidl?" Sir John felt a surge of excitement. Direct contact with Karin, at last.

The woman nodded her head. "Freidl, that was the name, *ja*. She was working as assistant with the British Possession troops, *ja*?"

"She was my assistant. And I'm anxious to discover what became of her."

"*Ach, so.*"

"Have you any idea where she might be now?"

The dentist's wife, who Jack thought perhaps doubled the roles of receptionist and dental nurse, shook her head slowly. "It was very many years ago."

"But you do remember her?"

"Oh, yes. She was a nice girl but very – how shall one say – very quiet and very – sad."

"In what way sad?"

"She was lonely always – most of the time reading or playing the records on her – "

"Gramophone?"

"*Ja*. Sometimes we would hear her crying in her room. She never go so much out."

Jack's heart smote him. "Did she have any friends?"

"I do not think so. She speak sometimes of perhaps to leave Bad Godesberg and return to her home."

"In Coblenz?"

"I cannot say where . . .."

"How long did you – I mean – when did she finally leave this house?"

"Not very long after we have taken over the practice. Maybe a month or so. The British Army people come to pay what they owe for her room and she has gone away."

"And you never saw her again? Never heard from her?"

The dentist's wife again shook her head.

Sir John got up, thanked the woman for her help and left the house. Half of him had hoped to hear that Karin had taken up with another officer in the Divisional Headquarters and continued to work for the British, happy and contented; the other half of him, the selfish, conceited, dog-in-the-manger half, had wanted to hear what he had just been told. Now he knew that she had been sad, missing him? But immediately other possibilities came to mind. Had something else made her unhappy? Had they persecuted her, perhaps, after he left? Had somebody got a knife into her? One of his brother officers, perhaps, or the GSO1?

No, the Judge ruled, it was undoubtedly for him that she had wept those lonely evenings after he left Godesberg. She was crying for a lost love. Her British officer had left and she was alone. The faint inner glow of pleasure at the knowledge that she had missed him was overlaid by the sharp stabbing of remorse.

Sir John walked slowly and thoughtfully to the station for the train back to Bonn.

THE Saturday of the weekend that Jack had agreed to drive Karin to her home proved a hectic day. His first task was to acquire some rations from the quartermaster's stores to take down to

Coblenz as an offering to Karin's family. He felt a slight tinge of guilt, as he signed for them as 'refreshments required for civilian artistes engaged to perform for Divisional personnel'.

He had to explain to the quartermaster's clerk that the usual soup and cigarette hand-out was to be supplemented this week by a special box of provisions for a bad case of hardship on the part of one of the soloists. It was a blatant lie, but Jack told himself that the Freidl family would be every bit as short of food as the musicians. Why shouldn't they have some?

The box of provisions, mostly tins of spam, soup, baked beans and spaghetti, would help Karin's family to produce a modest meal on Sunday, with something left over for themselves the next day. Two bottles of Mosel would also be thrown in, and some army cigarettes.

The next problem was how to smuggle Karin herself into the French Zone.

Jack feared that awkward questions would be asked if he was stopped with a female civilian travelling illicitly in British service transport. The French might report it to HQ BAOR and General Tom Harrington would be carpeted for condoning fraternization by his officers with German civilians outside their area. 'The French would say it was an insult to the dead of two World Wars,' he thought, 'and I'd be in the soup.'

The only answer was for Karin to become a British soldier for the journey.

At first he toyed with the idea of asking her to impersonate Corporal Bridges for the trip down the Rhine, and to carry the corporal's pay-book for identity purposes. But that would be asking Bridges to contravene Army Regulations and risk a court-martial, so he abandoned the idea. However, Corporal Bridges had to be entrusted with the plan, for a corporal's battle-dress with stripes was needed for Karin to wear, as well as a beret and a pair of army boots – and Bridges must provide them.

"Bit risky, Sir," commented the worthy NCO, when Jack outlined his plan.

"Why?"

"Abuse of His Majesty's uniform, Sir. Fraudulently posing as a member of His Majesty's forces. The fraülein could get into very hot water for that, Sir."

"I'll see she doesn't," was all Jack could find to say.

The corporal's remarks shook him, but he knew how desperately Karin wanted to go home, make sure her family were all right, and fetch her winter clothing. And he would do anything to make her happy. That was for sure. Also, it would be quite a bit of fun to play a trick on the French and something amusing to recount in the Mess – after they got back. If they got back.

Having registered his doubts, Corporal Bridges agreed to hand over his spare battle-dress, boots and beret, not entirely happily, but trusting in his officer's judgement.

Not wishing to alarm her unduly, Jack underplayed the risk to Karin.

Accordingly she agreed, with only a twinge of apprehension, to scrape her blonde hair back tightly under Corporal Bridges' beret and attempt to fill out adequately a battle-dress jacket, trousers and a pair of Jack's boots – for Corporal Bridges' feet proved to be several sizes too large.

That evening Jack attended the *Tanzabend* with some of his brother officers, including young Peter Franks, who alone knew of and was in some sympathy with Jack's private feelings for Karin. He was also privy to the following day's secret journey to Coblenz which they discussed in hushed whispers during the interval.

Karin, having already seen the show, chose to stay in her digs and write letters.

The *Tanzabend* was a smash hit with both troops and public, and Klaus Spiegel's ballerina wife Lili succeeded in driving the mostly male audience nearly wild with a succession of highly erotic performances, sometimes solo, sometimes partnered by Werner.

Dark, lithe and sexy, Lili Spiegel possessed long, firm and

shapely dancer's legs and thighs and wore some daring costumes, especially for a number with Klaus entitled '*Morgen-liebe*' or 'Morning Song'.

This was a misty, idyllic duet, danced to the music of Debussy, in which he appeared as a young hunter with bow and arrow and Lili, lightly clad in wisps of chiffon with bare legs and feet, floated about the stage in dim lighting as his quarry, half-girl, half-bird, spinning and twisting and revealing fleeting glimpses of smooth white flesh. Once hit by Klaus's arrow, she writhed and struggled before dying in his arms. It was all a bit reminiscent of '*L'après-midi d'un faune*' but Jack found himself becoming roused by Lili Spiegel's dancing and reflected that it was comparable to the erotic displays he'd seen on a visit to the Windmill Theatre, while on leave in London. But this was rather more imaginative and certainly better danced, for Lili Spiegel was a properly-trained ballet dancer with the skill and art to lose herself in the role and project tremendous feeling into it.

Jack had once seen a jerky old film of Pavlova's 'Dying Swan' dance without much emotion. It wasn't so much the scratched bit of film but Anna Pavlova's rather grim face and unattractive costume that repelled him. Lili's dying bird, however, really touched and excited him.

After the performance Jack went backstage to congratulate and thank the Spiegels for organising the show. He told them that he would like Klaus to come to the office the following Monday morning to discuss a tour round the area and a date for a repeat performance in Bonn.

Then Jack went to Karin's billet and supervised an anxious dress-rehearsal in readiness for the following day. Stripped down to her slip, Karin stood in front of a full-length mirror, where she wriggled uneasily into the rough and baggy khaki trousers and the battle-dress jacket, with its corporal's stripes on the sleeves. Once she was buttoned up, Karin laughed out loud at the absurd reflection she saw in the mirror.

Jack only smiled wanly, beginning to wonder if he was out of his mind in planning the trip.

"So I am, after all, a corporal in the English army," Karin giggled; yet at the same time a little pang of fear pierced her guts, for she sensed that tomorrow's exploit was dangerous, and she knew that it could land both of them in serious trouble.

Chapter 5

THERE was a slight early mist on Sunday morning when Jack drove off from his billet through the quiet streets of Godesberg. As he pulled up outside Karin's lodgings he noticed with mild apprehension that there was already some activity around HQ 12th Battery, where gunners were emerging from nearby billets and going into their messroom for breakfast.

Jack rang Karin's doorbell, hoping that when she emerged in her disguise she would not attract too much attention. After a while the front door was half opened, very tentatively, and Jack caught sight of Karin. It was the first time he had seen her completely disguised. He swallowed hard and stared, for there was something about the girl's soft body encased in a bulky, sack-like battle-dress that stirred him deeply. Her fair hair was brushed severely up and tucked neatly away, leaving her delicate neck and ears naked above the rough khaki collar. He found the sight oddly exciting; while the cheeky, jaunty angle of the beret on her head and the look of faint anxiety in her clear blue eyes aroused his passion. He wanted to tear the clothes off her, to reveal shockingly her woman's body beneath and then, chivalrously, to protect her modesty by carrying her upstairs to the bedroom, away from the leering eyes of the soldiers opposite.

To cover the embarrassment of this sudden surge of fantasy and the desire that assailed his loins, he just managed to croak "Good morning, Corporal Freidl. All set?"

Karin nodded, nervously glancing across the street to three or four gunners who were joking in a group outside their quarters.

"Never mind them," Jack whispered. "Tell you what . . . " He groped in his pocket for a packet of Gold Leaf and a lighter. "Light a cigarette. Look better."

"I cannot smoke, Jack. I shall cough."

"You must try. Just a puff, as you come out and get into the Jeep."

"OK. I try."

When Jack had lit one for her, she turned to close the front door, keeping the cigarette in her mouth while desperately avoiding a cough or splutter and screwing up her eyes against the smoke. Then, standing erect and proud on the doorstep, she took the cigarette from her mouth and surveyed the scene opposite with contempt, as though to a Grenadier NCO the Gunners across the road were the scum of the earth.

Her soldierly appearance was only slightly marred by the school satchel she carried in her left hand. This contained a summer dress and a pair of sandals, for Karin had pointed out to Jack earlier that to arrive at her parents' house wearing khaki battle-dress, boots and a beret would suggest that their daughter had been persuaded to betray her country by joining some British Women's Auxiliary Corps.

She glanced up at the weather, as a man would, and walked with exaggeratedly long strides down the steps, across the pavement and towards the waiting Jeep. Jack followed her. Corporal Bridges' uniform fitted her pretty well, although the trousers were a trifle baggy. But her battle-dress jacket and beret looked OK and her sun-tanned face suggested a healthy, outdoor young man. Only her voice and hands might possibly give her away.

Arrived by the Jeep, Karin took a final puff on the cigarette and flung it down in the road, squashing it with the heel of her boot. Then she got in. As Jack climbed into the driver's seat beside her, he felt an urge to fling his arms round her and kiss her passionately for the brilliant way she had managed the bizarre scenario – so far. As he pressed the starter, he marvelled at her coolness. 'This girl is a born actress!' he thought,

Engaging gear, he observed her more closely and then murmured urgently: "Where's your moustache?"

"Must I wear it?"

"Safer, if you do. Don't say you've left it behind?"

Karin sighed. "No, it is here . . . in one of these so many pockets."

"Wait till we get going, then you'll have to put it on."

"OK."

As they drove off, a couple of Gunners glanced casually at the Jeep but evidently noticed nothing unusual. In a minute or so, Jack turned out of a side street onto the road that ran parallel to the Rhine, headed south for Coblenz, and breathed again. They were well clear of the town.

"Now put on your moustache," he ordered.

Karin extracted from her breast pocket the rather bogus-looking little piece of *crêpe* hair on flesh-coloured tape and stuck it on with obvious distaste, for it tickled her nose.

"I look like Charlie Chaplin," she said.

Jack glanced sideways at her. "You look like Hitler."

Karin said "I am supposed to look like Corporal Bridges."

"No," said Jack. "Like Corporal Freidl, a treacherous German girl, who has changed sex and defected from the *Bund Deutscher Mädel* to join the British Brigade of Guards."

This caused Karin to double up with laughter, but she soon regained her poise and sat up straight, trying hard to look like a soldier, her jaw set, her eyes screwed up, her back erect.

AFTER an hour's drive down the Rhine, they paused to admire one of the series of mediaeval castles that stand high on the rocks overlooking the river. On the lower slopes to their right were acres of vineyards, where the grapes for the famous Rhine wines were already ripe for the *vendange*. Jack reflected that this was the kind of trip that, before the war, British and American tourists used to enjoy, sightseeing from an open charabanc. The scenery was impressive, and since the early mist had now cleared to release a warming sunshine on the sloping vineyards, both Jack and Karin felt a lifting of the spirits as if they were on holiday.

Spontaneously, forgetting their cares, they began to sing from the sheer joy of being young, alive, and together beside the Rhine. But as they approached a small village where some German vineyard workers were about in the street, Jack reminded Karin that she was supposed to be a man and warned her to drop her voice an octave. As they sped through the village, they launched into the Sharpless and Pinkerton duet from Act 1 of *Madame Butterfly* at the tops of their voices, Karin taking the tenor part and Jack the baritone. Once through the village, they burst into happy laughter again, causing Jack to swerve at the wheel and narrowly miss the kerb. A moment later a signpost for Andernach dampened their jubilant mood, for they were now less than a couple of miles from the border of the French Zone and possible trouble.

Thinking of the approaching hazard, Jack asked himself resentfully 'Why should French soldiers be strutting around the German countryside ordering people about, when their only contribution to the overthrow of Adolf Hitler was to sit behind the Maginot Line and allow themselves to be outflanked and smashed by the German army?' In reply, he had to admit that their people – some of them at least – had made a brave contribution in the secret war that had been fought out by the Resistance on dark nights, in the woods, on the roads, beside the railway lines, in the farms and on the village streets, armed with small arms dropped from the air, home-made grenades and sticks of gelignite.

The Maquis were heroes, but not all French men and women were *maquisards*. Thousands of them did nothing to trouble the German occupying forces and many hundreds actively collaborated. Nevertheless, to communicate such thoughts to a German girl, much as Jack loved and trusted her, would be a betrayal of his country's old alliance with the French in two successive wars, an act of disloyalty to the old *entente cordiale*. So he said nothing, and a moment later they were approaching a checkpoint by a bridge over a stream on the outskirts of Andernach, where an armed French *poilu* duly flagged them down.

The Jeep jerked to a standstill.

The unshaven, sloppily turned-out soldier came to the nearside of the Jeep to address Karin. "*Vos papiers*," he barked.

Slightly thrown, and not a little afraid, she said nothing but glanced sideways at Jack, causing the French soldier to repeat his question a bit louder.

"*Vos papiers, votre laissez-passer! C'est ici le zone d'occupation français!*"

Jack now went into his pre-rehearsed routine. Summoning up all the authority his rank and regiment could give him, he embarked on an explanation in reasonably comprehensible French as to how and why he was on an important but strictly 'top secret' intelligence mission from SHAEF, to investigate reports of some suspected Nazi activity in Coblenz. "I am," Jack said, lowering his voice as one about to divulge a profound confidence, "an officer of the Grenadiers of the English Guard, holding the special appointment of DADAWS to the Guards Division, which are the special Household Troops that guard and protect our sovereign, His Majesty, King George the Sixth and our beloved Queen Elizabeth."

To prove his point he produced and waved in the air the

memo. he had received appointing him to Divisional HQ, signed by the General. The sentry came round the Jeep's bonnet to inspect it. Next Jack produced a snapshot of himself, slightly masked by his Company Commander, escorting the King along the ranks of his platoon, on a royal inspection that had taken place the week before his battalion had sailed for Normandy.

"*Le roi d'Angleterre*," said Jack, pointing to the Monarch on the rather crumpled photograph, "*et moi*". Jack's finger indicated his own face and one shoulder just visible in the picture.

This seemed to satisfy the French soldier, but only as far as Jack was concerned. "*Et les papiers de votre camarade?*"

The soldier now moved back to the nearside of the Jeep and stood inches from Karin's face. Jack's heart missed a beat.

"*Mon camarade?*" Jack asked, feigning surprise. "*Vous avez besoin de ses papiers?*"

The *poilu* was now holding out his hand to Karin, waiting for her to produce some form of pass. Karin looked across in despair at Jack, who got out of the Jeep and hurried round to the passenger side, positioning himself protectively between Karin and the soldier. In his best French, Jack explained that his companion was a mere corporal, but then made the mistake of saying that he would normally be driving the vehicle and carrying no papers other than his pay-book. Naturally, the soldier then insisted on seeing the corporal's pay-book.

Jack decided his best bet was to stand on his dignity. "Now look here," he blustered, "you are making unnecessary difficulties." He added for good measure, "I must remind you that I am an Allied officer, not a bloody German civilian." He glanced past the man at Karin, hoping she would not be offended by that remark. A faint smile about her lips indicated that she was not.

Again the *poilu* insisted on seeing the corporal's pay-book, whereupon Jack demanded to see the soldier's commanding officer.

"*C'est insouffrable!*" Jack exploded, not quite sure whether the word was appropriate, although it sounded good.

But the *poilu* wasn't having that, and roughly tried to push Jack away from the vehicle, shouting at Karin "*Vous devez montrer votre laissez-passer. C'est un ordre, vous comprenez?*"

With that, he lunged towards Karin again but Jack seized him and dragged him away from the Jeep. A scuffle followed. In the course of the struggle, the *poilu* dropped his rifle and Jack, rather foolishly, kicked it with his foot across the road out of the man's reach. He'd seen it done with revolvers on the floors of saloons in Western movies. But the French soldier left his rifle where it was and came back at him with fists flying. Once more the two men locked in combat. The dust flew, as their feet agitated the dry road surface.

Suddenly Karin sneezed. The *poilu* spun round, letting go of Jack. Karin sneezed again, even louder, a high-pitched, unmistakably feminine sound.

In a flash, the French soldier had pushed past Jack and whisked off Karin's beret, allowing her flaxen hair to cascade down her back. There was a short silence. Then the sentry doubled up with laughter.

Jack attempted a conciliatory grin, while Karin sat immobilized by mortification. Then she began to replace her beret, tucking in her hair again with an air of cold indignation. Karin's French was limited, so that exact details of the following conversation escaped her. All she knew was that, as the *poilu* picked up his rifle, Jack was saying something about the British army's uniformed women's auxiliary; how the young lady was a member of their secret intelligence mission, someone to take shorthand notes and that, in case she should get separated from him and exposed to ill-treatment or abuse by the German population in Coblenz, his General had ordered that the ATS clerk accompanying him on the mission, should be disguised as a male.

The sentry was now nodding his head with evident understanding. Karin sensed that the crisis was over and flashed a radiant smile at him, and he returned it with a lecherous wink, a glance at Jack and a suggestive movement of the loins, as though to suggest that she was in for a good romp in Coblenz with her officer.

Jack patted the man on the back as he climbed back into the Jeep, and thanked him for his understanding.

As they drove away from the checkpoint, Karin was too shaken to express amusement and Jack knew better than to joke about the matter.

"If they will stop us again, I shall be afraid."

"They won't."

"We must not tell my parents about this *Vorfall* or they will be nervous and not wish me to come again to Coblenz."

Jack agreed. "It can't be easy for your family or anyone, living in the French zone."

This was borne out more and more by the grim atmosphere, as they passed through a couple more villages and a small town, before reaching the outskirts of Coblenz. Everywhere shutters were closed; houses, cottages and shops had a dead, deserted look. There were very few people about and those who were visible had anxious, unsmiling faces. Here and there a French soldier lounged against a wall, smoking a Gauloise, his rifle propped up beside him. It was austere and gloomy inside the French-occupied zone and Jack could see that Karin was worried for her family.

After a long silence she said "It is very changed here, since I came to teach in Mehlem."

There was a pause before Jack said "The French cannot be magnanimous in victory, because they lost the war. They are bitter."

"*Ja*, it is so," said Karin, looking around at the people in the village through which they were now speeding.

"It is easier for us," Jack went on. "We didn't have an enemy occupation. That is a humiliation we haven't suffered since 1066."

"Ah, you English, you are so lucky, *nicht war*? You live safely on your little island, and take care to have all your not-so-little wars abroad!"

With that, Jack had to concur.

Soon after midday Jack's Jeep turned off the main road and for about half a mile bumped over a rough dusty lane, through a thick wood of fir trees and tall pines.

"How far now?" he asked.

"Not more than a kilometre."

"Then you must change your clothes."

Karin said, "Where?" as the vehicle pulled up sharply. The lane was deserted, with not a living soul in sight. The only sound was the wind sighing in the tall trees.

"Over there," Jack suddenly commanded, pointing to some bushes a few yards from the road.

"You will guard me?" Karin asked anxiously, as she jumped from the Jeep, clutching her satchel.

"I will guard you," Jack reassured her, and she skipped away into the undergrowth.

After a matter of minutes she returned dressed as a girl, Jack stowed her discarded battle-dress in the back of the Jeep, and they set off again.

"We must remember this spot," said Jack.

"It is not so romantic," Karin murmured, misunderstanding him.

"I meant as a convenient dressing-room for you, *Liebchen*," he laughed. "You'll have to change back before we tackle that cursed French border again. Let's hope there's a different sentry on by then."

They drove on for a while, and soon drew up at the door of Karin's home. It was one of a scattered group of modest one-storey villas among tall pine trees, and stood some way up a rough gravel drive lined with rhododendron bushes.

'A bit like Virginia Water,' Jack thought, but doubted if the social life of suburban Coblenz was comparable to the bridge and cocktail parties of Surrey.

Frau Freidl, who must have been watching from a window, came out at once, and as Karin jumped from the vehicle, she flung her skinny arms around her daughter, folding her in a long, tearfully emotional embrace. She was a handsome woman in her late forties with fine features and clear blue eyes. Jack recognized immediately the source of Karin's beauty.

As soon as mother and daughter disengaged from their embrace, Karin introduced Jack, very correctly, to her mother as "Herr Major Hamilton", adding "*mein guter Freund, er ist auch mein Arbeitgeber,* my boss".

Frau Freidl was at a disadvantage, for her English was limited. But she managed to smile and say "She speak of you very nice, my daughter. Come please in."

"I am – very – glad – she is happy – " Jack said, slowly enough for her to understand.

When Jack lifted the small crate of provisions from the back seat of the Jeep and handed it to her, saying "*Etwas zu essen and zu rauchen,*" Frau Freidl took it with a slightly embarrassed nod.

"We are so grateful. We cannot – *so* – what we shall eat . . . *kriegen.*"

She looked to Karin for the word. "*Kriegen* – get – obtain – " Karin translated, unnecessarily.

"I understand," said Jack with a reassuring smile, as Frau Freidl carried the crate of provisions indoors.

Karin took Jack's arm. "Come now to meet my father and my sister – this way."

Jack followed Karin through the house and onto a wooden verandah overlooking the pine forest at the back, where Herr Freidl was sitting in a bamboo chair, from which he rose with some difficulty. Karin's rather plain elder sister, Lotte, who was also present, was sitting at a table with her three-year-old son, helping him to draw a dog with coloured chalks. Karin's father was a man of charm and good looks, although the war had taken a toll of his health. Jack already knew that he had been invalided out of the German merchant navy in 1941. He had contracted double pneumonia as a result of being four hours in the sea off Norway, when his ship was torpedoed. After partial recovery in a clinic, he had been given a job in the *Rathaus* in Coblenz as a forestry clerk, but his chest was still vulnerable to damp weather and an arthritic leg forced him to walk with a stick.

Although Herr Freidl spoke reasonably good English, Jack and Karin talked in German, mainly for Lotte's benefit. In spite of this, Lotte contributed little to the conversation and Jack wondered whether her almost sullen reticence indicated resent- ment or bitterness at her husband's death in 1942 in Italy.

After some twenty minutes of strained conversation about the weather and Karin's new lodgings in Bad Godesberg, initiated mainly by Karin, who was painfully anxious to make things go, Frau Freidl mercifully appeared on the verandah to announce "*Mittagessen*".

Karin helped her father to his feet and Jack handed him his stick. Lotte grasped her child by one hand and they all trooped indoors to the dining-room.

It was clear that Karin's mother had taken great trouble to make the occasion memorable, for the table was elaborately laid with the best linen, lace-edged cloth, lace mats and all the glass and silver she could muster. Cut-glass condiment sets, wine glasses and a large bowl of tulips adorned the table, all of which seemed sadly incongruous in view of the simple, improvised meal that followed.

From the rations provided by Jack, Frau Freidl had managed to make spam fritters, with a salad of lettuce from their own garden, mixed with chopped ham and salami sausage.

Throughout the meal, Lotte fussed over her fatherless child.

As the second bottle of Moselle was poured, conversation began to loosen up, and Jack launched forth about the splendid way the concerts and opera performances were bringing together the military personnel and the civilian population in the Cologne area and how much he owed to the help of Frau Pauels and Karin in bringing this about.

"Your daughter," he declared to Herr and Frau Freidl, "is a wonderful assistant and translator; I couldn't do without her." As he said this, he caught Karin's eye across the table and saw that she winked, almost imperceptibly, as though to say 'That's right, make out I'm just a useful assistant; then they won't ask awkward questions'.

Frau Freidl began to ask Karin about the concerts, what works were played and where. She was evidently interested when Karin explained how they had scoured the area for musicians and singers, and managed to put together four opera companies and orchestras, and a ballet company.

Jack remembered Karin telling him once that all her mother's family had been musicians and that her mother herself had taught the piano for a while at a local school.

"Hier haben wir gar keine Musik. Nichts."

Of course not, Jack thought; the French authorities would move slowly on that front.

HERR FREIDL questioned his daughter closely about living conditions in the Cologne area, about food supplies, bomb damage, water and electricity shortages. Were there many refugees in the towns, he wanted to know, and how many buildings were still standing? Between them, Karin and Jack managed to paint a picture of life around Cologne, Bonn, Godesberg and Aachen that showed how, in spite of the devastation of Cologne itself and large areas of Aachen, life in general was slowly improving.

"Here it is not so," said Herr Freidl and complained of the cold, restrictive atmosphere under the French authorities.

"We must not go out from the house at night, from six o'clock in the evening until dawn the next day," he explained.

"Good Lord!" Jack said with some surprise. "Do you mean to say you still have a curfew?"

"We must obey the orders of the French soldiers."

Frau Freidl added that a poster on the wall in the town square, signed by the local French commander, assured the people of Coblenz that anyone ignoring the curfew would be *erschossen* – shot. "That's barbaric," said Jack, "and the war is over. But I suppose the French suffered so much from curfews in their own country that it's not surprising they are turning the tables."

The slight silence that followed was broken by Karin, who suggested to her mother that, as it was a warm autumn day, they should leave the dining-room and have coffee on the verandah. The ersatz coffee served by Frau Freidl tasted even nastier to Jack than Ingrid Pauels' brew and he regretted not bringing some decent coffee down to Coblenz with the provisions. But it was wet and warm and good manners dictated that he should swallow what he could. Luckily he was able to tip the residue in his cup secretly into a tub of geraniums next to his chair.

After a while, Karin and her mother excused themselves and disappeared upstairs to sort out some winter clothing for Karin to take back to Godesberg. Lotte then muttered something, and left to put her child down for a rest. Jack and Herr Freidl were left on the verandah to exchange halting, sporadic remarks, each trying to assess the other under the cover of polite small-talk.

Most of the Germans Jack had encountered under the Allied Occupation fell into two categories: the unrepentant and the ingratiating. There were exceptions, of course, such as the tenor Otto Maier, who was by any standards an agreeable, friendly and natural chap – without any bitterness. This was usually true of active members of the armed forces on both sides; those who actually fight in wars tend to respect each other as adversaries.

Jack felt with regret that Herr Freidl belonged to the second category. After spending most of lunch thanking Jack profusely for being so kind to his daughter, he was now falling over backwards to ingratiate himself with his English guest.

At some point, when Goebbels was mentioned in connection with the pre-war Cologne opera, Herr Freidl uttered the usual disclaimer that echoed throughout occupied Germany in those days: "*Ich war nie in der Partei*" – I was never a party member. Jack knew and Freidl knew that every member of the German armed forces had been obliged to swear personal allegiance to Hitler. But Jack decided not to press the point.

When he offered the man his sympathy for being torpedoed and left in the sea, causing his current illness, Freidl brushed his experience aside and told Jack how much good Germans admired the English 'tommies' for their fairness and courage; how he himself had been wounded at Vimy Ridge in 1916 as a corporal with a Bavarian regiment; and of the great respect in which he and his family held the English king and queen and their family.

Jack wondered whether all this was a ploy, designed to ensure the continuation of his daughter's excellent job with the British in Bad Godesberg, or a safeguard against the possibility of Jack drawing his revolver and shooting the entire Freidl family just to establish who was boss (something that might conceivably take place in the gloomy, hate-ridden Soviet-occupied zone), or if there was no ulterior motive and it was just a case of plain good manners towards a guest in his house.

Before Jack could make up his mind on this question Karin, carrying a small suitcase. came out to the verandah with her mother. This gave Jack the cue he wanted to glance at his watch, for he was anxious now to get away.

"I hope to bring Karin home again before too long," he assured Frau Freidl.

"You must go now? So soon?" Karin's mother looked suddenly distressed and her eyes filled with tears.

"We must if we're to get back before dark," he said. Privately, he didn't fancy the risk of another scene at a French checkpoint, especially in darkness. But Karin's parents must not be unduly worried about their daughter's safety, so Jack found another excuse for going. Shaking hands with Herr Freidl, he said "I have things to arrange for tomorrow morning and Karin has a busy day ahead in the office."

"*Ja, ist wahr, Mutti,*" she nodded, "we must leave."

When Jack held out his hand to Frau Freidl, she squeezed it hard but could find no words.

Karin kissed her father, who hugged her with emotion, then turned to Jack and said "Look after my little girl, Herr Major."

"I will," said Jack, and Karin's father added "I am reassured that she is in good hands."

Whether Karin herself had revealed to her parents in her letters the true nature of her relationship with the kind British officer who had driven her down the Rhine to Coblenz for the day, Jack would never know, unless Karin told him. He would certainly never ask her. Perhaps they had guessed, or maybe on the other hand they could not conceive of their daughter entering into a romantic attachment with an occupying ex-enemy officer.

Frau Freidl's last words from the doorstep were the colloquial German phrase, which Jack always found so charmingly simple and apt. "*Kommt gut nach Hause.*" 'Come home well', or 'Safe journey'.

IT was almost dark when Jack pulled up at the door of Karin's digs. He urged her to slip in quickly and quietly, for fear of attracting the attention of the sentry on duty at the Gunners' HQ across the street, who just might report to his Sergeant the mysterious arrival at a civvy billet late at night of a civvy girl dressed as a soldier, escorted by an officer from Divisional HQ.

But Karin said she wanted to give him something, and begged him to wait while she fetched it.

Sitting patiently at the wheel of his Jeep, Jack thought with satisfaction of their success in getting back unchallenged across the French border, until he was made aware by rumblings in his stomach that he had had to miss his dinner. He'd have to beg a piece of bread and cheese from Otto, if the chap was still on duty. 'That's what comes of getting tangled up with beautiful fraüleins,' he thought with a faint smile. He recalled the excitement of the adventurous trip to Coblenz and of his darling Karin's courage and guts in undertaking such a hazardous journey in disguise, all for the sake of her parents. What was a missed dinner, compared with a romantic day spent in the company of a glorious Rhinemaiden?

At this point in his reflections, Karin returned and pressed into Jack's hand a thick envelope, sealed with wax. Then, with a cursory "*Schuss*, Jack," she hurried back into the house and closed the door.

Half an hour later Jack was alone in a corner of the ante-room, downing a *Stein* of delicious, ice-cold Löwenbrau and munching bread and cheese, as he opened the sealed envelope.

Most of the officers had gone to bed. Only the field security officer, ADOS, the education officer and the padre, in a far corner, were engrossed in a game of bridge, and they scarcely noticed the young Grenadier, as he gently and symbolically ruptured Karin's seal – a large ornate K – in order to invade the privacy of her innermost thoughts and feelings. Carefully he drew from the envelope a long, closely written letter and a small leather-bound book, its pages covered with handwritten poems, all initialled KF.

As he glanced at the closely written pages of poetry and began to translate, a strange mixture of excitement tinged with anxiety and a touch of guilt overcame Jack.

He needed no German dictionary to tell him that this was heartfelt, emotional stuff, written from the depths of the soul of a young girl in love for the first time. Spiritual and physical desire were both expressed:

Nur deine Haende moecht ich streicheln
und dir ganz nahe sein!
Deine dunklen Haare mit weichen
Lippen Kuessen: sei mein.

'Oh to stroke your hands and feel you near me, to kiss your dark hair with soft lips: be mine.'

In her letter Karin assured Jack that she dreamed of him every night, that he lay beside her in the dark, stroking her body with his strong hands, that when she gazed into his clear eyes, she could see Heaven, that her world was filled with happiness and the music of his laughter and the sound of his voice.

Jack lay in the dark alone that night, staring up at the ceiling of his small room in the officers' billet.

It was very flattering to have had pages and pages and pages of love poems written to him by a beautiful girl, he thought. It was something he'd never experienced in England. The nearest he had come to it was when a girl called Peggy Stuart, with whom he had danced cheek-to-cheek at a Pony Club dance in Berkshire one long-leave from school, had written him a letter the next day on dark blue embossed notepaper headed The Old Rectory, Harpinge, Berks, saying how much their dance had meant to her and would he like to come over for tennis on Sunday? He had accepted eagerly, but Peggy's mother had put him off at the last moment. No reason had been given but Jack guessed that either she didn't trust him with her daughter or, more likely – since she was an incurable snob – had her eye on someone with a title.

Karin's feelings were on an entirely different plane, and he wondered whether he was as much in love with her as she seemed to be with him. Everything pointed to it yet, in some ways, the setting, the odd situation he found himself in, the lack of other distractions, other girls, told him that this passion for Karin could be deceptive. If one day, say in a year or so, after he'd been demobilized, Karin suddenly popped up in London, rang him up and wanted to see him, how would he feel?

His thoughts wandered. Again he wondered how the Freidls would react if their daughter told them she had fallen deeply in love with an English officer. Maybe she had told them. Maybe she dared not.

Jack fell asleep. It had been a long, rather fraught day.

THAT evening, as Sir John entered the Bergischerhof Hotel, footsore from tramping round Godesberg and disappointed at his failure to find any trace of Karin, the receptionist handed him a postcard: a brown, official-looking communication that had come for him in the afternoon post. A quick glance at it raised his hopes. There were some words typed under an official heading: '*Abgabenachricht*', something about Fraülein Karin Freidl, and an address in Leverkusen.

The Judge opened his door hurriedly with the heavy hotel key and then flopped onto the bed in order to study the card, with the help of his German dictionary that was lying on his bedside table. After careful scrutiny, he realized that the clerk at the town hall in Coblenz had come up with some positive information. She'd found Karin Freidl, who was alive and living in Leverkusen, only a few miles up the river from Cologne. There was no doubt about it. The message on the card was quite clear. Fraülein Karin Freidl now lived at No. 23, Bismarckstrasse, Leverkusen.

Fraülein? So she'd never married; still Fraülein Freidl, after all these years. 'She's an old maid,' he mused. 'My Rhine-maiden, now a spinster of sixty-three or sixty-four. Unless Freidl is her professional name. She could be a writer of course; an authoress, or a singer or even a painter. Perhaps famous. Too famous and established to have taken her husband's name when she married.' As he took a bath and dressed for dinner, a whole flight of fanciful ideas about Karin's fortunes danced in his mind.

He was too tired to go out again to a restaurant, although there was a pizza bar just opposite the hotel, beneath what had been the main block of the Bergischerhof in 1945 but was now a huge insurance office building. Instead, he found a quiet corner table in the little dining-room, ordered the set dinner with a bottle of Mosel, and began to meditate on how he should approach Karin. There was no telephone number on the card from Coblenz but, surely, she would be in the directory. Then, after some reflection, he decided against telephoning. The shock might be too much – a strange voice from out of the past. Besides, he thought, she might be ill or . , . unstable in the mind. Better to go there personally, ring the bell and disclose his presence to her gently, on the doorstep. It would be easier, wiser. Yes, he would go to Leverkusen tomorrow, probably by taxi from Bonn. It would be expensive, but this was to be the key journey, the climax of his visit to the Rhine. He would do it in style.

Chapter 6

WHEN Jack arrived at the office on the Monday morning after the trip to Coblenz, Karin was already at work with Corporal Bridges. They were sending out tickets to the various units for another *Tanzabend*, the last show having been so popular that, this time, every unit in the Division had applied for a substantial allocation.

Karin showed Jack a copy of the poster to go out for display in all areas. It would certainly make sure the show was a sell-out. Klaus Spiegel had taken an extremely sexy photograph of his voluptuous wife, posed in her diaphanous, chiffon costume, alluring and unsettling, with a wicked smile on her face.

"That should get them in all right," said Jack, swallowing hard to steady his voice and conceal a surge of sexual excitement that suddenly hit him at the sight of it.

He glanced at Karin and noticed that she looked just a little flushed and perhaps mildly shocked by the daring photograph.

"Klaus Spiegel came here early this morning," she said evenly, "to tell you he has added two new items to the programme and will drop 'The Cuckoo Clock' dance, because he thinks it is too long and bores the soldiers."

"OK," said Jack, going through to his office.

Towards midday, Jack and Karin went into Mehlem for a regular weekly conference on concerts and opera performances at Ingrid Pauels' house, where Julius Heuss was now comfortably settled in Karin's old room.

There, it was decided to allow Karin, as a reward for her hard work, to choose the programme for a special concert by the Cologne Symphony in the second week of November. Her choice would, of course, be subject to the availability of scores and limited by the size of the orchestra. After some discussion, she chose to start with the 'Leonora' No. 2 Overture, followed by the Rachmaninov Piano Concerto in A Flat Minor and, as the main work, the Symphony No. 5 by Sibelius.

During the conference Julius Heuss got up and asked Ingrid if he might go to her kitchen and make some coffee.

When he was in the kitchen, Ingrid lowered her voice to say "He is so sweet and modest, you know. Three weeks already he is here but he still behaves as though Werner is at home and he is just a humble guest." She also said that Julius had no money and was constantly embarrassed at living in her house rent-free. "Always I must tell him his company is payment enough for me. And the joy of seeing how he recovers every day a little from the death of his dear sister, Margharete. I tell him also, he should remarry. Frau Professor would have wished it so. A man is never too old to marry again."

A short silence followed. Ingrid glanced out of the window, thoughtful for a moment, then looked back at Jack and Karin sitting side by side on the sofa, their note-books on their knees, like two children at school.

Heuss had just come in with the coffee, so Ingrid turned to him, as he put the tray down: "Willy Pohl or Krauss?"

"Willy Pohl," said Heuss immediately. "*Der* Krauss is a fine player but he does not understand Rachmaninov."

Ingrid turned back to Karin and Jack with a gesture of finality.

106

"There. We have a decision from the Maestro himself. There shall be no more discussion. We invite Rudolph Krauss to play on the 15th of November. Good?"

"Good," agreed Jack, and Karin took his hand and squeezed it. Feeling slightly self-conscious, he wondered if this signified approval for his willing co-operation with Ingrid and Heuss in matters musical, or possessiveness; or whether it was a spontaneous gesture of happiness and love? Knowing Karin as he now did, he felt sure it was the last.

"WHAT time does it start?"

Jack had not been listening. He was miles away, thinking about Karin.

There could be no doubt about her feelings for him. But what about his for her? Was this genuine love or just being 'in love', infatuation? . . . He came to, with a start.

"What?"

"This dance show you're dragging me to."

Peter Franks, downing a glass of port was at Jack's elbow. Round the large B Mess dinner table a handful of officers were dispersed in twos and threes, smoking and talking.

"Eight o'clock, at the Gunners' place near Gummersbach. We ought to be off or we'll be late."

"That's what I thought," said Peter, getting up and putting his napkin back in its ring.

Karin had told Jack earlier in the afternoon that she would rather not accompany him to the *Tanzabend* that evening, as by now she had seen it in Bonn. Besides, she had letters to write. So Jack had said to her that he would call on the way home after the show and he had suggested to Peter Franks that he might enjoy the dancing, explaining that the Company would do all sorts of stuff: rumbas, blues, exotic numbers, rather like the Folies Bergères.

"In that case," Peter had said, "I'll risk it."

ALONE in her bed-sitting room at the top of the dentist's house in Frankengraben, Karin was about to complete the third page of a long, newsy letter to her brother, Dieter. Reaching for another sheet of paper, she began to wonder whether her letter would ever reach him. Supposing he was suddenly transferred to another prisoner-of-war camp or even released before the letter could reach him? Then her thoughts strayed to Jack, who would be at the *Tanzabend* by now with his friend Peter Franks. A vision invaded her thoughts, her first sight of the young British captain, his dark, wet hair and broad shoulders showing above the surface of the Rhine that warm afternoon, addressing her in German, a friendly, hopeful smile on his face. Then she remembered her anxiety when she realized that she was illegally communicating with an English officer. He was not supposed to fraternize with her, nor she with him. They were recent enemies. At this point a sharp rap on her door made her start. Assuming it to be her landlady Frau Inner, the dentist's wife, Karin got up from her table and went quickly to open the door.

A man stood on the landing, only half visible in the dim light. He appeared to be in his late thirties, wearing a long belted coat and a peaked civilian cap. He wore steel-rimmed glasses. Karin had never seen him before and the rather cold, unfriendly tone of his voice, when he spoke, chilled her heart.

"Fräulein Freidl?"

"*Ja, was wollen Sie?*"

The stranger said he was from Cologne and that he wished to speak to her about an important matter . . . in confidence.

"*So, kommen Sie herein bitte . . .* " Karin stood aside and, as the man passed her, she caught a fleeting glimpse of a scar across his left cheek. She followed her visitor in and gestured to him to sit in her only armchair. "*Nehmen Sie bitte Platz,*" she said without warmth, annoyed by his terse and un-sympathetic manner.

Before he sat down, the man asked "You are the sister of Dieter Freidl?"

"I am."

The stranger sat down and stared at her for quite a while, without saying a word.

Karin noticed that his hands were shaking a little. He seemed distinctly ill-at-ease, so she said quietly that her brother was a prisoner-of-war, still held by the Americans in Italy, and that she had just been writing a letter to him.

The man seemed uninterested, but lit a cheroot while telling her that it was concerning her own conduct that he had come to see her. At this a cold shudder ran down Karin's spine. A sudden twinge of fear gripped the pit of her stomach and she turned pale.

THE Gunners, like Peter, roused to heights of enthusiasm by Lili's execution of Salome's 'Dance of the Seven Veils', had invited the Company to stay on for soup and sandwiches after the *Tanzabend*, before their long coach trip back to Cologne. Jack, however, had arranged to drive the Spiegels straight home after the show, as they were anxious not to be back too late. As they drove into the night, Jack tried to convince himself that he was being tremendously helpful and kind to the Spiegels in seeing them home. But in his heart he knew well that he wanted to see more of Lili and get to know her better. For the second time since June 1945, he found himself aroused by a German girl, just as he had been the first time he spotted Karin swimming in the Rhine.

Jack found it strange that any girl could go out on a stage to dance and writhe and twist about in a highly erotic manner, exposing much of her scantily clothed body to the gaze of a hall packed with men, and then come off stage to behave like a self-conscious, nervous child, speaking in quiet monosyllables and giggling awkwardly. Nothing, Jack thought, could be more seductive. He'd never found exciting the brash, loud, extrovert, jazzy sort of cabaret stripper in silver tinsel and fish-net stockings, who winked provocatively and belted out a blues number, while twirling her stockings and other discarded garments round her head in the process. That was, for Jack, always a yawn.

What he found devastating about Lili Spiegel was her illusion of modesty and innocence. Moreover, he was curious to discover more of the relationship between Klaus and Lili, an unlikely and oddly-matched couple. Klaus, from every aspect of him; his gestures, tone of voice, small mincing steps and tight little mouth, together with the movements of his head, meant he must surely be queer. A pansy. A fairy. After all, Jack thought, a hell of a lot of male dancers were. Yet he was married to this dark seductive woman. What did she see in him?

Jack was sure they had no children. But did they actually sleep together, make love in bed? Or was it a brother-sister sort of relationship? Were they, perhaps, two people thrown together by a common love of dancing? Anxious for company, needing to share their lives with a kindred spirit? Klaus was certainly six or seven years older than Lili, possibly more. He was her teacher, her trainer and dance instructor, her mentor. Was he playing Svengali to her Trilby?

They reached the outskirts of Cologne, and as they drove between the grim, dark outlines of irreparably damaged buildings, bumping over rough roads pitted with bomb craters and strewn with twisted, burnt-out and abandoned cars, Lili and Klaus became uncertain of the way.

"Everything is so changed, you see," Klaus explained, "with the *Bombenschaden*."

"I know," said Jack, forcing back a slight feeling of guilt. "Awful what bombs can do."

"If we can find the road to the railway station," Klaus said, "we must then take the third turning after the Eisenbahnplatz. The Goethestrasse is now blocked completely. Five big shops and a garage are piled up in the middle of the road. People have to climb over the rubble to reach their homes."

A fresh wind was blowing, and it brought into the Jeep a smell that Jack recognized: the sharp, unpleasant stench of burnt-out timber and scorched woodwork mixed with the faint odour of rotting bodies, human and animal, that still lay buried under mountains of plaster and masonry. It was a smell that characterized every badly bombed or shelled town that Jack had passed through, in France and Belgium and Holland; and again in the German frontier towns of Goch and Kleve, which his battalion had reached in the Allied drive to the Ruhr.

Soon Klaus recognized the jagged outline of the station, and after a few turnings they pulled up in the Adelstrasse by a square, featureless, comparatively new building of dirty white stucco with many small windows. It was almost the only block still standing in the area, and even that had a gaping hole down one side, with the outer wall torn away by bomb blast. By the light of a street lamp, what was left of the staircase could be seen, open to the elements, and also half a room, its wallpaper still in place, and torn, scorched curtains flapping in the breeze. The Spiegels' apartment was on the third floor.

Jack got out and helped Lili from the Jeep.

Klaus extricated himself from the back. "You will come up for a glass of wine, please?"

"Thanks," Jack replied with enthusiasm, though something warned him to add, "just for half an hour. Mustn't stay too long."

FIFTEEN miles away in Karin's bed-sitting-room her visitor got up from his chair.

"You are employed by the English army, yes?"

"How did you know that?" Karin asked, her heart beginning to thump and a dry feeling coming into her mouth.

"That is no concern of yours, Fraülein," the man said. "We are interested in German people who are in the pay of the

Besatzungstruppen. How much they earn, for whom they are working and in what capacity. That is all."

"I see," Karin said, feeling slightly easier. "Then I imagine you are from the *Stadtverwaltung,* an official person?"

The visitor evaded that question, but went on fairly convincingly to interrogate Karin about her job at the Entertainments Office.

"I help to arrange concerts and shows for the British soldiers and for our own people. I am secretary to the officer who does this, also I am *Dolmetscherin* to interpret for him."

"His name?"

"Captain Hamilton."

The man made a note of this and went over to pull back the curtain and look down into the street below, so that he was not looking at Karin when he asked suddenly "You are friendly with this Captain Hamilton?"

Karin felt another little pang of fear, but she managed to keep her voice calm and firm. "Captain Hamilton is a man of honour and very correct."

"But you are friendly with him beyond your normal duties?"

Karin caught her breath but said nothing.

"Please do not try to deny this, Fräulein Freidl. Telling lies will not help. Your relationship with the British captain is already known to our group."

Karin's mind raced back over the last weeks, trying to think of anyone who might have spoken of her feelings for Jack. Not Ingrid, surely, or Herr Dr Heuss. Otto Maier might have said something without thinking, or even Emmerich Karl, the conductor. But would they be so two-faced as to complain to the German authorities of her liaison with Jack? The people of Bonn and Godesberg were the beneficiaries of her musical co-operation with the English, hers and Ingrid's.

"What group?" Karin asked, still fighting to control a slight tremor of anxiety in her voice.

"That is not your concern."

"So you're not from the *Rathaus*, you're not an official?"

"I am a former prisoner-of-war, Fraülein. There are many of us returned now to our homeland after service with the *Wehrmacht* and we do not expect to see our women acting like whores with British officers."

"How dare you say such . . . " Karin began, but the stranger's voice cut in like a whiplash, high and shrill.

"You will be wise to end both your employment and your intimate friendship with Captain Hamilton at once or you will have reason to regret it."

The man was at the door now, his hand on the handle. He opened it and turned back to face Karin. Then, quite suddenly, in a flash so quick that she was barely able to take it in, his right forearm shot up and was lowered again and Karin just caught the barely audible words, as he murmured "Heil Hitler" and was gone.

Karin sank into the armchair, her face drained of colour, her heart thumping wildly. After a moment she got up and rushed to the window, drawing back the curtain just in time to see a large, rather ramshackle Mercedes touring-car disappearing down the dimly lit street.

MEANWHILE, Jack was accompanying the Spiegels up to their apartment. It was a long climb up three flights of circular stone stairs, with an iron railing. On the first landing there was a strong smell of boiled cabbage and the sound of a baby crying. Up one more flight and someone was scraping a violin, in competition with a barking dog. Jack observed, with a feeling of sadness, that the unseen fiddler would never qualify for the Cologne Symphony Orchestra. And they could do with some more string players. Pausing for breath at the third floor, Jack realized how horribly unfit he had become lately – drinking too much Moselle in the Mess every night and going everywhere in his Jeep, when he wasn't stuck to his office desk.

Only five months before, when hostilities ceased, he'd been as fit as a flea, as you had to be in battle.

Now he stood gasping for breath, as Klaus unlocked a door on the landing and stood aside for Jack and Lili. The studio flat consisted of one large room with a sofa, armchairs and a wood-burning stove at one end, and a small, round, scrubbed wood table. The rest of the room was a miniature dance-studio with a very old, well-worn area of parquet floor, a mirror entirely covering one wall and a practice bar. The other walls were bare, but for two or three reproductions of rather bizarre paintings by Braque and Picasso. Through a small arch were the kitchenette, bathroom and bedroom.

Klaus turned on a few dim lamps and placed a log in the stove, as carefully as though it was a bar of gold. Jack looked round, noticing that the dance floor was strewn with female apparel; tights, bras, blouses, bits of black muslin and chiffon and stage garments of all kinds, suggesting that Lili had been trying on costumes in front of the mirror where she practised her steps. Jack, already aroused by her overpowering sex-appeal, found this all highly erotic. Slightly ashamed of himself, he switched his glance to a small table beside the dance area on which stood a wind-up portable gramophone and a pile of records.

Lili had disappeared into the bedroom and Jack, accepting a glass of wine from Klaus, assumed she would not be partaking. But when Klaus failed to respond to his friendly "*Prost*" with a raised glass, Jack asked him if he were not having a drink. Klaus shook his head with a sad smile.

"If I drink wine, I become too – *dick* – thick – "

"Fat?" Jack volunteered.

"*Ja*, too fat to dance. Lili will drink a glass with you. Her body will come to no harm."

Sipping his wine, Jack wondered whether there was any likelihood of being offered something to eat, some 'blotting paper' for the alcohol. A crust of bread would do, he thought; anything.

Then he remembered that even bread was a precious luxury in Cologne, and resigning himself to going without sustenance, he settled down to discuss the *Tanzabend* with Klaus.

After a while the bedroom door opened and Lili emerged, clad in a towelling robe, loosely held together by a belt and plunging at the neckline, with bare feet. Jack had the impression that she was wearing nothing underneath. She picked up her glass of wine and sat on a chair opposite Jack, saying nothing, just smiling demurely and listening to the conversation.

Klaus was talking about a new dance he'd been working on for Lili, a technically difficult ensemble number called '*Zereissung*'.

"*Zerreissung?*" Jack repeated. "That means break, tear, rip . . ."

"Is good. We show you," said Klaus, refilling Jack's glass and muttering to Lili, "*Geh Dich umkleiden, vorführen, ja? Ich bereite die Musik vor.*"

Jack swallowed another glass of wine, his fourth, and found himself beginning to tremble with excitement.

Lili shot a quick 'Must I?' glance at Klaus, who again murmured "*Umkleiden*", upon which the girl rose obediently to her feet, moved across the studio and picked up from the pile of costumes strewn about the parquet flooring a long, black cotton robe with frayed edges and a lot of roughly stitched seams.

As Klaus selected a record for the gramophone and started winding it up, Jack poured himself a fifth glass of wine, realizing as he did so that he was getting pretty drunk; he was beginning to see double, experiencing that hazy, extra outline that appears around objects and peoples' faces, accompanied by a mild weakening of the knees. The room began to sway a little.

Klaus explained that the stage would be dark, with flashes of thunder and lightning, and the setting would represent a wood with the girl dancers grouped about the scene, covered from head to foot in painted cloth, their arms outstretched with sharp claws on their hands, to represent the jagged branches of trees. "Through the forest," Klaus went on, "will come a young woman, caught in the storm. She attempts to find shelter. But, as she runs through the woods, the trees impede her progress, the sharp branches rip and tear her dress, as she struggles on . . ."

Suddenly all the lights in the room went out, but for a dim, blue lamp over the stage mirror. Lili had appeared from the bedroom, wearing the long black garment and Klaus had switched off the lights.

The gramophone started playing some dramatic, turbulent music. Then, as it built up, Lili mimed the movements of a scared girl in a storm, clasping her arms around her, bending her head against the wind, lost and bewildered.

Jack was suddenly distracted from his hypnotic stare at Lili to find Klaus standing beside him, holding out his hand.

"Come, Herr Major, and help her."

"Help her?" said Jack, puzzled. "To escape the storm?"

He began to laugh rather stupidly, as he staggered to his feet.

"We have no trees on which she will tear the dress. The girls of the ballet are not here, so you shall be all the trees."

"You mean – I – *Ich muss zerreissen*, I must rip her dress? Like a tree?"

"*Sicher, sicher*," Klaus nodded, urging him on.

Jack couldn't believe his luck. His whole body was pounding with the breathless anticipation of a chance to touch Lili and gradually to uncover her lithe form as she spun around the dance floor in front of that vast mirror. It was a fantasy that had gripped him twice before, when he had watched her dance for the troops in various crowded halls. Now it was to become a reality. The music grew louder, the beat more frenzied, and Lili moved her supple body ever more seductively against the imaginary wind and rain.

"Go, Herr Major, be the sharp branches of the trees, tear at her, trap her, and she will escape and dance . . . "

In a haze of wine and disbelief, Jack lurched forward onto the dance floor, wondering what the hell Klaus was doing in encouraging him to take part with his wife in this dance, allowing a complete stranger, a British officer, to strip her only garment off her in his presence, and indulge in what was clearly developing into a minor orgy.

Lili was by now writhing and twisting very close to him, and he kicked off his shoes, threw off his tunic, tore off his tie, unbuttoned his shirt and lumbered towards her, eager to take his part in the proceedings.

Lili suddenly spun into a position close to him, her knees touching his. As she seized his right hand and placed it on a spot just below her left arm, where there was a small hole in her dress, he saw she was breathing heavily with excitement

"So, halten Sie mich fest – jetzt bin ich von einem Baum festgehalten – davon muss ich wieder frei."

Jack got the message that he was now supposed to represent the sharp branch of a tree, and so gripped her black garment by the small tear. Lili spun away from him with a sharp, ripping and rending of the flimsy material, which came away in his hand, exposing a vast area of her left side, completely naked. Wildly aroused, Jack took a pace towards his partner to rip some more off her but Klaus shouted to him to stand still and hold out his hand again, as a tree, to let Lili come to be caught again in its branches, to tear herself free and lose another portion of her covering. But Jack was completely out of control now. The music, the wine and the sight of Lili Spiegel with her black dress in tatters, exposing more and more of her gorgeous body, drove him beyond his last remnants of self-restraint. Klaus or no Klaus, Jack joined in the dance, chasing and cornering Lili from one side of the dance floor to the other, ripping off another piece of her dress as she sped away from him. One gleaming white shoulder was already bared and Jack went for the other, this time gripping her dress at the back with both hands and tearing at it with all his strength. As Lili spun round again, her firm white breasts became totally exposed. Then, suddenly and unexpectedly, as a lascivious grin appeared on her face, she seized Jack's shirt and tore it off his front.

Vaguely, through the roaring in his ears and the throbbing in his temples, Jack could hear Klaus applauding and crying out: "*Aber das ist grossartig, der Major ist ein fabelhafter Tänzer*".

Those were the last words Jack heard that night, for at that moment the room spun round, the ceiling came crashing in on him, and everything went hazy and dim, then black. Temporary-Major John Hamilton, Grenadier Guards, barefoot, tieless, with his shirt half off his back, crashed to the floor and lay still.

Chapter 7

IT took Jack some minutes to realize where he was, when consciousness returned and the events of the previous evening came slowly and painfully into focus.

Lying on his back with an aching head, the first thing he noticed was the little gilt bowl-shaped ceiling light over his head, which told him that he was in bed at his billet. It was daylight but very quiet; there was not a sound in the road but the twittering of birds and a solitary hoot from a barge on the Rhine.

As he tried to raise himself up to look at his travelling clock, an excruciating pain stabbed him in the head. He managed to see that it was getting on for eight o'clock before he flopped back on his pillow. The pain, combined with the sight of the clock which his mother had once given him, gave him a momentary pang of deep insecurity about his parents. Then he went on thinking about them, imagining them starting their day as they would be just about now, across the other side of the North Sea. He could see their sizeable, red-brick bungalow close to the golf-course at Sunningdale and his father in his dressing-gown, grey hair tousled, unbolting the French windows to let Sally, the King Charles spaniel bitch, out for an early-morning run; his mother, ready for a Red Cross committee meeting, busy at her desk; and Mrs Croft, the Hamiltons' cook-housekeeper, boiling their eggs for breakfast.

Jack felt ashamed, knowing how shocked his parents would have been to witness their son's behaviour last night, when he danced half-dressed with a semi-nude German woman in a sleazy flat amid the rubble of Cologne. It was not for this sort of thing that Arthur Hamilton, a respectable, retired solicitor, had encouraged Jack to join the Grenadiers, with whom he himself had served in France in 1917.

Jack thought of the formal photograph of himself, taken in 1939, in his Grenadier service dress and blue forage cap, which his mother displayed so proudly on one of her drawing-room side tables. Sybil Hamilton was a formidable woman with a will of her own, the daughter of a Cavalry general. He remembered how firmly she used to hug him in the hall at home before driving him to his prep. school, so there was no need to do so later, in the school lobby. It was an arrangement that suited them both. She would issue a stream of last-minute instructions: "Tell Matron I'll send on your tablets," "I've said you're to continue your music lessons," "Do write to your father sometimes; he so loves to get a letter." Never a word of affection; that was all packed into the bear-like hug. This happened after tea on the last day of the hols; his father would have given him a shy pat on the back and a ten shilling note after breakfast, before walking to the station to catch his train to London and Lincoln's Inn Fields.

These reflections were interrupted by a sharp stabbing in his head. He must have been concussed by his fall last night. So how did he get home? Did Klaus drive him back in the Jeep? They must have been alarmed when he fell and knocked himself out, and gone to get help. He could imagine Klaus, pale and nervous, banging on the door of the Military Police Headquarters near the Station. 'I have a British officer in my apartment who is drunk. Please come to remove him.' A sudden thought came to him, so he left his bed and staggered to the window. As he feared, there was no sign of his Jeep, which was normally parked in the street outside.

He returned to bed, now thoroughly alarmed and angry. He'd made a bloody fool of himself last night and fallen into a trap. Klaus had perhaps taken compromising photographs of him with Lili so they could blackmail him for food or cigarettes, or use their power over him to save their own skins from the de-Nazification Tribunal. But were the Spiegels Nazis? Were they capable of such behaviour? To give Klaus his due, it might be that allowing a minor orgy to take place with his wife was his way of thanking Jack for arranging the *Tanzabend* in the first place. So was it just a bizarre form of German hospitality? Some Germans would do anything to ingratiate themselves with their conquerors. 'No,' Jack thought, 'that's unfair. The Spiegels are not like that.' But by whatever miracle he'd managed to end up in his own bed this morning, one thing was certain. His trip with the Spiegels to Cologne last night must be known to his army colleagues. Peter Franks had known what his plans were and would have disclosed them, if questioned. Had there been a scandal and he'd been reported drunk and unconscious in a ballet dancer's flat in Cologne there could be awkward questions and possibly a Court Martial.

Breakfast was long since over when Jack reached the Mess and the German Mess waiter had already cleared the long dining-table. Jack found Otto in the pantry and managed to get a piece of toast and a cup of coffee, which he took away and consumed furtively in a corner of the ante-room, hiding behind a copy of the *Sphere* in case a senior officer should spot him and ask why he wasn't on duty.

The coffee went down well and Jack, feeling mildly revived, walked along the road to the Entertainments Office. Passing Corporal Bridges' desk on his way through, he noticed that his trustworthy assistant carried on typing with his head well down and failed to deliver the normal 'Good morning, Sir.'

That was a sinister omen. Jack sensed he was in bad odour. Or was it his guilty conscience? He didn't want to wait too long for an explanation. Karin was not in her room, so once he was safely behind his desk with the adjoining door open, he cleared an awkward frog in his throat and called through as casually as possible: "Corporal Bridges!"

"Sir." The typing stopped abruptly.

"Come in, will you?"

"Sir." Bridges came to stand in the doorway.

"Where's my Jeep?"

"In the Divisional Workshop, Sir, having the dent in the bonnet hammered out, Sir."

"What dent in the bonnet?"

"The vehicle sustained minor damage, Sir, last night, Sir, when you went off the road and turned over, Sir, on the way back from Gummersbach."

Jack tried hard to focus his memory but once again drew a blank around the end of his visit to the Spiegels' apartment. But he knew damn well he hadn't gone off the road or damaged the Jeep. "What's going on, Corporal Bridges?"

"In what way, Sir?"

"Why are you telling me all this – crap – about overturning the Jeep last night – coming back from Gummersbach?"

Corporal Bridges looked over the top of Jack's head at the wall behind him. "If you'll pardon the liberty, Sir, I think you'd better have a word with Mr Franks, Sir."

"Why Mr Franks?"

"He'll explain, Sir. He – saw you home, Sir."

"Oh, did he? – I see – all right, Corporal Bridges." Jack wanted this embarrassing interview to end. "You'd better carry on with whatever it is you're doing."

"It's a notice for the *News Guardian*, Sir, about the inter-unit cross-country run, Sir."

"Well, get on with it."

"Sir."

Bridges went out, leaving Jack little the wiser.

IT was your fault for telling Karin you'd come and see her when
ou got back from Gummersbach, then not turning up. She was
cared stiff by this chap who turned up at her billet, so she got on
er bike and cycled over to see if you were in the Mess and found
ne, playing a rubber of bridge before turning in."

"What in God's name are you talking about? What chap and
vhy was she scared?"

Peter Franks stirred his coffee, took a sip and put his cup
own on a table, stretching back with maddening leisure in a
eep leather armchair. Jack glanced round the crowded Mess,
vondering how much they all knew.

"All I know is that some character came to her room and
sked her a lot of questions about her job in your office, which
vorried her somewhat; and she felt pretty let down, you not
eing around when she needed you."

"Dammit, she didn't want to see the *Tanzabend* again; she said
ne would stay in her billet and write letters," he protested, as
nough that excused his failure to keep their rendezvous later.

Peter shrugged his shoulders and stifled a yawn.

"So who was this chap who came to see her?" Jack
ersisted.

Peter closed his eyes wearily. "She wouldn't tell me; just said
ne must speak to you about it, but when I told her you'd
olunteered to drive the Spiegels back to their flat in Cologne,
ne became even more alarmed; said the streets of Cologne
vere dangerous at night with bands of robbers and desperate
uffians armed with knives, sticking people up in dark alleys
or cash and cigarettes. There is also the danger of falling
nasonry. She said every time there's a slight breeze off the
thine a few more badly damaged buildings come crashing
own into the streets."

"So?"

"So, you ought to be bloody grateful for her concern, old boy."

Jack glanced round the ante-room, where a number of officers were helping themselves to after-lunch coffee, reading the papers or chatting.

"Peter," Jack said, lowering his voice, "I want to know what happened last night at the Spiegels."

"I'm about to tell you, old boy. Just keep calm and listen."

"Right."

"Karin seemed in such a state that I thought I'd better get hold of some transport and drive to the Spiegels' place to find you. Trouble was, neither of us knew the Spiegels' address."

"But you managed to get there?"

"Oh, yes. We got there all right," Peter went on, rather enjoying himself. "Luckily, your chap Bridges was at a social evening in the Corporals' Mess, so we were able to dig him out to look up the Spiegels' address in your office."

"It was locked," said Jack, trying to stave off the moment of truth.

"Bridges had the key."

"How did you get into Cologne? In your truck, I suppose."

"Precisely. Rather filthy in the back from carting coal around the area but the cab's all right. We just managed to squeeze in front, the three of us."

Jack swallowed hard. He was beginning to feel sick. "The three of you?"

"Karin, Corporal Bridges and me. We set off about twenty to one in the morning. – I say, what a mess it is, all round the Adelstrasse. I wouldn't care to live there."

Jack was trembling now. He dared not ask the next question until he'd got control of his voice. When he did, it came out an anxious squeak. "So then you – went up to the Spiegels' flat?"

Peter nodded his head, choking back spasms of mirth until

he finally burst into roars of laughter, causing one or two officers to look at him over their newspapers.

"What's so humorous, Peter? Hadn't you better tell me?"

Peter suppressed his amusement as he went on: "The door was opened by Frau Spiegel, wrapped in a rather dirty dressing-gown and trembling like a leaf. Herr Spiegel was hovering in the background, whimpering."

"So?" Jack asked, defiant but impatient to hear the worst.

"So," Peter continued, calming down a bit, "we went in."

"We?"

"Yes, we. We went in and there you were, stretched out on the Spiegels' sofa, out for the count and in a pretty tattered state."

"Did Karin come up to the flat with you?"

"Had to, old boy, to interpret. Bridges and I couldn't have discovered what had happened without her help. As far as I could make out, Klaus told Karin you'd been having dancing lessons from Lili, found the studio a bit warm, so took off your shoes and socks and your shirt, had drunk a bit too much wine and fell on your head trying to leap about like Nijinksy. – Is that true?"

"More or less," said Jack, now deeply depressed. "But I still don't understand this bit about turning over in the Jeep."

Peter Franks looked at his friend with a self-satisfied half-smile. "Don't you? Well, I'd better explain. When we got there, Klaus Spiegel told us he'd already telephoned the British Military Police to say that – "

"That what?" Jack asked, very tense.

"That a British officer had been injured in an accident. Naturally, the fellow was anxious to clear himself and do the correct thing."

"Did the MPs come round?"

"Fortunately, not until after Bridges and I had taken the Jeep round the block and overturned it on a pile of rubble. The story goes that the Spiegels found you, and to their eternal credit carried you up to the studio to bathe your bruised head and contact the MPs. By the time the bulls arrived, Karin had briefed Klaus and Lili to corroborate the story and put a blanket over you to hide your state of undress.

"You have good friends, Jack. Corporal Bridges, Karin, me, and the Spiegels. Mind you, I'm not sure you deserve us. – Get you another cup of coffee?"

Jack shook his head gloomily. "Did Karin say anything?"

"Not a word. She sat in complete silence between me and Bridges all the way back to Godesberg."

"Did she come in and – help – you know, get me into bed?"

"No. We dropped her off at the Mess to collect her bike, then she went back to her own place. Corporal Bridges said he thought she was crying but I didn't notice myself."

After a long pause Jack said quietly "Thanks, Peter. I'll go and see Corporal Bridges, put in an accident report and sign it myself. Don't want the fellow to get himself court-martialled for making a false statement."

Peter was privately amused by the irony of that remark, considering Jack had only narrowly escaped a court martial himself, thanks to the efforts of a loyal corporal, a brother officer and a Kraut girl friend. But he was sensitive enough not to rub salt in the wound. Instead, he got up, gave Jack a tap on the arm that combined sympathy, encouragement and just a touch of patronage, and went off to his billet to change for a game of squash.

JACK left the Mess at half-past two, imagining in his guilt that his escapade the previous night was being talked about in hushed whispers all round the Division.

As he walked into the office, Corporal Bridges greeted him with a polite but formal "Afternoon, Sir."

Karin was still not at her desk, a fact upon which Jack chose not to comment. There were several obvious reasons for her absence: the wretched girl had spent a long and distressing evening, beginning with an unwanted visit from some sinister fellow-citizen, and she was short of sleep; she was giving her job a miss today because some former German boy friend had come home from a POW camp and found her working for the Tommies; or she thought it wiser after all not to be employed by the British and had decided to quit. Whatever the reason for her absence from work, Jack knew he must go round and apologise. He decided to get it done at once.

Moments later Jack and Karin were face to face in her room at Frankengraben.

"Do you swear you've never met him before or seen him or – ?"

"I would not describe him as a stranger, Jack, if I knew who he was. Please try to be sensible." Karin's voice was sharp and cold, her tone unfamiliar to Jack. 'Not unnaturally,' he thought, 'she's angry and scared and it's my fault.'

"I can only say that I'm deeply sorry for what happened and sincerely grateful to you and Peter and Corporal Bridges for getting me out of that place. I only wish to hell I'd come straight back here instead of. . . It was most unfortunate this man came to see you on the one night when I was somewhere else." Jack tried to take Karin in his arms but she slipped free and moved across the room to the window. Jack followed her.

"I do love you, *Liebchen*, honestly I do. I dream about holding you in my arms and loving you properly. Perhaps if you'd let me I wouldn't get into a state when people like Frau Spiegel arouse my passions. Do you understand what I'm trying to say, darling?" Jack asked.

Karin's eyes widened at this admission that Jack's behaviour had been every bit as bad as she feared.

She said nothing so he went on, "After all I'm a normal, healthy male; you must realize what I feel about you, it's – I . . ." He gave up.

A short silence, and then Karin said, "Please leave me now, Jack. I would like to think about things. I need a little time by myself."

"OK." Realizing it was time to disengage and hoping for the best, Jack gave a shrug and a sigh. "Take a few days off from work," he said, "I'll tell Corporal Bridges." With that, he left her and walked back to the office.

The next morning a note was delivered by hand in Karin's handwriting. It read 'I have taken your kind offer of a few days away from the office to go to my home where my mother is not very well. A friend has arranged for me to get to Coblenz by barge. Karin.'

That was all. No message of love or affection. No mention of when she would come back.

IT was as well for Jack that the rest of the week was exceedingly busy. There was a big party at the general's *Schloss* for a visiting American press delegation, at which a string quintet was to play during dinner. Jack had put this together with volunteers from the string section of the Bonn Symphony Orchestra and had taken responsibility for getting them to the *Schloss* and back. There was also the senior chaplain's farewell party at the officers' club, for which a conjuror had to be transported from Düsseldorf.

Jack slept late on Sunday, waking at midday, and decided to go for a solitary walk along the Rhine and up into the mountains above the river. He was in no doubt at all that he had behaved badly and in his depressed mood felt that almost certainly he had blown his affair with Karin for good. Why in God's name did she have to turn up at the Spiegels' and find him there, half-dressed and unconscious?

Now the girl had gone off to Coblenz to see her parents and doubtless pour out her soul to them: how she'd found him dead drunk and snoring like a pig in his braces on the Spiegels' sofa after what must have looked like some sort of triangular roll-in-the-hay with a couple of depraved ballet dancers.

As he trudged miserably on up the hill, he could imagine the scene at Coblenz. She would tell her parents how she'd been fooled by a swine of an English officer, who pretended to be in love with her, but only wanted her in his bed, hadn't the guts to restrain his sexual passion, so satisfied himself with a nymphomaniac ballet dancer. Just as Jack arrived at the highest point on top of the Petersberg it started to rain, causing him to think of all those French movies in which jilted lovers walk alone through the rain with tears and raindrops competing to wet their cheeks. He could hear the mournful music on the sound-track and almost see the camera tracking back, as it held his tragic face in close-up. Perhaps, he thought, as he turned to descend the hill, he should take positive action now, as in a film. Should he drive down to Coblenz, seize Karin from the bosom of her family and bear her away to Godesberg, a knight on a charger? No, he thought, such a gesture might end in failure. If Herr Freidl ordered him out of the house and slammed the door in his face, not only he, but the entire British Army of the Rhine, would be gravely humiliated.

Another option was to write her a long, affectionate, apologetic letter, asking her to understand and forgive. He would write in German and hope that a few minor mistakes might charm her into making it up with him. '*Du muss mich vergeben, sonst ist mir das Leben . . . unertraeglich . . .* forgive me or my life will be unbearable.'

This course of action seemed the most practicable, and he brightened up at the thought of putting it into effect.

As soon as he got back to his billet Jack had a bath, changed and went over to the Mess, where he found an unoccupied writing desk in the ante-room. There, intermittently sipping a whisky and soda, he scratched away at his literary olive branch.

After several false starts, in which half a dozen crunched up bits of notepaper hit the wastepaper basket, his missive was finally finished.

My Darling Karin,

In case you can't guess how sad, angry and humiliated I'm feeling, I shall try to explain it to you in writing. What happened on

Thursday night was disgraceful and must have made you feel you have been wasting your time these last five months on someone unworthy of you. I know it is not much of an excuse, but my intentions were strictly honourable. I simply wanted to – had to – take the Spiegels back to Cologne after the *Tanzabend* and they were polite and hospitable enough to ask me up to their flat for a drink. I had not eaten anything for some hours and must have drunk a little too much of their wine. When Klaus encouraged me to dance with Lili, I was foolish enough to try and somehow lost my balance and fell. One obviously can't dance successfully in an Army tunic with trousers, braces etc. so I took them off, which accounts for my odd state, when you, Peter Franks and Corporal Bridges came to find me! I'm afraid it must have looked like some sort of a Roman orgy.

I miss you terribly and find the days long and dreary without your smiling face and sweet laughter in the Entertainments Office. Will I ever see you again?

I am very sorry to hear your mother is ill. I do hope she will recover soon, so that you can return to us. We need you here. (Corporal Bridges, Ingrid, Julius and I.)

Your own concert looms up. Don't forget it's on Nov. 15th. I feel sure you will be back in Godesberg for that, with I pray a forgiving heart. For mine is breaking without you.

Your penitent, loving friend, Jack.

P.S. Remember me to your family.

Reaching for an envelope, Jack realized he didn't know Karin's address in Coblenz and reflected that, anyway, it would be a risk to post his letter into another Zone of Occupation. The French would be sure to lose it. So he drove to the Frankengraben and dropped the envelope marked 'By Hand' through the Inners' letter-box. That done, he returned to the Mess to dine with a couple of brother officers, whose conversation about the brothels they'd visited on a recent forty-eight hours leave in Brussels jarred his nerves. After a while he said he was tired, and went to bed early. He still felt hurt, angry and had a distinct pain where his heart was.

"DO you love her?"

"I think I must, Ingrid. I miss her so much. I can't help thinking about her and hating myself for being so stupid."

Ingrid looked hard at Jack, and said meaningfully "I would not like little Karin's heart to be broken."

Jack thought of the passionate poems Karin had pressed into his hand after their trip to Coblenz and wondered yet again whether she had by now suffered a change of heart.

He had used Karin's programme for the forthcoming concert as an excuse to go to Bonn and confide his misery to Ingrid. They were sitting in her salon in semi-darkness, for the autumn day was almost over but economy dictated the latest possible lighting of the lamps. Outside in her small garden a few leaves were falling from a walnut tree and Julius, wrapped up with a warm scarf, was raking them into piles for burning.

"I feel like driving down to Coblenz right away. Tomorrow."

"No," said Ingrid firmly. "Do not be so impulsive. Your letter will be waiting for her, when she comes back. You must be patient. *Sei geduldig, mein Freund.*"

The wisdom of giving Karin time to sort out her feelings for Jack during her few days away from Bad Godesberg was apparent. She was plainly upset, hurt and disillusioned by what had happened but Jack thought his letter ought to help her get his exploit into perspective and decide whether her love for him was strong enough to understand and forgive. It wasn't as if he was having an affair with Lili Spiegel. – How could he? – She was married.

Ingrid rose and walked to the window to watch Julius outside in the garden.

"When a young girl of Karin's temperament loves, my dear, she loves with very great passion and fire and much jealousy. She believes you belong to her, body and soul, and she cannot bear that any other woman shall attract you or interest you in anyway."

"Nobody else does," Jack said.

"Good," Ingrid continued, "We Germans love with very great emotion and . . . how shall I say – *geist* – spirit."

"I know," said Jack. "*Gründlichkeit.*"

"You know the word?" Ingrid was smiling now. "Then you will understand how Karin feels."

"I do."

When Jack got up to leave, a strong shaft of golden light from the setting sun was shining through the open window on Ingrid's fascinating, lined face, like a sculpted bronze head in a museum that has been singled out for dramatic display by brilliant lighting. Jack could see what a beautiful creature she must have been in her younger days – and still was. Perhaps Karin would one day grow into a handsome, middle-aged woman like Ingrid, with all the wisdom and depth of feeling that older women seemed to contain.

Jack thanked her for listening to his tale of woe and for her comforting words.

"If she loves you, she will be back, my dear," said the *diva*, as he left the room. "Just remember that."

On the way back to his billet, Jack reflected on his decision not to tell Ingrid about the visit Karin had had from a possible blackmailer. He thought that he had made the right choice, for it would only have worried her.

DRIVING through Cologne in the back of a taxi on his way to Leverkusen, Sir John knew there was one place from his past that he would not wish to revisit even if he were able to. He could just envisage, dimly, that sleazy dance-studio where he had been 'entertained' by the Spiegels, high up in a half-destroyed apartment block in the Adelstrasse, close to the railway station. It would be impossible to find it now. The bomb damage around that area had been so intense that over the intervening years it must have been totally rebuilt. The Adelstrasse might well have ceased to exist, or have been renamed Truman Allee or something similar.

Also, the Judge reflected, he was not at all keen to be reminded of an evening of which he was not proud. His behaviour had been unworthy and he had managed, that night, to hurt Karin deeply and all but destroy a budding romance before it had had time to flower.

As the taxi driver reached a roundabout on the northern outskirts of Cologne, where several huge tower blocks threw their shadows over the crowded pavements, a sign to 'Leverkusen 8 KM' caught Hamilton's eye, and he felt a pang of anxiety and excitement, mingled with fear.

In a matter of twenty minutes, possibly less, he should be standing face to face with an elderly woman called Karin Freidl, once the girl who had loved him and whom he had loved in his fumbling, cowardly way but possibly destroyed by his selfishness and lack of maturity. What would he find, awaiting him at that address in Leverkusen, a few miles up the Rhine from Godesberg, where he and Karin first met one sunny afternoon, forty-five years ago?

To ease his anxiety, Sir John slid open the glass partition to talk to his driver. Commenting on the scenery, he told him that he had swum in the Rhine as a British officer of the Occupation Army over forty years ago.

The man gave a wry smile. *"Das Könnten Sie heute nicht, der Fluss ist viel zu schmutzig."* – Not now, the river is far too dirty. And the Judge realized that industry had as thoroughly polluted the Rhine as every other great river in the world. His driver was right. A swim in it today would be lethal.

As the taxi reached the fringe of Leverkusen Sir John saw his driver consult a street map and then turn off the main boulevard into a winding side street, which curved steeply down towards the river. The street merged into a broad quayside along the west bank of the river, where several Rhine barges were loading coal at a depot. There were a number of large warehouses and yards along the river front, where coal, pig iron and steel from the Ruhr was being loaded on to barges for transport down the Rhine to

Mainz, Mannheim, Karlsruhe and into the Black Forest region. The slopes above these quays were dotted with small, humble dwellings, little terraces of workers' homes, not unlike those to be found in Welsh mining villages.

While the taxi bumped and wound its way along a narrow street Sir John's heart sank until, after a final glance at his map, the driver found the Kaisergasse and stopped outside No.16.

After a moment of apprehension, during which he thought of making a run for it, Sir John eased himself out of the taxi and stood for a few seconds looking up at a drab little red brick house, blackened by smoke, with its paintwork peeling and its brickwork crumbling.

There was no bell or knocker, so he banged on the door. A dog barked inside and then a woman appeared, fiftyish or possibly younger, but aged by poverty and ill health. She was thin, and wore slippers and an apron. From the ladle in her hand he deduced she had been disturbed while cooking.

Sir John cleared his throat and asked in his best German if Fraülein Karin Freidl was at home.

The woman looked instantly suspicious and on the defensive. "Why do you ask?"

"I am anxious to see her. Does she live here?"

"She has a bad throat."

"May I speak to her, please?"

"Who are you?"

"I am an old friend of Fraülein Freidl. She will remember me."

"Are you from the school?"

That made some sense. Perhaps Karin had gone back to her old profession of teaching. Too old now to get a decent job. Forced into lodgings in a dump like this, teaching the children of Rhine bargemen.

"I am not from the school. Why do you ask?"

"She has missed school three days. Her throat."

"Is she in bed?"

"No. I will call her."

The woman turned into the narrow hall, and called out "Karin. *Komm her!*"

Jack asked the woman her name and she was just in the act of replying "Frau Freidl" when a little girl of six or seven peered from behind her mother's skirts; an angelic-looking child with fair curls and light blue eyes who sucked her thumb while treating the stranger to a dazzling smile.

"*So, da ist die Karin . . .* "

And Frau Freidl of Leverkusen took her little daughter's hand protectively against whatever threat this elderly, grey-haired Englishman posed to her youngest child.

PERHAPS, Sir John reflected, as he headed back to Bonn, the authorities had been over-zealous, but he had to give them full marks for trying. For him it was a deep disappointment, a depressing let down, and he was no nearer to finding Karin than he had been when he left London.

Rather than do nothing, he decided to telephone Coblenz and report politely on the Leverkusen *débâcle*; he did not want to alienate the authorities, in case they stopped trying. Meanwhile he would try to find the house in Mehlem where Ingrid and Julius Heuss had lived. Some neighbour might have survived who remembered Karin. It was worth another trip while there was still daylight.

Chapter 8

A FEW days passed and still Karin had not returned to Bad Godesberg. Jack was becoming convinced that her concert would have to take place without her. For Karin to miss the evening of music chosen by herself, demonstrated to him more than anything the depth of her anger and disappointment in him.

As he passed the lettered pigeon-holes on his way into the Mess for dinner, he glanced anxiously to see if there was anything for him; a reply from Karin to his letter, perhaps, if Frau Inner had chanced to forward it to Coblenz.

There were two letters in the cubby-hole marked H, and Jack seized them eagerly. One was for Captain A.G. Horlock, the Divisional Field Security Officer and the other an internal memo. for Captain P. Harper, the Education Officer.

Jack replaced the two envelopes and continued into the ante-room, inwardly despising himself for his foolish optimism. All the same, he told himself, the absence of a note from Karin did not necessarily mean she was still at Coblenz. Perhaps she would have found the constricting family atmosphere, with a lame father, a depressed and gloomy sister with a bawling child, and the probing of her mother into her private affairs, too much for her – especially after the freedom of her life in Bad Godesberg.

But if she left home again, where could she go, other than back to her job? Of course she would return. She must have got over her pique by now and at any moment she'd reappear in the office, contrite and a little tearful, to fall into Jack's outstretched arms.

On the other hand it was possible that, encouraged by her family, she had decided that the British were, after all, two-faced people. So she might have set off in search of a job in the American Zone, in the Frankfurt area, where more affluent conditions prevailed, with better paid jobs and a chance to work with generous and friendly Yanks. 'After all,' Jack thought, 'many GIs have German names and some of them are only second or third generation American immigrants. Karin could have gone to join her American cousins, to be spoilt with compliments and nylon stockings, never again to return to the British Zone!'

'But what about the music?' he thought. All their efforts together, with Ingrid and Julius, to revive the opera and the concerts? Would she really throw all that away, because of a tiff over one unfortunate incident at the Spiegels?

Curiously, it did not occur to him to think of the threat to Karin that had come on the night of his fiasco with the Spiegels. Shame at her discovery of his predicament blotted out from his mind the possibility of any cause for her disappearance other than his own bad behaviour.

Jack resisted the strong temptation to go round to her billet and see if she was there. If she was back, she must be allowed time to unpack and get herself settled in again. When he went into the office tomorrow morning, he would know soon enough what sort of mood she was in and where he stood with her. Meanwhile, one more lonely evening in the Mess had to be faced, no doubt to be followed by another anxious and sleepless night.

At dinner Otto informed him that most of the officers, including Mr Franks, were out, so Jack swallowed a whisky and soda and sat down by himself at the long table.

After a moment the Divisional Education Officer Philip Harper appeared, murmured "Mind if I join you?" and without waiting for an answer dropped into the chair next to him. Jack would have preferred to dine alone, but he could hardly say so, and in ordinary circumstances Harper's company was not disagreeable. He was a quite friendly if somewhat pedantic man, and no fool. He'd been Intelligence Officer to his Artillery Brigade in battle, spoke several languages and was widely travelled.

After tasting his consommé in silence, Harper opened a conversation with a request to pass the pepper.

"Looking forward to your demob.?" he asked, sprinkling his soup.

"Not much." Then, realizing how terse he must have sounded, Jack added "Are you?"

"I've got another six months."

"I get out in the new year. Wonder what sort of a world we'll find waiting for us," Jack said.

"A better one than we left behind, I hope," said Harper, "or the General Election will have been fought in vain."

Jack had suspected for some time that Harper was a Labour supporter and this remark made his Conservative hackles rise. No doubt, part of his irritability was due to his anxiety about Karin, but in any case he felt a deep resentment at the recent election landslide. He was convinced that it had been caused by the itinerant Army Bureau of Current Affairs. This was manned by officers who had taken no part in the fight, had escaped the rigours of battle and instead had spent the last year or so beavering away delivering lectures to units in the field, persuading the troops to demand a new Utopia after the war; a classless society, an egalitarian socialist Welfare State.

Their propaganda, Jack felt, had caused the war-weary troops to 'vote against the sergeant-major', as someone had put it, and sweep Churchill and the Tories out of office to make way for a new Socialist government under Clement Attlee.

"If the Labour Government has achieved nothing else so far," said Jack, feeling the need to be fairminded, "at least they're sticking to their anti-Colonial principles and planning to give India back to the Indians."

"They have no choice. Gandhi's policy of civil disobedience and passive resistance has made sure of that."

"Do you think it'll work? Indian independence?"

To Jack's surprise, Harper expressed certain reservations on the subject. "I know India," he said; "I was out in Calcutta and Bombay before the war. In my view, there's a very real danger of long drawn-out and extremely bitter civil war between Moslems and Hindus, unless great care is taken with the granting of Partition. That's to say, the planned creation of two separate states."

Jack hadn't thought of that. "You mean they might slaughter each other, the two rival religious groups? Nehru's boys and Jinnah's boys?"

Harper sipped his Moselle and nodded. "We could see bloodshed on the sub-continent, if it's not handled with considerable tact and statesmanship. Let's hope Mountbatten can steer it through."

"Quite," said Jack.

They went on to discuss other topics of the day, including the Nuremberg War Crimes Trials and the dropping of the atomic bombs on Hiroshima and Nagasaki, which had brought about Japan's unconditional surrender and the last-minute salvation of about six million multi-national occupants of Japanese concentration camps, by then nearly all at the point of death.

Philip Harper proved to be a stimulating dinner companion, and by the end of the meal had effectively taken Jack's mind off his own troubles.

But this relief from worry proved only temporary. For most of the next morning Jack sat alone at his desk brooding, with only half his mind on the job.

Around midday Corporal Bridges came back from a visit to the Gunners at Reifenfeld to help arrange their sports day, and looked in on Jack. "One minor query, Sir."

"What is it, Corporal Bridges?" Bridges looked a trifle uneasy, but after a pause cleared his throat. "About Fraülein Freidl, Sir."

"What about Fraülein Freidl?"

"How long is she going to be absent, Sir?"

Jack exploded at the touch of this match to the gunpowder of his irritated temper. "She is not absent, Corporal Bridges," Jack shouted furiously.

"No, Sir."

"I object strongly to that word."

"Sir."

"She's not AWOL, like some bloody guardsman!" said Jack, even as he realized that the man had a point.

Shaken, Corporal Bridges said "No, Sir," again, feeling as though he'd just stepped on a landmine, but also that he now knew more exactly the quality of his senior's affection for his supposedly unfraternal secretary.

"Fraülein Freidl has gone to Coblenz, with my permission, to see her mother who is ill."

"I see, Sir. More like compassionate leave, Sir?"

"If you insist," said Jack. 'After all,' he thought, 'she is on the staff payroll and technically, as an employee of the British Army of the Rhine, she bloody well is absent. If she was an ordinary guardsman, she'd be on a charge. But she's not, bless her, she's just a girl, an adorable, lovely creature, whom I have shamefully wronged. I ought to be on a charge, not her.'

Coming sharply back to reality and irritated to find the worthy corporal still standing before him, he snapped at him "What's that in your hand?"

"It's the programme for the concert on the 15th, Sir. It ought to be sent off to the printers today, Sir."

"Then send it."

"Do you wish to check it before it goes, Sir? It's the pieces chosen by Fraülein Freidl, if you remember, Sir."

"Yes, Corporal Bridges, I do remember."

Jack glanced at the sheet in Bridges' right hand. "Isn't that her handwriting?"

"Sir. She wrote it out herself the week before last."

"Well, there won't be any spelling mistakes," said Jack, "and there are no alterations that I know of, so bung it into Brühl's Printing Works at once."

"Sir."

Bridges went out, leaving Jack even more morose than before. 'If Karin doesn't come back for her own concert,' he thought, 'the whole exercise will be totally pointless."

Later that afternoon Otto telephoned Jack to say that a lady had arrived at B Mess asking for him and would he come over. In no more than three minutes Jack was racing up the steps of the Mess building, two at a time, only to stop short, slightly out of breath, just inside the door. The only female in sight was a woman in khaki uniform, her back to him, studying the noticeboard.

As Jack stared at the unknown back, cursing inwardly, she turned round to face him; a plain, hard-faced female in her thirties with horn-rimmed glasses and short-cropped hair under an ATS cap.

Seeing Jack gazing at her with his mouth open, the woman advanced, at which Jack noticed she clasped in her hand a clipboard – the symbolic prop carried by all busy, efficient ladies of the Armed Forces.

"Major Hamilton?"

"Yes?"

"Staff-Sergeant Broadbent, ATS, HQ 30 Corps."

"Yes."

"Wasn't sure where your outfit operates from, so I asked the Mess chappie."

In spite of Jack's profound disappointment, he replied civilly enough. "In fact my office is just two houses along the street but it doesn't matter. What can I do for you?"

"Ping pong balls."

"I beg your pardon?"

"We need some for our billet and the Commandant told us to get in touch with the army welfare people at Division. So here I am."

"I see."

"We've got a ping pong table; quite a decent one actually, but no balls."

"No balls!"

"That is correct."

Jack suppressed a savage guffaw, along with the urge to tell her that he declined to provide her with balls himself. Instead, he said "Come along to the office and I'll hand you over to my assistant, Corporal Bridges. He'll fix you up."

"Good-oh," said the female warrior with an eager nod of the head. She led off at a brisk trot, while Jack, by contrast, left the building sedately, in a considerably more subdued mood than when he had entered it a few moments earlier.

THE following afternoon the printed programmes for Karin's concert arrived. Jack left Corporal Bridges to get them distributed while he drove into Mehlem to see Ingrid and ask her if she had any news of Karin.

It was almost dusk when Jack drew up outside the white stucco house where Frau Pauels had locked Karin in her room that June morning. It didn't seem like five months ago. Much had happened since. He rang the bell and waited. No banging on the door in the name of the British Army this time or shouting 'Machen Sie auf!' through the letter-box.

A bolt was drawn back inside and the door opened slowly.

The hall was so dark that, at first, Jack could barely make out the lean figure who stood outlined in the dark shadows.

A deep, shaking voice said in a whisper "Come please in, Jack. There has been some bad news." Julius closed the door behind Jack and switched on a dim light, so the latter could see the sadness and worry on the old man's already lined face.

"What's happened?" Jack asked. "Where's Ingrid?"

"She is up in her bedroom with the curtains closed. She will remain quiet for a while."

"Why?"

"Today has come news from the Red Cross people in Holland. Werner's body has been found . . ." The old man broke off to get control of his voice. "They found his remains – in the Waal river, near Emmerich – deep in the mud. – He was identified yesterday – "

"Oh, God! Poor Ingrid! She never gave up hope . . . "

"Now she is inconsolable."

"May I go up to see her?"

Julius shrugged his shoulders, so Jack went slowly up the stairs to the bedroom and knocked gently on the door.

A weak voice inside asked "*Wer ist da?*"

"It's Jack. May I come in?"

A long pause, then from inside "*Moment, bitte.*" He waited until he heard "Come in now, please." Then he opened the door, to find Ingrid on her bed, propped up on pillows and wearing a robe, her tear-stained face dimly lit by the bedside lamp. The curtains were closed and it was plain that she had been crying. After all those months and weeks of pent-up tension and uncertainty about Werner's fate, grief now had overcome her. Jack went over to the bed, bent down and put his arms round Ingrid's shoulders, resting his chin on the top of her head. It was an awkward gesture, but it touched Ingrid's heart and caused her to dissolve into tears again.

For a time nothing was said, while Jack massaged her back gently and muttered "There, there. I'm so sorry . . . "

The nearest thing he'd had to the experience of comforting a bereaved woman of middle age was an occasion years before, when Nanny Sutton's brother was killed in a car crash. Jack had been eight at the time and he could still remember his combined feelings of fear and embarrassment at seeing a grown woman crying.

After a while Ingrid pulled herself together and managed to say "You are so dear to come and see me."

"Not at all."

"I have always feared this moment, you know. It was hard to believe my Werner could be alive still. But I have lived in a foolish dream. Now I know for certain . . . perhaps it is for the best."

Jack perched on the edge of her bed and took her hand. "I know it's not much comfort, Ingrid, but you can surely be very proud of your husband, knowing that he. . . died for his country."

Ingrid nodded her head, too moved to say anything.

He did not tell her his thoughts on the irony of war. For Jack had a friend, Guy Baring, in the Leicester Yeomanry, which had shelled Emmerich for days at one stage during 'Operation Market Garden'. It could have been Guy who gave the order to fire the barrage that blew Werner Pauels into the Waal river. Who could say? And here Jack was, sitting on the dead man's bed, trying to console his widow. Such was the lunacy of war.

It was impossible to confide in Ingrid at this moment his worries about Karin.

LATER that evening Jack was interrupted in the middle of a game of backgammon with the Senior Chaplain by Otto, who came hurrying into the ante-room. He whispered dramatically to Jack that a woman was in the lobby wishing to speak with him. She appeared distressed. "*Etwas zerstört*," Otto added.

Jack jumped to his feet, muttered an apology to his ecclesiastical companion and followed the mess waiter out of the room.

Frau Inner stood in the hall, plainly agitated.

"My husband decide I must inform you, Herr Major. The Police have been just now to the house. Fraülein Freidl's bicycle has been found on the road, two miles out on the way to Mehlem. There is no sign of her but the machine is not damaged."

Jack thanked the woman for telling him and told her to return home and keep in close touch with the police. Meanwhile he would alert the military authorities. Frau Inner nodded, and vanished into the darkness outside.

As Jack returned to the backgammon board and told the Senior Padre of his anxiety, his heart was thumping hard.

The Chaplain was aware that Jack employed a female German interpreter in his office but knew nothing of the nature of their relationship. "Let's hope the woman turns up unharmed, old chap," he murmured, drawing on his pipe. "Too useful to lose."

Jack made an excuse, said he was tired, and asked the padre if they might play backgammon again another night.

By midnight he was in bed at his billet, staring up at the ceiling, unable to sleep. A connection between Karin's mysterious visitor and the discovery of her bicycle abandoned on an open road late at night was sickeningly obvious, and gave him considerable cause for alarm.

The next morning, half expected but none the less chilling in its implications, it came: an unsigned, anonymous note, scribbled on a message pad of the sort issued to officers of the *Wehrmacht*. The note was addressed to '*Hauptmann Hamilton, beim britischen Militarkommando am Rhein*'. There was a Cologne postmark just visible by the stamp and the missive had been delivered by a despatch rider from Guards Division Main Headquarters. Someone there had scribbled under Jack's name 'Try B Mess, Div. HQ.

As Jack tried to control his shaking hand and read the contents, he sensed trouble.

'Frl. Freidl will remain in our hands indefinitely if you will not be standing tomorrow at midday on the point here indicated. You must be alone if you wish to see Frl. Freidl again.'

Jack turned the note over to find on the back a crudely drawn map of the area of Cologne close to the Hohenzollern Bridge. A junction between two streets had been marked with a cross. Jack sank into his chair and let the note fall on his desk. In the silence that followed in the empty office, Jack could almost hear the pounding of his pulse as the blood rushed into his head.

So Karin was not with her parents, nor in the American zone. Some bloody gang of Krauts had seized her as a hostage, and the likelihood induced in him a mixture of cold fury, mingled with deep apprehension. 'They must be people who know that she works for the British Forces. And they know my name, maybe forced it out of her,' he thought.

He went over in his mind Karin's story of her sinister visitor on the evening of the *Tanzabend*. What a bloody fool he was not to have taken it seriously! How many days had the poor girl been held captive without his giving a thought to the possibility of her being kidnapped? What might they not be doing to her?

Having witnessed the cruel revenge meted out to French female collaborators when he passed through the liberated villages and towns of Northern France, he could imagine how some Germans, bitter in defeat, might punish their own kind for working with the enemy – even under military occupation. They might shave her head, whip and torture her for her friendship with a British officer and then hold her as a hostage to make demands on the officer concerned.

Action had to be taken at once to find and release Karin from captivity. That was certain, but what action should he take? And who, if anyone, should Jack consult? He knew that he alone was to blame for what had befallen her; he had, by his friendship with her, placed her in danger from her own countrymen. If he went to the GSOI or the DAQMG they would smile cynically and say 'We warned you not to get involved with the Krauts. It's their business. Nothing we can do.' Then an idea struck him. He remembered the incident the day after Karin's arrival at the office when Ingrid stopped her coming to work. On that occasion it was the Provost-Marshal who had instructed his Military Police to provide the Task Force for Jack's visit to Ingrid's house. He was a good chap, Major Sallis, sympathetic and ready for a fight. Jack decided to show the Provost-Marshal the note and take his advice. At the same time he told Frau Inner that the matter of Früalein Freidl's disappearance would be investigated by the British Military authorities, who would keep her informed.

When he had told Sallis his story, the P-M said "It sounds as though these chaps mean business, Hamilton, in which case they'll be armed. There are plenty of German weapons still around. *Wehrmacht* soldiers back from the front stowing their Schmeissers and Mauser revolvers away for future use. We can't guarantee 100 per cent disarmament."

"I can't risk anything happening to Karin. She could get killed if there was a shoot-out."

"I agree," said the P-M. "That's why for a start you must go alone to meet these people in Cologne. Find out who they are, what they want and just how dangerous the situation is for your – German friend."

AFTER a moment's thought Jack took Corporal Bridges into his confidence. He had to, really, for Karin's continued absence from work needed an explanation. Corporal Bridges was strongly opposed to the idea of Jack going to the rendezvous unaccompanied but accepted it as a preliminary 'recce' and not a case of going into battle – not yet.

At eleven o'clock on the following morning Jack put his

service revolver under a ground sheet in the back of the Jeep and set off for the suburbs of Cologne. His heart was beating as he drove along the road towards Bonn. It was like the war all over again, he thought, but in a way more exciting, for now he was more personally involved. He was a knight in a shining Jeep off to rescue a Damsel in Distress, from an enemy that was more repellent and snake-like, or dragon-like, than any of the soldiers he had fought against in battle.

It was a dark, overcast day with a slight drizzle that heightened the gloom and ugliness of the jagged, wrecked buildings and the numerous piles of rubble. As Jack drove up to the rendezvous on what had once been a street corner, he noticed two men standing by a newspaper kiosk, evidently deep in conversation.

He pulled up, switched off and waited. After a moment one of the men came over to him, glancing sideways in both directions. He was middle-aged, wearing glasses, a long coat and a peaked civilian cap.

"*Hauptmann* Hamilton?"

Jack nodded.

"We will sit please in your vehicle."

"Please do."

The second man, young, unshaven and wearing a tattered army tunic and no cap, responded to a nod from his friend and joined him. They climbed into the Jeep.

"Drive please towards the bridge."

Jack complied, and they bumped along through a devastated area of Cologne, Jack receiving directions from the first man until he was ordered to stop in a dark alley under a railway viaduct.

"We are an organization of former war prisoners, Herr *Hauptmann*, and we do not accept your right to associate with Fräulein Freidl while her brother is still in the hands of the Americans."

"So what do you propose to do about it?" Jack asked, trying to sound casual.

"Normally she would receive a form of punishment. But there is a way this can be avoided."

"Oh; how?"

"There is a price for her release. The matter can be negotiated."

"I'll bet it can," said Jack grimly. "But it's not money, is it? It's food and cigarettes; am I right?"

"You are right, but there is more."

"What?"

"A British Army vehicle, handed over to us intact with the supplies listed here, correct papers, a British uniform with identity card and certain signed orders." The man handed Jack a piece of paper.

"Ah, now I begin to understand," Jack said, glancing at the paper. It was pretty much as he had guessed. Their price was a trailer-load of supplies and authority to obtain more from the British Army, which they would sell on the black market.

Jack told them he would need time to organize such a deal but he did not turn it down out of hand, for the extortion attempt must be handled with extreme caution if Karin was to emerge from her ordeal unscathed.

He asked the men for their names, but was told simply "We are Franz and Ulrich and you will meet us here with your answer. How soon will this be?"

Jack gave himself twenty-four hours and a rendezvous was fixed at the same spot under the railway viaduct for midday on the following day.

The Provost-Marshal agreed with Jack, when he reported back, that any attempt to trap the men with their British vehicle and haul of illicit supplies when handing over Karin would put her at too much risk. He had no doubt that these were bitter, desperate men with nothing to lose, probably ex-SS personnel who would not hesitate to shoot their way out of a corner. There were many repatriated German servicemen about and many of them could not easily accept the Allied occupation of their country nor settle down to civilian life.

Jack and Major Sallis agreed that before any undertaking was reached, proof must be received that Karin was safe and unharmed. It would be a help to know exactly where she was being held but this was unlikely to be disclosed.

The P-M told Jack to go alone to his second rendezvous, as planned, to arrange details of a handover in the next few days. Meanwhile, the Field Security people would provide an Intelligence officer, disguised as a German civilian, who would tail Ulrich and Franz from the rendezvous to their address or addresses, which just might lead them to Fraülein Freidl.

At twelve o'clock the following day Jack pulled up his Jeep under the viaduct and waited. There was nobody in sight. Five minutes went by, then ten, and Jack began to worry. 'The buggers have suspected a trap,' he thought, 'or lost their nerve.' A train rumbled over the viaduct but was soon gone; silence fell. Some pigeons fluttered in the girders above Jack's head. Then came the sound of a car, missing on one cylinder, coming gradually nearer. A battered Mercedes tourer with two men in it went past Jack's Jeep and stopped a few yards further on, just past the mouth of the tunnel at the far end, close to where two old women in headscarves with shopping baskets were chatting outside a small shop. The two men got out and walked back under the viaduct to the Jeep.

"Everything is arranged," Jack told them.

"*Gut so . . .* "

"A British 30-cwt truck loaded with the provisions you have demanded will pass this spot, exactly where we are now, at three o'clock in the morning next Wednesday. The driver will be alone in the cab, in possession of the papers and requisition forms you asked for. You will signal the vehicle to stop and stage a hijack of the truck. The driver will have been instructed to jump down from the cab and offer no resistance. He will run towards the Hohenzollern Bridge ostensibly to get help, but you will have driven the truck away before he can return to the scene with assistance. In this way the loss of the truck and goods will be attributable to a German black-market gang and the driver will not be blamed, although somebody's head will roll for allowing the vehicle out at night unescorted."

"Is good," said the man called Ulrich with a ghost of a smile.

"There must be no British troops or armed men involved," said Franz.

"None," Jack assured him, and was not lying. "Only I myself will be here at this spot in my Jeep. But I shall be in radio contact with our Military Police."

"Why so?" asked Franz anxiously.

"Because Fraülein Freidl is to be standing alone at the entrance to this tunnel at three minutes to three, one hundred and eighty seconds before our truck passes under the viaduct. If she is there, I shall pick her up in my Jeep and the hijack will proceed normally. If she is not, I shall immediately radio a warning to our military police that a hijack is taking place at this spot and they will close in on you very quickly. Is that understood?"

"*Stimmt*," muttered Ulrich.

The two men drove away, apparently satisfied with the plan.

THAT evening Major Sallis came to see Jack in the Mess with important news of Karin.

"Where? Is she all right?"

"Depends what you mean by all right," said Sallis. "A couple of our Intelligence chaps, dressed up as old crones, tailed our friends all day and most of the evening. Evidently the two villains went round and round Cologne and the outskirts, going into small shops, meeting people in parks on bombed sites and open spaces collecting orders for black-market goods, to be delivered when their deal with us is concluded."

"But what about Karin?"

"When they'd finished taking orders, Ulrich and Franz ended up somewhere near the old *Rathaus*, abandoned their car in a side street and clambered over mountains of wreckage, closely followed by our chaps. Finally, they went down into a little hole under the ruins of a large office building. The spot was marked by a small red lamp indicating steps down into a cellar, where there was a bar, a few tables and a woman playing an accordion. It was called the Himmelkeller, a broken-down night-club. There were a handful of Kraut ex-soldiers in there and one or two civilians. Also three girls – probably working as hostesses. From the photo you gave the FSO of Fraülein Freidl the Intelligence chaps had no difficulty in recognising her as one of the girls."

"My God!" was all Jack could say but his heart missed a beat. Could the bastards have forced the gentle Karin into a brothel?

"That's where she is, old chap, and that's where they're holding her. But we'll work something out. Whatever happens, this hijack must go ahead."

"I suppose it must," Jack said but he knew it was going to be hellish dangerous for Karin.

"Why can't we take them everything they want? And then round them up at the night-club afterwards?" he asked, after a short pause.

The question was rhetorical, for he knew what Geoffrey Sallis would reply. Indeed, Sallis confirmed that if they were to do that, it would be a much bigger operation, requiring permission from higher authority that would most certainly be refused. If a senior officer heard of the affair, Jack would be extremely lucky to get away without a severe reprimand at the least, and there would be no possibility of him being allowed to keep Karin on as his secretary after her release.

The principal consideration was Karin's safety, but the only hope was to go on with the plan on their own. Jack would carry out the hijack, as agreed; but the back of the lorry would contain dummy cartons, except for a few genuine goods at the tail. It was to be hoped that the Germans would not want to examine them until they had handed Karin over and got well away from the scene, by which time the Military Police would have closed in on them.

It was a risk that had to be taken.

JACK was more nervous that night than he'd ever been, even on the eve of a big battle. He decided not to go to bed. Instead he spent the evening playing bridge in the Mess, and stayed until all the officers had turned in and Otto had closed up the premises for the night. After that he strolled along the river in the darkness and counted the hours until his mission was scheduled to start.

A meeting point just outside Bad Godesberg had been arranged with the FSO for Jack in his Jeep to join up with the 30-cwt truck provided by the Military Police, with all the appearances of a normal supply vehicle. They would rendez-vous at 2.30 a.m. and proceed in convoy to Cologne.

The truck driver was a corporal of the Intelligence Corps who had been thoroughly briefed as to the charade of the hijack, a fact that if known to the Germans would have alerted them to possible trouble. As it was, it was to be hoped that they thought Captain Hamilton simply wanted his German girl friend back safely but, as his affair with the fräulein was frowned upon, dared not ask the British Forces for help; so that he was prepared to organize the theft of a lorry full of military supplies, and to sacrifice some innocent RASC driver who would be hijacked in the small hours and probably then court-martialled by the British authorities for carelessness.

It was a pitch-black night as Jack's Jeep, followed by the 30-cwt truck, both using sidelights only, approached the district of the Cologne Hohenzollern Bridge and the entrance to the short tunnel under the railway viaduct. Jack peered forward through the gloom, hoping to see Karin standing by the tunnel mouth. He slowed down and signalled to the truck behind him to overtake him, then moved slowly on along the road at fifteen m.p.h.

Aware of something on the kerb, Jack flashed on his headlights just long enough to pick out Karin in the beam. She seemed at first to be standing alone, as requested. But as the Jeep came closer, he saw to his horror that she was being firmly held by someone, a murky shadowy figure placed between her and the bridge, who was pointing a gun at her throat.

Jack's immediate instinct was to stop, jump out and bellow at Karin's captor that the girl was supposed to be on the road alone, that the agreement had therefore been breached and the deal was off. But caution prevailed. Jack decided not to risk a sudden flare-up but to play it cool.

He pulled up, got out quite calmly and walked over to the place where Ulrich was holding the terrified girl in a tight grip, with a Mauser's barrel pushed against her neck. In the dim light from the Jeep's sidelights Jack could see that Karin's eyes were staring in fear and her cheeks were tear-stained, but she could not utter a sound for Ulrich's other hand was clapped firmly over her mouth.

"That's not what we agreed," Jack said, trying to sound cool.

Ulrich viciously dug his gun-barrel deeper into Karin's neck. "We have to be sure you have not cheated us," he said. "Franz will examine the lorry. If the correct provisions are in the back and the documents we demand are handed over with the truck, Fraülein Freidl will be released."

At that moment there was a scuffle just ahead and some shouting, as Franz ordered the driver out of the truck's cab at gun-point, whereupon the Intelligence corporal carried out his pre-arranged role of abandoning the vehicle in mock alarm and running off into the night to get help. Jack's throat went dry and sudden panic overtook him, for now the moment that was crucial for the success of the operation had arrived. But with a gun at Karin's throat, what chance was there? Clearly, the Germans were not taking it for granted that all was going according to plan, as indeed it was not, and it looked as if they planned a check with Teutonic thoroughness, before letting Karin go.

Out of the corner of his eye Jack saw Franz, less than sixty yards away along the tunnel, climb up to the tailboard of the lorry and pull back the rear tarpaulins to look into the back.

In a matter of seconds he was yelling out to Ulrich "*Diese Kaste ist leer, es ist nichts drin!*"

In a flash Ulrich grasped the situation, let out an oath of fury and started dragging Karin across the road towards the Mercedes tourer that was parked in a shadow across the road. Karin struggled and shrieked in terror but Jack could do nothing. He stood for a fraction of a second, rooted to the spot. Everything had gone wrong so swiftly, he'd had no time to react. A moment later he grasped what had to be done and dashed to his Jeep where he managed to get his service revolver out from under the seat and aim it across the street at Ulrich.

"Stop and let go of her or I'll shoot," he shouted. "Stop, damn you."

But he couldn't risk a shot. Karin was in his line of fire as she stumbled after her captor and was then thrown bodily into the car. Ulrich crashed into gear and drove off at speed, pausing only for a second to collect Franz, who had now jumped off the tailboard of the lorry and, as it passed him, hurled himself into the car.

Jack ran after the Mercedes and took aim at the offside rear tyre, pressing the trigger. A shattering bang echoed under the railway viaduct as the touring car sped on towards the tunnel exit. Jack sprinted after it and fired again. This time he hit the nearside rear tyre which deflated with a loud swish of air. The car lurched violently to one side but did not stop, so he ran on in pursuit, firing two more shots at the car's wheels. The

Mercedes was now unable to increase speed owing to the punctured tyre but it still kept moving. Then Jack heard shots coming from the far end of the tunnel and was suddenly blinded by headlights coming towards him from the other direction. The Mercedes seemed to swerve, slither and skid across the road, finally crashing into a wall.

Jack reached the wrecked car just as Major Sallis loomed up from behind the headlights. In an instant both he and Jack were dragging Karin from the wreckage while two Redcaps pursued and quickly caught up with Ulrich and Franz who had tried to run for it. Jack saw them both punched in the face then handcuffed. A third MP was climbing up into the hijacked truck which remained parked and unmanned exactly where it had originally stopped. Karin was unconscious but alive and bleeding profusely from a nasty cut on her forehead. The impact of the crash into the wall had thrown her head first against the sharp perspex sidescreens. Jack managed to lower Karin gently to the pavement and attempted in the dim light from the cars' lamps to press his handkerchief to her badly gashed forehead and stem the flow of blood.

"You're safe now, *Liebchen*," he murmured to her but her eyes remained closed and she did not reply.

Meanwhile, the Military Police took charge of the lorry and bundled Ulrich and Franz into their own truck to be driven away to MP Headquarters, where they would be charged with attempting to steal a British Army vehicle. No mention would be made of the involvement of a German girl or of a British officer from the Guards Division.

"I'll drive her to the Medical Officer at once and do something about that cut," Jack said to the Provost-Marshal, who had just seen the villains driven off and was getting into his own staff car.

"Good idea, Hamilton. I'll give you a hand."

Jack threw his greatcoat over the girl. Karin had come round now and, totally dazed, was staring wide-eyed and uncomprehendingly at the two officers as together they lifted her up off the road and into the front seat of the Jeep.

"Get some iodine on it or some sort of antiseptic, old chap."

"Yes, I will."

Jack extended his hand to the Provost-Marshal.

"I'm sorry about all this but thanks for helping me out and thanks for keeping it under your hat. I'm very much in your debt."

"My pleasure," said Major Sallis. "Just look after your fraüleins more carefully in future, eh?"

Jack winced and took the full weight of that remark on his guilty conscience, as he climbed into the Jeep beside Karin and drove away into the darkness.

WHEN Karin had been attended to by the MO and had been helped to tidy herself up, Jack and she finally arrived at No. 1, Frankengraben. Jack was obliged to ring the bell and rouse Frau Inner, for Karin had lost her bag and keys when she was snatched from her bicycle. Jack thought it prudent not to mention the details of her lodger's abduction to Frau Inner but to suggest that Karin had been knocked off her cycle by an Army vehicle and that the driver had taken her to the British Military Hospital where she had stayed to be treated for her injuries. And Karin made no attempt to contradict this story.

When the dentist's wife left them to go back to her own bed, Jack stayed with Karin for some time.

She was strangely cool and uncommunicative. Something was very wrong. There was no gratitude for rescuing her from a bunch of thugs, no warmth, no affection. Perhaps, Jack thought, she was still in shock from her terrifying experience or even concussed. That would account for it. All the same he sensed resentment, almost anger.

"Leave me now, please, Jack. I shall be OK," was all she would say.

"Very well, if that's what you want, I'll go."

Jack could not conceal his bitterness and disappointment at her mood. But he knew damn well what it was all about. She was still upset by his performance at the Spiegels' flat. That was obvious. And the less said about it the better. He bent over and kissed her gently on her cheek but she made no response.

At the door he said "Don't come into the office until you feel up to it."

Karin made no reply, so Jack left the room, closed the door and walked wearily down Frau Inner's stairs again and out into the street, where he got into his Jeep and drove back to his own billet.

Chapter 9

"HAS our little Karin returned yet?"

It was the afternoon following Karin's rescue from the black marketeers, about which Ingrid knew and would know nothing. Jack felt the episode was over now and nobody had been seriously hurt. There seemed no point in needlessly distressing the elderly singer further, during her grief over Werner's confirmed death. But he had felt once again drawn to her for comfort and sympathy in his anxiety over Karin's continuing coolness towards him.

Jack had found on arrival at the office after breakfast that despite his offer of a few days off, Karin had arrived for work that morning as though nothing had happened. She had apologized to Corporal Bridges for her absence in Coblenz, telling him, to account for the plaster on her forehead, that she had been knocked off her bicycle, unaware that Bridges himself knew all about her abduction and rescue.

Nor did she refer to the matter when alone in the room with Jack – as though she was as anxious to forget the whole ugly incident as Jack was. Perhaps she felt if news of it got out it would discredit her fellow countrymen, or perhaps she felt too shamed and embarrassed by it to want to talk about it to anyone, even Jack.

All in all, Karin had continued that morning to be polite, cool and thoroughly uncommunicative.

"And have you made up your quarrel?" Ingrid asked.

Jack shrugged his shoulders and moved to look down from the bedroom window into Ingrid's garden. "I don't know. It wasn't really a quarrel . . . more a misunderstanding."

Ingrid looked up at Jack with moist eyes and said "I should like very much to see the child, if she can be spared for an hour or so."

"She doesn't know about your husband yet. I was planning to tell her this evening."

"Let her know and bring her to me, Jack, please."

"I'll go to fetch her right away," Jack said and Ingrid nodded, sinking back wearily onto her pillows.

When Jack reached the office in Godesberg and told Karin the news about Ingrid's husband, she dropped everything and hurried out with him to the Jeep.

No longer silent or moody, she asked anxiously, as they drove along the road to Mehlem, how the news had come through, the details of Werner's death and how Ingrid was bearing up.

Jack answered factually, formally and without emotion.

Within half an hour of leaving Plittersdorferstrasse they were sitting bolt upright in two chairs, slightly apart, facing Ingrid's bed. They might have been a young couple being interviewed for a job as domestic servants.

"Jack has been so sweet and strong and comforting," Ingrid was saying. "I have been crying in his arms just like a baby."

Jack shifted in his chair, a trifle embarrassed, but pleased to be praised in front of Karin. Ingrid went on, now in the role of a vicar, Jack thought, delivering an address to a bridal pair at a wedding.

"When you lose someone very dear and close to you, my children," she said, "you will come to realize what a precious treasure is love and companionship – something we must all hold on to, once we have found it, and never lose."

It dawned on Jack, to his even greater embarrassment, that Ingrid was doing a great propaganda job on his behalf, telling Karin she was a damn lucky girl to have a nice young British officer to love and that she should not risk losing him by sulking with hurt pride.

Karin must have grasped the intention of Ingrid's homily but she showed no signs of a change of mood, not glancing at him once during the discourse. Instead, she suddenly rushed over to the bed and flung herself into Ingrid's arms, murmuring with deep emotion "*Ach du – arme, liebe Freundin, ich bin zu Tode betruebt . . .*" and smothering her with kisses.

Cynically, Jack thought, from his upright chair, 'That's all very well. I've just done all that. She's trying to score an equalizer.' Then he withdrew the thought as childish tit-for-tat, and unfair, in view of Karin's emotional and volatile nature.

After a moment Ingrid reached out past Karin and beckoned to Jack to come over to the bed again. "*Komm, du auch.*"

Jack obeyed, and Ingrid took his hand, holding Karin's with the other while she played, quite beautifully, the scene when the wise older woman tries on her deathbed to reconcile the young lovers who have quarrelled.

"Listen, my dear children. My Werner is dead and no power on earth can bring him back to me now. I am content to live on, as he would wish me to, cherishing his memory and setting his example of love and loyalty. Shed no tears for me. Rather, shed tears for your own love, my dears, that seems to have gone astray. Reach out for that affection and respect you have built up between you, hold on to it firmly and never let it go."

The tears were rolling down Frau Pauels' cheeks now but, oddly, Karin remained unmoved. Jack wondered whether she, too, realized the ageing Soprano was singing a great deathbed aria, which required only a score by Giacomi Puccini to make it into a world-beater.

Delivered of her oration, Ingrid patted the two hands she was holding dismissively and let go of them. Then she said "Now you must run along, my darlings, and get on with living your own young lives. Julius will come up and sit with me for a while. It was sweet of you both to call."

Karin bent over and kissed Ingrid on the cheek. Jack followed suit, kissing her on the forehead. Then he followed Karin to the door and went out, leaving it open, for Julius was already lurking on the landing outside and indeed, might well have been listening.

The drive back to Godesberg took place in silence, until Karin asked to be dropped at her billet, having finished her work in the office. They would meet at work tomorrow, the day of the concert.

The following morning passed with barely a remark between them, until around two o'clock, when Jack asked Karin if she would be sitting with him at the concert.

She said "Of course, if you wish me to."

"I do."

And that was that.

JACK fetched Karin at seven o'clock. Once more they drove in silence on their way to the Divisional College, where they joined a crush of civilians and military personnel thronging the foyer. Corporal Bridges was standing just inside the entrance with a couple of guardsmen volunteers, handing out programmes. As he gave her a leaflet and murmured "Good luck, Fräulein," Karin beamed at him. Jack laughed, and commented that it sounded as though Karin was about to perform on the platform herself.

"If the people do not like the music I have chosen and the concert is a failure, it will be my responsibility," she said, rather crossly, looking around the packed entrance hall.

"Sorry I spoke," said Jack, and followed her sheepishly down the aisle to their seats.

They sat for a while without speaking, Karin studying her programme unnecessarily hard, Jack thought, for she knew every item on it. He looked round the packed hall, noticing many familiar faces that belonged to the Divisional personnel who were usually to be seen at opera performances and concerts these days; the genuine music-lovers of the Divisional area.

Suddenly, the chattering stopped and the audience fell silent in the tense moment that immediately precedes the entrance of the leader of the orchestra. Karin reached out for Jack's hand and squeezed it. It was something she had not done for a long time, and at her touch Jack felt a warm glow inside him. A ripple of clapping heralded the arrival of Ernst Kleber, the Leader of the Cologne Symphony Orchestra, and then came Emmerich Karl, dapper, smiling and confident, mounting the podium to a storm of applause.

His baton went up. Silence fell. The opening bars of Beethoven's *Leonora* No. 2 Overture filled the expectant air with glorious sound.

Once or twice Jack glanced sideways to catch a quick glimpse of Karin's enraptured face, eyes glistening, sensuous lips slightly parted, as she concentrated on the music she had chosen, music she loved with dedication and passion.

The Overture ended with an outburst of tumultuous applause and then, as Emmerich Karl went off, three soldiers in battle-dress came on to roll the Bechstein Concert Grand to the centre of the platform, ready for the Rachmaninov. To facilitate this, some of the orchestral players left their desks, and beyond the resulting gap Jack caught sight of Ingrid and Julius at the far side of the platform.

The sight of that greying, elderly couple sitting close together, each comforting the other in their personal sorrow while sharing a total devotion to music, seemed to Jack rather touching. He pointed them out to Karin and she waved across to them, but they were too far off to see her.

"I am so glad they have come. It will take her mind off Werner."

Jack agreed. He looked across at his two older friends again, aware of a sentimental feeling for them that was growing on him, so that they were beginning to seem like substitute parents.

For most of his thinking life, Jack had been guiltily aware of something lacking in his feelings for his own parents, but the fact was that in a way they were strangers to him. His formative years had been shaped by two nannies, a governess and a series of expensive schools. 'The parents' were a man and a woman in whose house he had lived, who had told him what to do and where to go and sometimes took him to a theatre or a cricket match in the holidays. He had kissed his mother dutifully at bedtime and on his way to day school in the morning. His father had patted him tentatively on the shoulders if he'd done well, and ticked him off if his school report wasn't very good.

Jack had respected and slightly feared them but he could not pretend to 'love' them. Not as you love a pretty girl, or Nanny Sutton, or even your best friend at school. He imagined his parents loved him in their own, rather formal, dutiful way but it was not something of which he had a strong conviction. There had been some conventional expressions of affection in his mother's recent letters; phrases like 'I pray every night that God will protect you and bring you back safe'; and soon after he'd landed in Normandy his father had written 'Your mother and I are so proud to think you are risking your life to serve your country', but he could not imagine either of them saying things like that to him out loud. They would surely be far too embarrassed, and so would he.

But Ingrid wouldn't, he thought, nor would Julius. They were emotional, sentimental, elderly Germans given to excesses of feeling, as so many Germans were. It wasn't really fair to compare them with his mother and father. Still, he felt that

Ingrid and Julius loved him genuinely, not for what he could do for them as a British officer, but for what he was and for his friendship. And he believed that Karin loved him in the same way.

NOW the piano was in position, the orchestra rearranged and a hush fell, soon to be shattered by another burst of prolonged applause, as Karl led on Willy Pohl the soloist.

Herr Pohl was short, bespectacled and slightly bald, and Jack found it difficult to imagine him flying a Messerschmidt 109 in the skies over Britain in 1940. But he was only thirty-two, and Jack wondered if it was his life spent hiding from the Gestapo after he quit the Luftwaffe that had aged him before his time.

Pohl bowed and sat down. Then he adjusted his stool, flicked his borrowed tails behind him, flexed his fingers and nodded to indicate his readiness. Karl's baton went up and the Rachmaninov Piano Concerto in A Flat Minor began.

Midway through the first movement Jack began to feel a lump in his throat; he found his emotions were profoundly stirred by the combination of the music, his fondness for Ingrid and Julius, and lastly the heart-warming fact that Karin's coldness was melting. A sense of belonging and being loved swept over him and tears welled up in his eyes.

Perhaps it was his suppressed love for uninhibited sentiment and human emotion that touched him deep down in his soul. As an Englishman, brought up in the public school stiff-upper-lip convention, he had accepted that uncontrolled expressions of emotion were not considered good form. One did not cry openly at sad films or plays, not in the world he grew up in. One blew one's nose and pretended to have a cold.

When the interval came, Karin immediately began to talk about the music. They remained in their seats while she discussed the performance warmly and naturally as if nothing had gone wrong between them. Jack replied enthusiastically, but while he spoke of crescendos and codas, his heart was rejoicing that the storm with Karin appeared to have blown over, and once again he felt the searing passion for his lovely Rhinemaiden, the longing and desire to possess her, that had first hit him that June afternoon when he first set eyes on her.

It wasn't long before they were enveloped once more in a great wave of splendid sound, when after the intermission the Sibelius crashed forth from the orchestra, causing Jack's scalp to tingle and Karin to feel cold shivers up and down her spine. They clasped hands, like a couple of children in the presence of God, and Jack knew from the sharply delicious pain of Karin's nails digging into his palm that he was forgiven for his recent transgression and that the trauma of her kidnapping ordeal was behind her.

By the time the Sibelius ended in a great crescendo of brass, woodwind and the thunder of the timpani, they were limp and breathless, unable to applaud at first and afraid to speak for fear of bursting into tears. They stayed in their seats until the hall was almost empty.

As Jack once more became aware of his surroundings, he also saw one thing very clearly. Karin was the only girl he could ever share his life with now. Whatever obstacles might stand in his way, he wanted to marry Karin Freidl.

"Shall we make a move?" he said quietly, after a few moments, taking her arm.

Karin got up from her seat and together they walked slowly out of the Divisional College Hall into the cool night air.

HAVING arrived at the dentist's house in Frankengraben, Jack and Karin crept into the hall and climbed the stairs silently and stealthily, taking care not to allow a creaking floorboard to waken the dentist or his wife.

Once safely up in Karin's top-floor room, they breathed a sigh of relief. For if Karin was caught by the Inners with a man in her room at that hour of the night, she would be thrown out and the matter reported to the Billeting Officer. That would do Karin no good, nor Jack either, for that matter.

Karin switched on a small electric stove that glowed in the dim light – for only a crimson standard lamp and an amber bedside lamp illuminated the room.

On a large, deep rug beside Karin's bed was her most treasured possession, a square wind-up gramophone, and around it was a sea of records, scattered far and wide across the floor. Apart from collections of most of the Wagner operas in gold-embossed cases, she had accumulated a large number of other works.

When she asked Jack what he would like to hear, he suggested something dreamy and romantic, like Delius or Debussy. He had always found that school of music highly erotic. It was conducive to love-making and tonight, he thought, just might be the night. Karin kicked off her shoes and knelt down to scrabble about among her records, while Jack fondled the back of her neck, making her shudder with delicious, sensual pleasure.

"If you do this to me, *mein schatz*." she chided him, "I cannot find a record to play for you. Please, Jack – *lass mich* . . ."

Jack let go of her with a smile and a moment later Karin found Ravel's 'Daphne and Chlöe', which he knew and loved.

By the time she had put on the record and wound up the gramophone Jack was kneeling on the floor beside her. From behind her back he put his arms round her and fondled her breasts.

"I get for us some *glühwein*," Karin said, suddenly disengaging from him and making for the kitchenette in her stockinged feet.

"Don't worry about *glühwein*," Jack murmured, anxious not to lose the moment.

"But it is a cold night," Karin called back, "and it will warm us up. I have it all ready."

"OK."

Jack shrugged and got up to sit on the bed, at the same time removing his shoes and socks.

Karin returned with a thermos flask and two glasses on a tray, which she placed on a table. "I make it this morning and it stay hot for us."

By the time she had removed the stopper and poured Jack a glass, he had removed his jacket and tie and unbuttoned his shirt. Karin gave him his glass of wine and sat beside him while he drank it.

The warm glow produced by the mulled claret and the sweep of Ravel's music made Jack fall back on Karin's bed in a state of near-ecstasy.

He wanted desperately to fulfil his long imagined fantasy, the dream that had pursued him almost every night since he first caught sight of her lithe body swimming past him in the Rhine, back in early June. In his dream she would fly past him across a vast, empty beach in the moonlight, a wispy figure in flowing chiffon, almost nude. He would chase her into the sea, catch up with her in the warm, salt water, and hold her to him. As she cried out in her ecstasy, he would make love to her underwater, the movement of the waves gradually stripping the chiffon from her shining, foam-covered body.

Jack now sat up and took Karin's glass from her, placing it carefully on a table. With a smile he turned her gently round to face him and began slowly and methodically to unbutton her blouse. She made no move as he slid it off her back and released the straps of her brassière.

Gently, he took her bare shoulders and held her against him. Still she made no move, simply closing her eyes and allowing him to run his fingers softly up and down her back. Finally Jack fell against the pillows of Karin's bed. "You still have too many clothes on, *Liebchen*."

Karin hesitated a fraction of a second, then got up and switched off the bedside lamp, so that in the dark Jack said

"I'm not shy, if you aren't – no need to – where are you? Karin?"

No reply came. Then Jack heard a rustling sound across the room. Karin's voice came from over by the window. She said quietly "I am obeying your orders, Herr Major."

Jack rolled over, swiftly shed his shirt and trousers and slid under the duvet. The growing excitement and delicious anticipating he felt while lying naked in Karin's bed, waiting for her to creep in beside him, was almost too much for him, as had been the case that first night he kissed her at Frau Pauel's house. Anxious not to allow his desire to overflow again, Jack quickly filled his mind with as many unromantic, unerotic thoughts as possible in a desperate attempt to temper his throbbing passion. He closed his eyes and thought of boiled cabbage, ugly fat women with warts, playing football in the mud at school, and discordant modern music.

But Karin was soon beside him under the duvet. Reaching out in the dark to feel her, his hands discovered that she was not wearing a nightdress. Instead, she had wrapped herself in some kind of soft, silky material, a headscarf perhaps, or just a large handkerchief, held round her by a silken cord. Whatever it was, it barely covered her body but the juxta-position of the sensuous material and her warm, bare flesh, exposed between gaps in the covering, inflamed Jack even more.

He attempted to draw her towards him, murmuring softly "Oh God, how lovely you are."

But Karin made no complementary move towards him. Instead she remained on her back, but held out her hand to take his. "I would like us to lie like this, Jack, close beside each other and . . . we can stroke each other and . . . be very loving but not . . . "

"But not what?"

"Not – really make love . . . just be together. Please, Jack, not now, not yet – I . . . "

169

Jack felt himself suddenly flush with anger and bewilderment. "This isn't very fair of you, Karin. I mean here I am – "

"Please, Jack. You must try to understand. I feel strange . . . I am not . . . I do not know how to say it but . . . it is too soon – "

"Are you afraid of having a baby, Karin?" Jack had already prepared for any eventuality. His tone was almost harsh. "If you are, you can trust me. It will be all right. I promise."

"It's not that, Jack," Karin said, turning away from him. "I do trust you. It's just that I feel tonight . . . somehow . . . I don't know. – Oh, please don't . . . make me . . . please . . . "

Suddenly Karin crumpled up, convulsed with sobs. Her whole body shook, as the flood-gates opened and all the tensions and fears and doubts of recent weeks came pouring out.

Jack reached out for her, touching her gently on her shaking shoulders. "Of course, darling, I understand," was all he could manage to say, but it was enough. She turned round in the bed, sobbing her heart out, and clung to him violently, her wet, salty tears soaking his chest.

"I was so afraid . . . and I did not know whether you loved me or – if I should be left in that horrible place . . . with all those people . . . to die alone . . . and never to see you again . . ."

Jack held Karin tightly as he calmed her, stroking her back and murmuring to her as to a weeping child. "I would never have left you with those thugs - we did everything possible to get you away. I was worried as well, terrified that you might be harmed. – I'm so sorry – *mein Schatz* – but it's all over now and you're safe."

Karin's sobbing soon reached a climax and then she began to quieten down until she was lying still in his arms.

"There," Jack whispered. "you're all right now. I'll look after you."

After a while Jack realized that his passionate desire for her had also diminished, changed into tenderness and pity, and he was able to continue to hold her and stroke her gently and soothingly, more as a mother than a lover.

As Karin became quiet and relaxed in his arms he began to reflect on her sudden change of mood. Had she intended to give herself to him, then changed her mind out of some deep fear that once she had yielded to him his love might somehow fade away?

Or was she simply a well-brought up religious girl, who would go most of the way, but stop short of sex before marriage? Perhaps marriage or the commitment to it was a precondition of total intercourse.

Or was it simply the recent humiliation of being kidnapped that was the trouble, as she said?

As these thoughts chased round in Jack's mind, Karin became drowsy and was soon asleep. Thus they lay in each other's arms, until a clock somewhere chimed seven and Jack slid quietly from the bed. It was time to go, before the dentist or his wife rose to make coffee or put the cat out.

Just able to find his clothes by the first daylight breaking outside, Jack kissed Karin, who was only half awake, on her forehead and whispered to her, "*Sei ruhig, schlaf gut, mein Liebchen . . .*"

Then he crept from the room, out of the house and into his Jeep to drive away in the grim, grey dawn back to his billet in Plittersdorferstrasse.

Chapter 10

IT was the last week of November, and Karin was watching a
dress rehearsal of *The Magic Flute* in the College Theatre,
when Jack slipped into a seat beside her in the darkened
auditorium. Julius was on stage coaching a young bass
Gerhardt Froebel from Aachen, who was singing Sarastro for
the first time. It was a role that Heuss had sung dozens of times
before and knew inside out. Mozart's invocation of Isis in the
second Act ended with Heuss climbing on stage and applauding the young singer: "*Ist gut, sehr schön, nur einige kleine
Einzelheiten, ja, hören Sie mal. . .* "

Jack had come to the rehearsal to present Karin with two
items of news about himself, both of which he feared would
upset her. Since that evening in her room when she had broken
down and cried in his arms he had played his hand most
carefully, never forcing himself on her, being on hand at all
times, considerate, thoughtful and chivalrous, but behaving as
the Germans themselves would say *ganz herrlich*.

She was still recovering from a shocking experience and he
knew that only time and care could rebuild her trust and her
love for him.

A memo from the DAQMG's office that morning had informed him that he was due for demobilization on February 6th. He was also entitled to a forty-eight hours' leave.

While Heuss was giving the singer his notes, Jack decided not to mention his demob. date; not just yet, although he fully realized the moment of truth had now arrived. If he was due back in England so soon after Christmas, he must decide pretty soon whether to propose marriage to her or not.

A short spell of leave seemed a good opportunity to get right away from Bad Godesberg and his emotional entanglement for a few days and think things out calmly and clearly.

It might of course be the perfect opportunity to take Karin away to some picturesque country *Gasthaus* in the mountains, where under a spotless white duvet, as vast and as light as a cumulus cloud, they would finally and unreservedly make love, with the sound of robust voices singing down below in the *Bierkeller*, accompanied by an accordion, a tuba and a violin. But a holiday in any public place with Karin would not do. Fraternization was still strictly forbidden.

'Besides,' he thought, 'there is no guarantee that she would not insist on separate rooms. Only marriage could overcome that obstacle.' And if they did marry, how would Karin fit in with his life and surroundings? Would she be happy in Virginia Water? . . .

Jack took the plunge. "I'm taking a forty-eight hours' leave I'm entitled to. Probably up to Brussels."

Karin looked round at him, her eyes shining. "*Aber das ist fabelhaft*. I have never been to Brussels. – There are so many things to see and . . . "

"*Liebchen*, I cannot take you with me. I would have to stay at the Eye Club. It is a club for British officers. A German girl would not be allowed to go there. In fact I'm not sure you're even allowed to leave Germany."

Karin's reaction was first of bitter disappointment, followed by reasoned acceptance of the situation.

Jack explained that most of his brother officers had been to Belgium to revisit the capital city they had liberated a year earlier and to go back over the battlefields where so many of their comrades had died.

At this Karin fell silent and Jack knew that she could hardly argue against it. All the same, he felt ashamed at his own cowardice in not admitting to her that he needed to get away and think out his feelings towards her on his own.

Instead, he said "I shall leave on Friday afternoon and be back late Sunday night. Just the weekend. That's not long. I'll bring you back something nice."

Karin nodded sadly, and returned her eyes to the stage where The Queen of the Night was rehearsing her 'Vengeance' aria.

JACK drove alone in his Jeep to Brussels, via Aachen, where he purposely turned north up the old 'centre line', the route into Holland that had been taken by the Guards Armoured Division after the liberation of Brussels in September, 1944. As he drove through Maastricht and Hechtel, up through Eindhoven and Grave to Nijmegen, he found the very names striking cold fear in his heart, as memories of bitter fighting came back to him, with the screaming of mortar shells, the grinding of Sherman tanks manoeuvring in the narrow streets, and the sight of ashen-white badly wounded guardsmen.

Monty's bold and imaginative plan 'Operation Market Garden', to seize the bridges over the Lower Rhine by a combined air drop and armoured advance had gone tragically wrong and Jack's battalion had suffered considerable casualties in a desperate battle to seize the bridge at Nijmegen. They had succeeded, but the armoured advance was then halted before they could reach Arnhem and a long, dark, muddy and static winter had been spent at a place called Gangelt on the Dutch-German border, where constant shelling, mortaring and patrolling made conditions rather like those of the 1914-18

War. It was only when the spring of 1945 came that the Second Army moved out of Holland, crossed the Rhine into the Reichswald Forest and in May made its last lethal lunge towards the Ruhr.

At Nijmegen Jack took a look at the intact bridge, which the Germans had failed to blow up and the Grenadiers had seized, allowing the Irish Guards' tanks to advance across it. Then, deciding that he had satified his curiosity enough, he headed south again for Brussels.

Jack had felt a certain compulsion to revisit those scenes of battle, which at first he had excused to himself as a need to pay silent tribute to his fellow Grenadiers who had died there. This was a perfectly genuine sentiment. But the truth of it was that he was also deeply proud of having taken part in one of the more dramatic and important battles of the recent war and he wanted to revisit the scene before his own fading memory and the redevelopment of the town erased forever those few dangerous but historic days of his life.

An hour or so later he was in the busy streets of Brussels, remembering the happier scenes of Liberation Day, when pretty Belgian girls, weeping tears of joy and relief, clambered up on to the tanks and greeted the astonished guardsmen with champagne and kisses.

Jack found the Boulevard d'Anspach and checked into the Eye Club, had a bath, and lay on his bed with an entertainments guide for theatres and cinemas, to decide how to spend his first evening. He decided to give the opera a miss and take in a show. A good dinner, eaten alone, was rather pointless and anyway the food in Belgian restaurants was still pretty foul – except for the little tucked-away, hole-in-the corner *marché noir* establishments, where a waiter kept a look-out down the street outside, while you devoured your black market steak.

In the main restaurants rationing was still very much in force. Fortunately, as he left the Eye Club Jack decided he was not particularly hungry.

While walking through the streets of Brussels in search of entertainment, still keyed-up by the day's recollection of the traumas of war, Jack found that the rumble of trams and the bright lights had an unsettling effect on him.

Crossing over the Boulevard Adolphe Max near the Bourse, Jack turned down a side-street into a busy brightly-lit square and soon spotted a large *théâtre variété* where a show was running entitled *Revue de la Victoire*.

He went in to buy a ticket, noting that the show had already started. A rollicking 'Can-Can' was going on when Jack made his way through the semi-darkness to his seat in the stalls; on stage, the girls were shrieking, kicking and doing the splits in the usual hackneyed way, to Offenbach's well-worn music from *Orpheus in the Underworld*.

The musical *scena* that followed a short acrobatic interval was a different matter altogether. Jack stared at the stage in amused disbelief. Accompanied by grim, subdued music, a dim light came up on a scene that depicted some sort of detention camp with barbed wire, huts and a searchlight tower, all suggested by cardboard cut-outs. The centre stage was occupied by three upright stakes. Three Belgian Resistance fighters in berets were being interrogated against a wall by a couple of German ss men in uniform. The dialogue was familiar: "Where did you get the guns and ammunition? Who is the leader of your group? What is the code name of your radio operator?"

Jack became aware that their voices were somewhat high-pitched and realized with a shock that both the *maquisards* and the ss men were portrayed by girls.

After a while the Resistance men were still refusing to divulge the required information, so the ss boss said sharply to his companion "*Amenez leurs femmes!*"

At this command the latter went off stage to drag on three women in peasant costume, who allowed themselves, with very mild, simulated resistance, to be roped to the stakes.

Obviously, there was a shortage of men in what was predominantly a 'girl' show. In fact, there were just two males in the programme: a middle-aged conjuror and a thin young man with long eyelashes who had already appeared, dressed in tight silver tinsel trousers, a bumfreezer jacket and a silver top hat, who had played the clarinet very fast, while turning cartwheels. Presumably these two solo performers could not be expected to act small parts in a sketch, so the Scena, called in the programme, 'La Loyauté', had to be cast from the chorus line.

With the three wives tied up, the interrogation continued: "*Je demande les noms de vos camarades.*"

The three *maquisards* shook their heads in refusal, so one SS man walked over to the stakes and ripped the tops of the three wives' dresses down to their waists, before whipping them – extremely gently – across their bare shoulders. The girls let out comic little strangled cries in rhythm with the whip lashes. '*Non*', '*Non*', '*Non*'.

After two or three more questions, refusals to answer, and whippings of the wives, the orchestra suddenly struck up the Belgian National Anthem, the camp scene faded out and a sort of throne began to descend from the flies, on which sat a semi-nude girl dressed as the spirit of Free Belgium, wobbling slightly as she was lowered into view. Below her, on stage, the rest of the cast, the *maquisards*, their wives and the two SS men, came down to the footlights and cheered as a loud female voice through a microphone cried out '*La Belgique ne capitule jamais aux atroces allemandes. Vive La Belgique*'.

The whole house applauded and cheered. Then, as the next act, the conjuror, came on and started manipulating cards, many conflicting thoughts raced through Jack's head.

'Rather doubtful taste,' he thought, 'now the Germans have been kicked out of Brussels and the war is won, for the Belgians to start commercializing Nazi brutality on the stage. But then, why not? They've suffered that kind of thing for five years. What's the harm in paying tribute to the guts and courage of the Resistance people and their womenfolk? But what would Karin say, if she'd seen that item in the show? Or Ingrid, whose missing husband was in the Waffen ss? Was Werner Pauels capable of whipping defenceless women? No. It wasn't his job. He was simply a colonel in a crack regiment, a proud, if misguided, soldier of the Fatherland. – But there were those who had done such things without compunction.'

As Jack walked back to the Boulevard d'Anspach it began to rain. A slight drizzle started to wet the cobblestones, causing the tramlines to shine in the light of the street lamps.

There were a handful of officers still at the bar of the Eye Club when he came in, but as Jack didn't know any of them he decided to turn in; it was well after one-thirty and he'd driven a long distance that day, all the way up to Nijmegen and back, to add to the journey from Godesberg to Brussels.

Jack got into bed and lay on his back. Across the street the lights from a large neon sign advertising soap powder flashed on and off, illuminating the ceiling. The sound of an accordion and drunken singing wafted up from a nearby café. To his amazement, Jack realized that he felt desperately lonely and homesick: not for England and his parents and pre-war friends, but for Bad Godesberg, for Ingrid and Julius, Peter Franks and Corporal Bridges, and above all for Karin. He was missing the life he'd grown used to: the excitement and fun of living and working beside the Rhine, able to carry on like an old-world impresario controlling musicians and singers and running three or four opera companies and of loving Karin.

It was not until the café closed and the neon sign was switched off that Jack finally slipped into a deep sleep.

He dreamed that he found Karin alone and naked in a large field of wild flowers, picking daisies and buttercups and that she smiled at him and took his hand.

A sudden crash and a tinkle of glass woke him with a start. Outside in the street there was a shrill altercation. A woman was screaming at someone and two men's voices could be heard in angry conflict. Jack went to the window to look out.

It was daylight and a church clock opposite said nine-thirty. On the street corner a car had collided with a tradesman's van. There were broken lamps and dented wings; it was nothing serious.

Jack fell into bed again, realizing with a stab of disappointment that his meeting with Karin in that field was all a dream. Things were still the same. And he still had another day's leave to get through in Brussels.

LATER that morning Jack went to see the famous Manikin Piss, the little fountain statue of a cherub peeing, which had been dressed up in a Welsh Guards uniform after the Liberation. Then he did some shopping. He bought a few little things to send his parents and grandmother in England, a scarf for Ingrid and a tobacco pouch for Julius. He hesitated a long time over what to get for Karin.

For some minutes he stared into the window of an expensive jeweller's, looking at the rings that flashed their brilliance at him from their velvet resting-places. If he were to buy her an engagement ring, what would he choose? The prettiest was an eternity ring of light blue sparkling stones that would match her light blue eyes. He stood for a long time gazing into the shop window. But somehow his will would not propel his steps into the shop. 'In any case,' he told himself, 'I can't afford to buy her a ring – and I certainly can't afford to get married.'

The age during which he learned his profession as a barrister stretched away into the distance; it seemed so long that he could not visualize what might happen at the end of it. A career? Yes, that was something he could imagine, but a house and wife and family – all that seemed to belong to different, older people – not himself. Yet the Karin of his dream the night before seemed close beside him, beckoning him to her. So close and yet so unattainable, so passionate and yet so likely to be lost. He sighed, and walked on.

A moment later he went into a shop to buy her some scent. He chose a small, very expensive, bottle of Lanvin's 'Arpège'.

As he handed the Belgian francs across the counter for his purchase, a soft, rather sexy English voice behind him said "I'm after 'Arpège' too. It's divine, isn't it?"

Jack turned to see a beautiful, pale face with scarlet lips smiling at him from under a khaki beret, worn well back to display a high forehead. She was a strikingly lovely, raven-haired English girl in the uniform of the FANYs, about twenty-five years old and possessed of superb legs, encased in very sheer nylons. Jack recognized her at once as a girl he'd seen chauffeuring the GOC round the Divisional Area. Everyone knew her by sight but nobody outside A Mess knew her name.

"You're General Tom's driver, aren't you?"

"That's right."

"Is he in Brussels?"

"No. I'm here on leave."

"So am I."

Jack stepped aside to allow the girl to make her purchase, which she accomplished in perfect French. Then he said "Are you on your own in the big city?"

"More or less. I came down with Priscilla Fielding; she's in the WAAF and works for Air-Marshal Cooper at SHAEF, but she's engaged to a Belgian, so I shan't see much of her till we go back together on Friday."

This lovely face provided relief from the problem of thinking about Karin. "How about a drink?" he asked. "There's a bar across the street, if you've got time."

"Thanks; I'd love one."

They sat down at a table on the pavement and Jack ordered a lager for himself and a gin and tonic for his guest. Then they exchanged names and vital statistics. Not their physical measurements: Jack didn't need to be told that hers were well nigh perfect with very nice, full breasts, a pure ivory skin and those sensational legs. She was, Jack thought to himself, what

Peter Franks called NFO – Not Fair to Officers. Tempting. Jail bait.

He discovered her name was Audrey Cornish, that her home was in Devon, that her only brother Martin, in the RAF, had been shot down and killed in his Mosquito the previous year on a raid over Brittany, and that she'd been studying for the stage at the Webber-Douglas when war broke out.

They discussed what Brussels had to offer and Audrey asked Jack how long his leave was.

"Only forty-eight hours. Got to drive back tomorrow."

"What a shame."

"I know. What are you doing tonight?"

"Nothing."

"Could we dine – somewhere? I would be glad of some company; I mean, someone – nice . . . "

"I'd love to."

Jack gulped, and turned round in his chair to ask the waiter for the bill. In doing so, his knee came into delicious contact with a khaki-clad thigh, causing him to mutter untruthfully "Sorry; not much room at this wretched little table . . . "

Audrey gave him an amused smile.

She was staying at a hostel off the Boulevard Adolphe Max, and Jack said "I'll come by for you, as the Yanks say, at seven. OK?"

"I'll be ready."

After they parted Jack walked through a park strewn with autumn leaves, his mind in a turmoil. He knew he was in love with Karin, he must be, to feel so bloody miserable without her. Yet here was this ravishing English doll, his for the asking for all he knew – he'd know in a few hours' time – and the thought of an evening with Miss Cornish made him tremble with excitement. 'It's sex, of course,' he told himself, 'rearing its ugly head again. Makes it so bloody hard to recognize true love, when it comes along.'

The Grill Room of the Hotel Liègeoise near the *Bourse* was

almost empty and the atmosphere faintly depressing. As Jack and Audrey followed the *maître d'hôtel* to a corner table under a palm tree, a three-piece orchestra was playing, thirty years out of date, the First World War hit 'Roses are blooming in Picardy'.

Among the handful of other diners in the place were two American officers, a few tables away, entertaining a couple of heavily made-up ladies of the town, who were dressed in tight satin and cheeky little hats with veils. A good deal of jolly laughter wafted over with the cigar smoke.

As the evening progressed, Jack discovered that Audrey had been to one or two of the concerts in Bonn. He mentioned, without too much modesty, his own personal contribution to the musical revival in the Divisional Area and was soon recounting his early experience with Ingrid Pauels, when she locked Karin in her house to prevent her from working for the British.

Audrey must have put two and two together, for after a while she asked "Is she very beautiful, your – secretary?"

"I think so," said Jack, quickly swallowing some wine.

There was a slight silence. It wasn't part of Jack's plan to spend the evening telling Audrey about Karin. If he said no more she might be tactful enough to drop the subject and ask no further questions.

By now the Grill Room orchestra was playing a selection from Noel Coward's operetta *Conversation Piece*, which, coupled with a second bottle of extremely fine Hock, encouraged Jack to take the plunge and ask Audrey if there was anyone special in her life.

She smiled and twiddled the stem of her glass before replying "I was rather in love once – still am, I suppose. But he's married."

"Happily?" Jack asked.

"No, but . . . let's not talk about it."

Jack wondered whether this was the truth or a standard device for warding off unwanted suitors.

"If you're still keen on this chap . . . and he's keen on you, maybe he'll get a divorce one day. Will you wait for that?"

"I don't know," she said with rather a sad smile. "One doesn't get any younger."

Privately Jack thought she'd still be a pretty good proposition in ten or fifteen years time, but what he said was "This war's played hell with so many marriages. Thank God I didn't marry and leave a wife behind to look for diversions because she'd got bored and lonely."

Audrey stared into space for a while. Then she said "I suppose I should be grateful not to have a husband on active service overseas, with all the temptations that men always . . . " She broke off.

Jack said "If I was a husband, serving overseas, and I met you in a shop in Brussels, as I did, I'd be bloody well tempted, as I am now, wife or no wife."

Audrey reached out to lay her hand on his. "That's a very sweet thing to say."

"I meant it."

"What about your lovely fraülein?"

"We had words. She didn't want me to come to Brussels without her, although she knew I couldn't bring her."

"How sad." Audrey looked genuinely upset for him.

Jack felt he was being disloyal to Karin, exploiting the coolness with her in order to get on terms with an attractive English girl. All the same, he was only a healthy, normal young man and could hardly be blamed for assessing his chances of seeing this gorgeous girl again. Even getting her into bed. But he knew it must be now or never.

THE bill was paid, the waiter tipped and Audrey was on her feet, collecting her shoulder-bag, ready to leave.

Jack knew there was little or no chance of bed tonight, anyway. It was never possible at the Eye Club and he was pretty sure that no man would be allowed within miles of the hostel for Service girls where Audrey was staying. The best chance of continuing the relationship was to get a little more wine down her, then escort her chivalrously to the hostel, part at the door with a tender but passionate embrace and hope to leave her wanting more.

"Why don't we go back to the Eye Club for a nightcap?" he ventured, "Or to your place?"

"Do you mind if we don't? I've got to be up early in the morning. Thanks, all the same."

"OK," he replied, trying to keep the disappointment out of his voice.

"Don't bother to see me back," Audrey said, but she didn't need much persuasion to be driven home in the Jeep.

Outside the hostel Jack took her hand and kissed it, like an old world courtier. Then he said "Thank you, Audrey, darling – if I may call you darling - you've given me a wonderful, exciting evening."

She smiled at him, and then she suddenly grabbed him to her, pressing her parted lips to his, so he could feel her tongue stabbing between them deliciously.

After a minute she let go of him and said quickly "You must go now or you'll catch cold," and disappeared into the building.

It was a fairly cold evening for early November but as he stood, dazed, looking up at the hostel building, Jack was on fire, throbbing with unfulfilled desire. It would be impossible to get any rest after this, if he was to go to bed now. He got back into his Jeep and instead of going to the Club, he set off for the red light district of Brussels.

UNDER the garish blue neon sign for La Pyramide, an arrow pointed down an iron spiral staircase, into a small courtyard below street level where beaded curtains covered a narrow doorway.

From inside Jack could hear the low murmur of female

voices, speaking very fast, and a gramophone record of Edith Piaf singing '*La Vie En Rose*'.

He brushed aside the curtains and went in. In the dim, murky light, he could just make out a small bar and a few tables, at which reclined a dozen or so girls in cheap, revealing evening gowns. There was one black girl in silver *lamé* with long earrings, extremely elegant and chic, and a couple of others from the Middle East who were sallow-skinned with Semitic profiles. The rest were presumably Belgian or French.

Anxious not to waste time drinking and chatting at the bar, Jack made a quick decision. He noticed one particularly striking girl, medium built with well-rounded breasts that were barely covered by a low-cut halter-neck dress of black satin. She had long, silky hair down her back, large brown eyes, and she was smoking with a cigarette holder. She had what appeared to be a touch more class than most ladies of easy virtue; she looked as though she might have come from a good family but had fallen on hard times. She was sitting alone at one of the small tables and Jack noticed that she wore a small gold crucifix on a chain, so that Our Lord's cross rested comfortably in the fold of her ivory bosom.

Jack walked up to the girl in black, cleared his throat and said "*Excusez-moi, Mademoiselle, mais je voudrais bien passer une demi-heure avec vous. C'est possible?*"

The girl looked up and smiled charmingly. "*D'accord, M'sieur. Mais ça va couter mille francs et tu dois achêter une bouteille de champagne, tu sais.*"

Jack knew his half-hour of pleasure would cost him champagne as well as the girl's fee, so he nodded to the old Madame, who was watching him carefully from behind the bar, and asked the girl her name.

"Yvette. *Et toi?*"

"Jacques."

Yvette had noticed Jack's uniform and now switched into English. "You are English soldier. I like English soldier."

Jack smiled, and told the girl that not too many months ago he and his division had been the first Allied troops into Brussels and had liberated the capital. The thought flashed through his mind that this might procure him a small discount but he certainly wouldn't dare to suggest it.

The Madame of the establishment agreed to serve the champagne in one of the private rooms behind the bar and moments later Jack and Yvette were alone in a musty room with a large full-length mirror, lots of cushions, a wardrobe and a double bed. In the ceiling a cut-glass dome illuminated the room with a garish bright light.

Jack quickly turned it off and switched on a small, crimson-shaded bedside lamp, which at once created a dimmer, more erotic atmosphere and concealed the squalor of the scene.

Next he closed his eyes and asked Yvette to undress completely but to put on a single garment, a slip or even a bath towel, and hide away all the impedimenta of shoes, stockings, suspender belt and pants. Then, to be in bed, well covered up, by the time he opened his eyes. And no conversation. Yvette did as she was told. Jack waited, his head turned away.

When he opened his eyes, Jack was pleased to find that Yvette was in bed wearing her slip with the straps down.

Trembling slightly, Jack got in beside her, clasped her to him very gently and began to stroke her smooth thighs and back slowly and sensually. Accustomed to rougher, more peremptory treatment from the cruder type of customer, Yvette could not help murmuring *"Mais tu me caresses bien, Jacques. Tu me plais, sais tu?"*

Jack had been driven to La Pyramide by a desperate surge of passionate longing for Audrey Cornish's body, built up during a long, intimate dinner, so it would not be unnatural to close his eyes and try to imagine he was stroking Audrey. But he had come to Brussels because of his love for Karin and it was to Karin that he now turned in thought. But for some reason, the illusion failed to work. Try as he would, he could not envisage

Karin beside him in bed, naked, warm and yielding. It wasn't long before his roaming hands reached Yvette's firm and shapely breasts and began to stroke them and cup them in his hands, and the vision that came to him was of Audrey. It was Audrey's body in his arms, Audrey's unknown back, thighs, buttocks, Audrey writhing and undulating in his firm grasp – Audrey drawing him into herself – Audrey . . .

It was all over. Jack was fulfilled, his lust had been tamed and it was time to swallow a quick glass of champagne with Yvette and get out.

Jack always felt a cheat after making love to a prostitute or a dance-hostess. There seemed something dishonest about paying a strange girl to lie in his arms and be ravished in the form and image of somebody else. But it happened, and perhaps it had to happen. Jack bade all present a polite "*Bonne nuit*" and left La Pyramide with a slight feeling of shame.

When he got back to the Eye Club at two-thirty in the morning he had a bath before getting into his clean, laundered sheets, and very soon fell asleep.

Chapter 11

ON the morning after his return from Brussels Jack found awaiting him in the Officers' Mess an envelope marked 'By Hand' in unfamiliar handwriting. It contained a printed invitation card from 'The General's Personal Staff', requesting the pleasure of Major J. Hamilton's company at the Bergischerhof Hotel, Bonn at 8.0 p.m. onwards. Dancing and Buffet. The date for the party was that very evening. Jack's first instinct was to sit down and write a polite refusal. But, as he turned the card over, he noticed some handwritten scribble on the back.

'Do come if you can. We're going to dance to a marvellous jazz guitarist called Eddie Christiani. Should be fun. Remember me? Audrey Cornish.'

Inviting Jack was plainly a late decision on Audrey's part. She hadn't mentioned the dance over the weekend in Brussels, so she'd probably asked him in place of some partner who'd let her down at the last moment. Could it be the married man she said she loved? Or some jerk around the General's HQ; an ADC perhaps?

The thought of dancing with Audrey was certainly very tempting, with the chance to get his arms around that shapely ody and hold her close and tight. That's all dancing was, he reckoned: licensed hugging to music; legitimate body contact etween the sexes.

Then Jack thought guiltily of Karin but told himself in ustification that one evening out with another girl was nothing o make a fuss about. But he knew in his heart that this was ot an adequate excuse for trying his luck with the general's lamorous girl driver. Torn by indecision, he opted for a 'wait nd see' policy. He would not reply to the invitation but plead ater on that it had come too late to be answered. He could hen decide at the last moment, depending on Karin's reaction, vhether to go to the dance and, if not, write Audrey a belated pology.

In the event Jack was not able to consult Karin about the ritish Headquarters' dance, for she was not in the office that norning and Corporal Bridges had heard nothing from her ince the weekend. Jack wondered if she'd gone to Coblenz gain, while he was away. Perhaps Frau Freidl had suffered a elapse.

Jack concluded that he ought, in fairness to Karin, to go to er lodgings, in case she was there, and tell her he'd been vited to a dance tonight at the British headquarters. He'd say was something he really should go to; as a member of the Divisional Staff he ought to look in just for a moment.

Then he thought 'No. Why should I discuss it with her? I on't have to get Karin's permission to accept an invitation rom my brother officers. I can tell her I went, tomorrow norning.'

But Karin did not show up at the office at all that day. nstead, there was a note from her saying 'Ingrid's party is onight, at 8.0 p.m. You must be there; you are expected.'

'Damn!' thought Jack. 'Why do the two events have to take lace on the same night?' He would have to go to Ingrid's – but e was not going to miss the dance, even if he had to leave early. On his way back for lunch he posted a note for Karin through her

letter-box. 'Thanks for telling me about Ingrid's party. I am ver
sorry I shall arrive late, as there is a do at HQ that I shall have t
look in on first. Please give my apologies to Ingrid, and tell her
look forward to coming on later in the evening.'

At 6.0 p.m. Jack left the office for his billet to bath an
change for the party.

THE Bergischerhof Hotel was ablaze with light and from th
ground floor rooms the sound of chatter, tinkling glasses an
the rhythmic beat of a guitar filled the night air.

Jack jumped out of his Jeep, demobilized it by removing th
rotor arm and putting it in his pocket, took a deep breath an
hurried in through the hotel entrance.

The Bergischerhof was a medium-sized pre-war touris
hotel, which the Division had requisitioned as a billet for arm
personnel. Tonight every corner was crammed with Allie
Service people of all sorts. They were mostly from the Guard
Division but Jack spotted a number of American uniforms a
well as RAF, WAAF and some khaki-clad girls of the othe
Women's Services.

The restaurant and bar had been cleared for dancing and th
floor was jammed with couples, hardly able to move but goin
through the motions of a steady foxtrot. Some were wrappe
in each other's arms, cheek to cheek; others danced a shad
more distantly, conversing politely, as their feet moved to th
compulsive rhythm of the guitar.

Standing at the edge of the dance floor and looking aroun
the crowded room, Jack was struck by the cleverness o
dispensing with a band. Instead, a dark, rather good-lookin
man was strolling around the floor among the dancer
strumming his guitar and singing, in a strong accent, th
popular Cole Porter number 'My Heart Belongs To Daddy'.

As Jack stood watching the scene in wonder, a voice besid
him said "Didn't think I'd see you here, Jack." Jack looke
round. It was the DAQMG, Geoffrey Wynn-Davies.

"Hullo, Geoffrey," he said.

"Got Fraülein Freidl with you?"

"No."

"Saw you had her in tow at that concert a few weeks ago. Just wondered."

"She wasn't asked to this hop," Jack said. Looking at the American uniforms among the dancing throng, he went on "I was told this party was for the General's Staff only. Didn't know General Tom had so many Yanks on his staff."

"We were all allowed to invite two guests. The Yanks are special guests of the G1."

"Oh." Then Jack said "I could do with a drink."

"So could I," said Wynn-Davies, and the two officers edged and elbowed their way through the crush round the bar, where they managed to get a glass of champagne each.

When Jack asked about the guitarist, the DAQMG told him that he was a Dutchman and that the Coldstream had picked the fellow up in the streets of Grave as a suspected fifth-columnist. But their Intelligence Officer had discovered that he was the famous Eddie Christiani, Holland's most celebrated jazz guitar player, whose records sold all over the world.

"The Second-in-Command of the Coldstream battalion concerned happened to be a jazz enthusiast, you see; knew all about Eddie and persuaded the Commanding Officer to take the chap on as an interpreter."

"Did he go into battle with them?" Jack asked.

"Certainly. Arthur Morris had him in his squadron; told me he was bloody brave."

"What's he doing now?"

"When the fighting ended, they tried to repatriate him to his home outside Eindhoven, but he begged to be allowed to stay on. I think he's become the battalion band now. He's on the Coldstream payroll. They hire him out for parties."

Turning away from the crowded bar to watch the dancing, Jack's eye suddenly caught a glimpse of what he was looking for. Audrey could just be seen in the middle of the crush on the floor, dancing cheek to cheek with her eyes closed, locked in the arms of a Scots Guards captain with a ginger moustache. For a moment Jack stared, a feeling of injured betrayal sweeping over him.

Audrey's scribbled message on his invitation card had given him the foolish and false impression that she would be awaiting his arrival at the dance with breathless expectation, keeping herself for him tonight. And there she was, locked in the arms of that jerk with the ginger moustache.

The last thing Jack wanted was to betray his interest in Audrey to a stranger. At the same time, he felt a need to discover more about her and, in particular, to learn what the ginger-moustached captain meant in her life.

"Who's that chap dancing with Audrey Cornish? Any idea?"

Wynn-Davies peered into the crowd. "That's poor old Charlie Eddington. Staff Captain at 5th Guards Brigade."

"Why 'poor old Charlie'? I'd have thought he was to be envied, dancing with that particular *numero*."

"He's Audrey Cornish's latest admirer," said Geoffrey, lighting a cigarette. "She's got plenty of 'em, God knows."

"I'm not surprised," said Jack, his eye still fixed on Audrey, who was now leaning back and laughing. Her smile as she laughed was dazzling.

"Charlie's got a perfectly good wife at home in Cheltenham. Splendid girl called Susan. She was Susan Courtney, Oliver Courtney's sister. Rather rotten for her."

"Oh!"

"Everybody thinks he's making an idiot of himself."

Jack sensed a tone of envy in Geoffrey's voice. 'Sour grapes,' he thought. The guitar stopped and most of the dancers applauded and, sweaty and thirsty, headed for the bar.

Jack saw Audrey lead Captain Eddington off the dance floor by the hand, as a Nanny would lead a child across a busy street. Possessively, she steered him through the crush until

Jack lost sight of them. He decided to find Audrey as soon as possible and ask her for a dance. Even if Eddington was the married man she had said she was in love with, Jack dared to hope she would agree to at least one dance with him. After all, she had invited him to the party.

Jack manoeuvred himself into a position where the couple were likely to run into him, as they made for the bar. They did. Jack feigned surprise.

"Hullo," he said cheerfully. "Didn't think I'd ever find you in this crush."

Audrey's face lit up with a smile that rocked Jack back on his heels. It made him feel, although he had to admit that it was probably without justification, that his arrival at the dance was the big event of the evening for her.

"Oh, I'm so thrilled you could come!"

She introduced her companion. "Do you know Charlie Eddington? – This is Jack Hamilton. He runs all the music and entertainment and things – don't you?"

"I try to."

Captain Eddington nodded.

"I was praying you'd be back from Brussels in time to get the invitation," she went on, "and you have."

"How about a dance?" asked Jack, glancing at Audrey's partner. "If you can be spared, that is."

"Could you spare me, Charlie?" Audrey turned to her escort with a deadly serious expression that rapidly changed into a mischievous, provocative smile.

Charlie Eddington seemed unamused. "Suit yourself," he muttered, and walked away.

"That means I can be spared," said Audrey, and she flung her arms apart in a gesture that said 'Take me, I'm yours.'

Jack gulped and said "Good."

Eddie Christiani downed his drink at the bar, swung the guitar that hung on a strap round his neck back into position and struck up again. This time it was a rumba, 'South American Way'.

"Come on," said Audrey, grabbing Jack's hand and dragging him into the *mêlée* on the floor. Before Jack could collect himself, she was gyrating and wiggling her hips like Carmen Miranda.

Not a very skilled dancer, Jack nevertheless attempted to execute a variety of South American steps, with some difficulty holding Audrey at arm's length as she spun and wriggled with total abandon. She moved beautifully, Jack thought, like a professional. Ought to be on the stage. That thought brought back a fleeting vision of Lili Spiegel. But he told himself that you couldn't 'sit out' with Lili Spiegel and have a conversation or a joke as you could with this girl.

When the rumba ended, with applause and some cheering, Eddie Christiani slipped smoothly into the haunting tune 'Dancing In The Dark', and someone dimmed the lights.

As Jack and Audrey danced the first few steps of the romantic slow foxtrot they remained slightly apart, with four or five inches between them. Slowly, imperceptibly, Jack drew her closer to him. She did not resist, and Jack registered a feeling of triumph when simultaneously as though by some mutual, unspoken consent, their bodies touched. Jack felt Audrey go slightly limp as her cheek touched his, while her right hand gripped his left a little more tightly. Nothing was said. They danced cheek to cheek to the music, waves of desire travelling between them, until the tune ended and they both surfaced to the reality of the dance, the applause, the sudden brightening of the lights.

"Why don't we go and sit out for a bit. I'm boiled, aren't you?" Audrey said, blowing her hair off her face.

"A bit," said Jack, slightly weak at the knees.

As they left the dance floor Audrey murmured "I feel like stripping off my uniform; it's roasting me alive."

They found a quiet corner just inside the front entrance where Audrey sank into a leather chair and tore off her tie, unbuttoning her collar and the first two buttons of her shirt.

"That's better," she said, fanning herself with a copy of the *Kolnerzeitung* she'd picked up from the table.

They sat for a while in silence. Then Audrey asked "Did you enjoy that concert the other evening?"

This took Jack a bit by surprise. "Do you mean the one on the 15th? The Rachmaninov and the Grieg Symphony?"

"That's right."

"Did you go?"

"I certainly did. And I saw you there."

No mention of Karin, Jack noted. Tactful girl. He was beginning to like her now, as well as desiring her. So she was fond of music, too.

Audrey repeated her question. "Well, did you?"

"What?"

"Enjoy the concert."

"Of course. I helped to organize it. Did you?"

"Enormously."

Jack thought 'This isn't the right script.' But communication, once established, had to be kept going at all costs.

"Which piece did you like best?" he asked.

"The Rachmaninov, I think. And the slow movement of the Sibelius. That was so lovely, it made me want to cry."

Jack felt uneasy. Audrey was showing signs of a serious side to her nature. That was dangerous. He'd much rather she continued to flirt, not start being quietly romantic, thus posing a threat to his feelings for Karin. Then a thought flashed through Jack's mind. 'What if she doesn't find me attractive? Doesn't want to get involved with me in that way? After all, I'm not Robert Taylor. Or is this talk of the concert a subtle way of landing me in her net? She knows I love a German girl, who loves music. What better way to break that up than by professing a love of music herself, while subtly indicating the possibility of a roll-in-the-hay?'

'No,' he thought, 'that's not fair. It's also extremely vain, on my part. She's a bloody attractive girl having a marvellous time, surrounded by as many men as she can cope with – all panting for her. Why shouldn't she exercise her sexual skills on all and sundry? – Better to seduce or, at least, scalp the whole field,' he thought, 'than break up one marriage; poor old Charlie Eddington's. – No, that's not fair, either. Charlie Eddington's breaking up his own marriage; Audrey isn't. Nobody ordered him to take up with the general's chauffeur.'

At that moment a rather limp, effete-looking major in the Household Cavalry came by, recognized Audrey and murmured in a lazy drawl "Good God, I do believe it's Audrey Cornish. Didn't know you were out here."

"Rupert, darling! How extraordinary!"

"Isn't it?" said the major.

Audrey decided to hold on to him by introducing him, so she said to Jack "This is a very old friend of mine from pre-war days, Lord Rupert Talbot-Carey. Jack Hamilton."

"Hullo," said Jack.

"Great party," said the major, taking a pace as if to move on.

But Audrey was too quick for him. "Isn't that guitarist simply wonderful? So much better than a band, don't you agree?"

Lord Rupert paused. "Absolutely first-rate. Chap can play anything."

"Makes you want to dance, doesn't it? I can't keep my feet from tapping." Audrey tapped her feet restlessly and hummed a few words of the Cole Porter song, 'Anything Goes', which was currently audible from the dance floor.

' . . . if driving fast cars you like or low bars you like or pink gin you like or just sin you like or Mae West you like, or me undressed you like, nobody will oppose . . . '

The words were accompanied by a seductive movement of the shoulders, which plainly had the desired effect. Lord Rupert glanced towards the restaurant, as though to make sure he was unobserved, then almost guiltily down at Audrey's shapely legs, which were now being revealed to a generous extent. "I say, would you care to take some exercise?"

"If by that you mean would I care to dance, the answer is yes, Rupert dear, I would."

She turned to Jack and said "You will excuse us, won't you?"

"Naturally," said Jack, summoning all the dignity and indifference he could manage, in spite of the shock and disappointment. He now knew for sure that he'd simply been guilty of over-optimism and wishful thinking. He was not the only fish in the sea. There were shoals of them in there, on that dance floor and standing round the bar, and Audrey could take her pick. Yet why had she invited him personally? She must have found him attractive in Brussels; or did she simply need a partner for the dance, someone unattached, unmarried, or was it just that she could not let one scalp escape her?

Jack decided he'd had the best of the evening. There was no future in it now. He'd had his dance with Audrey and there was nobody else with whom he had the slightest desire to dance, so he got up from his leather chair in the foyer and went out into the night.

The cool air outside brought him back to his senses and he began to experience a strange, sentimental longing for Karin. As he walked along the Acherstrasse to where he had parked the Jeep, he found himself comparing her with Audrey. They were both beautiful girls, in slightly different ways – one dark, one fair. One English, one German. They both had gorgeous bodies but here the comparison ended.

Audrey was a typically English girl with a county background, living it up out here in Germany in a way she'd never been allowed to in Devon, with parents and aunts and uncles cramping her style. 'She's obviously thrilled to discover the power she has over men, the ability to arouse them. Perhaps her aim is to find herself a husband. And what better fishing ground than the British Zone of Occupation in Germany, an area crawling with healthy, lusty eligible young officers, well out of sight of their families, sex-starved and highly vulnerable? Karin, on the other hand, is a more genuine, sincere person. She would never encourage a chap she didn't care for. She cares for me, that's obvious – in spite of our little differences. If she has a fault, it's that she's just a bit 'pi'. That's to say, she has very high standards of behaviour. Almost a puritan, and I can't imagine her giving herself to anyone who just happens to come along. She loves music and beauty and, with her, passion runs very deep. But then so might it with Audrey. Who can tell?'

INGRID'S drawing-room was full of people when Jack reached the house, rang the bell and was met at the door by Karin. Seeing him on the doorstep, she stopped short and looked at him without expression. There was an awkward silence, until she said "You are late – but come in."

The drawing-room door was open and a babble of voices and the sound of singing greeted him as he followed Karin into the room. Emmerich Karl was there and one or two members of the Cologne Opera orchestra plus several of the singers, including Otto Maier, all talking in small groups. Willy Pohl was at the piano, sight-reading a piece of music, while Julius and Ingrid sang together a number from an old Hungarian operetta.

The song ended to some applause.

"Why are you not here earlier, my dear?" Ingrid cried out, "We are missing you," as she left the piano to come over and greet Jack with an affectionate hug.

"I'm awfully sorry," Jack said, taking both her hands. "Didn't Karin tell you? I had to go over to headquarters today. The General gave a party to say goodbye to one of his ADCs."

With a dead straight face, Karin announced in a loud voice "The English army General has a girl chauffeur who loves Jack so much that he must go over there this evening or she would shoot herself like Hedda Gabler."

With that she burst into hysterical laughter that grew louder and more uncontrolled as tears rolled down her cheeks.

Jack never quite knew what it was that prompted him at that moment to do what he did. Was it a sudden need to enter into the spirit of her teasing; or an attempt to shock her out of her mounting hysteria?

For whatever reason, he seized Karin firmly round the waist and carried her to the sofa where he turned her over his knee and spanked her.

When the general laughter at this spectacle had died down and normal conversation was resumed, Jack helped Karin to sit upright and wipe the tears from her cheeks. He put an arm round her shoulder and squeezed it. "If you were referring to General Harrington's lady driver, darling, her name is Audrey Cornish."

"I know." Karin was quite calm now.

Jack went on "I met the girl for the first time in Brussels last weekend, so just what exactly did you mean?"

Karin shrugged off the question but Jack pressed on. "How did you know I knew her? – Are you going to tell me?"

At first Karin looked as though she was not prepared to reveal the source of her information. But then she assumed an expression of casual unconcern. "I should go this evening to fetch some music from the office for Herr Pohl to rehearse and bring it here tonight," she said. "Corporal Bridges told me to look on your desk for it and I see there a card to invite you to a party this night also. I am curious and I see on the back some writing and I ask Corporal Bridges who is this Audrey Cornish and he say she is the General's girl chauffeur at Headquarters and – how he has put it – she is – pin-up girl – very pretty. So I am angry that you see this woman."

Jack could only stare at her and say "I asked Miss Cornish to dine with me in Brussels for company, because I happen to dislike dining alone. I would far rather have dined with you. Surely you know that?"

"How could that be so," Karin retorted, "when I am not allowed to go with you to Brussels?"

"I know, *Liebchen*, I'm sorry."

Anxious to terminate this enquiry, Jack took Karin's hand to lead her over to the piano.

"Let's find out what Julius and Ingrid are going to do for an encore. Come on."

As Jack came up to Ingrid, who was peering over Willy's shoulder at the music on the stand, Willy Pohl was starting to play the same song as before.

"That's a great melody. I'm delighted to hear it again," Jack said. "What is it?"

"It is from the operetta *Maritza* of Kalman. Come and sing it with us," Julius replied.

"We shall teach you the words in German, Karin. Come, my dear, we shall all sing together and make ourselves more happy," Ingrid added.

Once more Pohl struck up the song from *Maritza*. As he played, Jack noticed that a candle was burning beside Werner Pauels' photograph on the piano and a single crimson rose stood nearby in a glass holder. Reminded of Ingrid's recent bereavement, he rather regretted indulging in horseplay with Karin and felt he must somehow change key, quickly.

Standing close together beside the keyboard, their bodies touching, Jack and Karin joined in the song. Jack glanced sideways once or twice to find Karin's eyes fixed on him, a look of deep longing in them, as she sang the words of the Kalman waltz in her charming, tuneful voice.

Then Ingrid clapped her hands and ordered everybody to come over to the piano. "*Kommt, meine lieben Freunde und Gäste, jetzt mussen singen wir alle zusammen.*"

Willy Pohl struck up 'Tannenbaum' and they all started to sing lustily in chorus. And so the evening progressed with music and laughter and happiness.

The contrast with the party going on a few streets away, inside the Bergischerhof Hotel, struck Jack as very marked. At their HQ the victorious Allies were drinking looted champagne, lusting and dancing to numbers from Broadway shows; in the other, vanquished German musicians were trying to re-establish their shattered lives with Mosel and Central European operetta. Jack could say a lot for both; after all, he now had a foot in both camps. But for how much longer? And although Karin stayed close to Jack, never letting him out of her sight, he felt that something, and he did not think it was just Audrey, had interposed itself between them.

STANDING on what might have been the very spot where once he and Karin had paused to watch Ingrid Pauels pursue the fugitive tenor Otto Maier along the platform, Sir John looked round him at Bonn's modern, post-war *Bahnhof*. Outside, the building was the same as it had been when he knew it before: an ugly reddish-brown stone edifice built in the 1890s, with a clock on its façade. But inside it was now full of shops, a restaurant, a large *Reisezentrum* on Platform 1 and smooth escalators down to the U-bahn. Fast comfortable Intercity trains with restaurant cars glided smoothly in and out on their way to Cologne from Munich, Nuremberg, Mannheim and other German cities, and smart German state railway officials in red-topped caps operated computers in small control cabins on each platform. It was very different from the bomb-damaged wreck of a station he could remember in 1945, when it had been crowded with limping, bandaged prisoners-of-war, exposed to the wind and weather by huge gaps in the glass roof overhead.

Half an hour earlier, Sir John had left the Bergischerof after arranging with the Records Office to continue the search for Karin.

Meanwhile, he had decided to try and find Ingrid Pauels' house in Mehlem, which he recalled had been somewhere near the Post Office. The name of the street he could never forget for it was appropriately Wagnerian – Nibelungen Allee. He thought he remembered that it ran parallel to the river. Ingrid herself would, surely, be long since dead – and Julius too – but someone in those houses might just be ancient enough to remember them.

Judge Hamilton soon found No. 42. The numbering had not been changed during the last forty-four years and the house was instantly recognizable by its shuttered windows and the monkey puzzle tree in the back garden. With an eerie sense of timelessness Sir John stood for a while and looked up at the first floor window of the room in which Ingrid had locked Karin all those years ago.

Sir John took a deep breath and put his finger on the front-door bell, pausing an instant before committing himself. As he waited he imagined the dim outline of Ingrid opening the door to him. She would be very old now – in her nineties and she would not recognize him.

'I am Jack Hamilton' he would say. 'Do you remember me? I used to come to this house soon after the war, when we started up the Bonn Opera. Jack – I am Jack.' – Perhaps the old lady would frown and shake her head . . .

His reverie was interrupted by the front door opening, revealing a thin pale woman with a bad cold, probably in her forties, carrying a baby.

She knew nothing of Frau Pauels. Her husband would be out all day, working at the local garage. They had bought the house in 1981 from a family called Schroeder and she understood the house had been empty for seven years before the Schroeders bought it.

Sir John asked the woman if there might be anyone in the neighbourhood over sixty-five or seventy, who might remember Frau Pauels.

The young wife pointed across the street to a small rather gloomy house with ivy growing up it and a sadly neglected front garden. "*Versuchen Sie Frau Kremer, gegenüber, vielleicht kann sie sich erinnern.*"

Jack crossed the road and rang the bell. After some time an old crone appeared in an apron, her face extremely lined and her back very bent. Sir John's hopes rose. The woman must be well into her eighties; more, perhaps.

The crone cupped her left ear to hear and understand his careful questions, asked in his best German. He concluded by saying "*Ihr Mann war ein Oberst in der Waffen ss und ist im Krieg gefallen. Aber Frau Pauels hat später einen alten Musik Professor, den Kammersänger Julius Heuss, geheiratet.*"

The old woman seemed to understand, for she nodded her head and in a weak, almost inaudible whisper, said "*Ja, Pauels, ja . . . sie sind beide umgefähr neunzehn hundert fünf und sechzig gestorben.*" She added that they were both buried in the churchyard further down towards the river, on the corner of the Geigerstrasse.

Jack thanked her and moved on. The least he could do for those two old friends of bygone days was to pay a visit to their graves.

Some minutes later he was reading the inscription on the headstone under a cypress tree:

Ingrid und Julius Heuss
Mit Gott zusammen, Aug. 1965.

ON Sir John's return to Bonn, after his nostalgic but fruitless trip to Mehlem, a telephone message from the Coblenz town hall awaited him. The receptionist produced the message from his pigeon-hole together with his room key, but a glance at the clock showed Hamilton that it was too late to return the call. The *Stadtverwaltungs* office would be closed by now, until the following morning.

Still smouldering from his wasted journey to the riverside slums of Leverkusen, the Judge felt a need to fill in his evening with some diversion, in order to take his mind off his disappointment and also to pass the time. It was frustrating enough having to wait until the morning to learn whether or not the Coblenz officials had made any real progress towards tracing Karin. But there was also the possibility they might send him scurrying off again tomorrow to West Berlin to interview some twenty-three old Fraülein Freidl working as a secretary in the Allied Control Commission . . .

He dined early and went out into the *Münsterplatz* in search of something to do.

There was a little studio theatre opposite his hotel, entered by a winding staircase past walls plastered with play posters. It appeared a typical 'fringe' theatre of the kind to be found in every major town and city in Europe. Here tonight, there was a visiting French company from Toulon, which was doing a Marivaux play in French. From the still photographs on the wall outside, it looked a reasonable production. There would be elegant costumes and witty language. It would be better than an aimless walk round the town at night, and Sir John went up the stairs with alacrity, into a small room with a tiny stage at one end.

The play came up to his expectations.

The next morning Sir John 'phoned the Coblenz town hall at the earliest possible moment. This time the news was definitely promising. Just outside Coblenz, in Andernach, there was a paediatrician, a Dr Hans Freidl, known to have been practising there for some years. Dr Freidl had been told of the English gentleman's enquiries and had said he could probably help. But, the girl clerk went on, the Herr Doctor would prefer not to discuss the matter on the telephone. Would Sir John, therefore, be good enough to travel down to Andernach and visit him personally?

Sir John did not much like the sound of that. He could still remember the Christian name of Karin's brother, who had been a prisoner-of-war in 1946 and must have been back in medical practice long since. But his name was not Hans. It was Dieter. Of that he was certain. Anyway, this could not possibly be Dieter, who was four years older than Karin and would be retired by now. Dr Freidl must be a relation of the Freidl

amily, possibly a cousin, and perhaps anxious not to break
ad news over the telephone.

All the same, it was a lead that must be followed up at once.
He decided to check out of the Bergischerhof in Bonn and find
small hotel or an inn to stay in, either in the small town of
Andernach or in the city of Coblenz.

He finally decided to stay in Coblenz, which was just as
vell, for on his arrival there he found that Dr Hans Freidl was
way for twenty-four hours on a seminar for paediatricians in
Mannheim.

He told the secretary he would call back the next afternoon,
nd after checking in to his hotel, spent the evening at a
oncert given by a visiting orchestra from Holland.

RONICALLY, the applause ringing in his ears momentarily
eightened the sense of guilt and remorse that had been a
requent companion during His Honour Sir John Hamilton's
ourney to look for Karin. Then his memories vanished and he
ound himself in the *Konzerthalle* in Coblenz, applauding with
he rest of the audience the Sibelius Symphony No. 5.

When he had left the concert hall and was making his way
ack to his hotel, for some reason that he could not explain, a
reat feeling of sadness overcame him.

Lying awake for some time in the solitude of his room and
stening to the constant flow of traffic outside, the occasional
acket of a motor scooter or the rumble of a train, Sir John
ried to analyse this feeling. Oddly, it was not that he was
issing Christine now, any more than he had during the first
ve or six weeks after her death, although it could have been
ecause small hotels abroad meant holidays shared with her
nd, on occasions, with Giles. But it was not that. He decided
hat it must be something to do with Karin; possibly the
memory of her and his drive in the Jeep down here, to the
eighbourhood of this very town Coblenz, to visit her parents
hat Sunday over forty years ago. Perhaps it was the un-

certainty of whether he was doing the right thing in trying to find her and unearth the buried past.

Within a matter of hours he might know the answers to all his questions. Whether Karin was alive and, if so, where was she? How was she?

Again the spectre loomed of a frail, emaciated, unhappy woman, short of money, bitter, ill, her life ruined. – Better that she were dead than that . . .

Chapter 12

CHRISTMAS was fast approaching and a flurry of snow had already settled high up on the peaks of the Siebengebirge.

On the morning of December 5th, after a fine performance of *The Magic Flute*, followed by another evening of *glühwein* and kisses in Karin's room, Jack had found a memo. in his pigeon-hole at the Mess, notifying him of the details of his demobilization on February 6th.

A strange feeling of depression, almost of bewilderment, came over him. It was hard to grasp the fact that within two months he would be on his way back to England, back to civilian life. At that moment, his present life: the Rhine, the music, and Karin suddenly assumed a feeling of dreamlike unreality, which would soon give way to the reality of his home, his parents and his future career.

After receiving congratulations from a number of brother officers, notably Peter Franks, who still had a further four to six months to go, Jack found himself wondering whether the confirmation of his impending demob. was, in fact, a reason for celebration.

One thing was certain and that was that Karin would be deeply saddened by the reminder of the impending separation. He would have to talk to her about it, of course. It would be unkind and unfair to allow her to go on believing in a long, uninterrupted romance, unless it were to end in marriage. As he sat at the Mess dining-table, spreading marmalade on his toast, Jack tried to imagine marrying Karin Freidl at Sunningdale.

Sunningdale? No, my God, it would be in Coblenz. The Freidls would have to hire a hall somewhere, arrange a service at the local Lutheran church, and give a reception. – How many of his friends and relations would feel like travelling across Europe to Coblenz in war-damaged trains to see him spliced to a Kraut?

Perhaps the Freidl family would understand if he took Karin over to England with him or arranged for her to come, once he was back in civvy street. They could then just invite her parents and sister over for the wedding – and possibly Ingrid and Julius – and even her brother, Dieter, if the poor bugger got himself released from his POW camp in time. They could be married quietly and without too much fuss in Sunningdale, to be witnessed by family and close friends only.

'What am I thinking of? I can't marry Karin. I daren't. I'm not even sure if I'm really in love with her. Could I expose her to all the hatred and ostracism she would have to endure?' He saw himself arriving to play golf at Swinley Forest with his German bride . . . all the whispering and muttering among the women players in their locker-room and the caddies and all the retired colonels in the bar. 'Maybe,' he thought, 'I'm using the possibility of anti-German prejudice as an excuse to get me off the hook. And yet, I do love her; I adore being with her; I'm sure I could share my life with her – happily and faithfully. – But would it last? – No, it wasn't on. – Or was it?

He started to think of all the qualities that made German girls into good wives. He didn't care much for the term *Hausfrau*, which suggested to him a stout, humourless woman with coils of blonde hair twisted round the top of her head, stirring a pot of *Gemüsesuppe*.

Karin had qualities, Jack felt, of deep loyalty, of correctness of behaviour, undoubted efficiency, probably a love of children and, above all, an undeniable love for him. She would surely make a good wife. – But what sort of husband would he make? He needed to do a lot of careful thinking.

JACK decided to break the news of the details of his demobilization to Karin the following morning, in the office, but on his way to work the pain that it was going to cause her made it seem too difficult. He told himself there was no hurry, and this was perhaps just as well, for when he got into work, he found Karin already in an emotional state.

When she asked if she might come into his room and show him something, he noticed that her eyes were moist, but she did not seem unduly sad.

"There is a letter has come from Dieter, my brother," she said, sniffing back the tears. "I'm so sorry. I cry a little, because he is safe and well. See, there is a photograph of him, taken only a month ago, at a transit camp in Naples. Look."

Jack took from her trembling hands a thick letter with the Red Cross franking on it, written in meticulously careful handwriting. The back of the envelope informed the world that it came from Dr Dieter Freidl, Asst. Arzt, USPWE 327, 81-G/650086, Napoli, Italy.

Jack drew the photograph from the envelope. He noticed that Karin's brother was quite a good-looking chap; he was wearing glasses and looked untidy and scruffy, not surprisingly, after several months as a prisoner-of-war. He'd been photographed, presumably by a fellow prisoner, standing outside a medical tent in bright sunlight, looking intensely bored. Jack wondered what Dieter would have to say if he knew his younger sister was working for, and in love with, a British officer.

"He says he will be released some time in the new year," said Karin. "They cannot get them all home for Christmas, because there are not enough ships to – how do you call it?"

"Repatriate them?"

"*So.*"

"Well," Jack said, replacing the snapshot and handing back the envelope, "at least he's safe. And he doesn't look too badly nourished. I don't think the Americans go in for starving their 'Kriegies'. Especially not medical personnel."

"To me he looks very thin, but he will soon put on some weight, once he is home."

"I'm sure he will."

With Dieter home, Jack reflected, Karin would have someone else to care for and confide in. Surely her brother would fill any gap made by his disappearance, so this could be the right moment to break the news of his departure. But once again Jack shelved the dreaded scene.

On the following day, the weather turned very cold and Bad Godesberg was soon under four inches of snow. Jack's Jeep had to be dug out of a drift most mornings and but for its four-wheel drive he would have been rendered virtually immobile.

Jack was in the office with Corporal Bridges, going through various dates for concerts and variety shows for publication in the *News Guardian*, when all the office lights suddenly went out and, owing to the heavy snow-laden sky outside, they found themselves plunged into virtual darkness.

"Bugger!" shouted Jack.

"Must be a power failure, Sir." Corporal Bridges turned to go out and check the rest of the street, when the office was suddenly illuminated by the soft, warm glow of candlelight.

Ingrid and Karin had come in together, each bearing a large pine wreath, mounted on a cardboard base, with a tall, red candle protruding from the centre. Attached to each wreath was a card. It was the traditional German table piece for *Weinachten*.

Ingrid placed hers on Corporal Bridges' desk and Karin put hers down on Jack's.

The effect was extremely pretty, and especially charming when the two ladies kissed Corporal Bridges, greeting him with the words, "*Lieber Gefreiter*, Bridges, *wir wünschen Ihnen eine sehr glückliche Weinachtszeit.*"

Bridges was touched and a little embarrassed, but he carried it off very well, smiled, returned the kisses, and said "Well, I'm sure that's very, very nice of you, ladies. All the very best for Christmas to you and yours!"

Corporal Bridges returned to his own room to sit at his desk and read his greeting card, as Ingrid and Karin came into Jack's office and Ingrid closed the door.

"I will give a small party at my house on Christmas Day and you are invited, Jack. *Eingeladen.*"

Karin, who seemed to be in on some secret, added "It will be a very special occasion, so you must not refuse."

"I shan't," said Jack.

Ingrid went on "We shall have a *gans* – how is that?"

"Goose," Karin translated.

"A goose, and what else we can find to eat and a bottle of port wine that Werner has always kept in our cellar, and we shall play some music and sing and try to cheer ourselves up. *Ja?*"

"We shouldn't need cheering up," said Jack, "not on Christmas Day."

The brief silence that followed this remark indicated to Jack that he'd been somewhat insensitive. Of course, Ingrid would need cheering up; she would be thinking of Werner, and Karin of her family in Coblenz and of brother Dieter in his prisoner-of-war camp. "I'm sure you will make it a very happy party," he added quickly.

A FEW days later, the Emmerich Karls invited Jack and Karin for a Sunday morning drink at their house at Brühl.

Emmerich Karl was an excellent conductor but Jack found him arrogant and conceited, unlike most of the other musicians he had to deal with. He felt that Karl's invitation was made in a formal and condescending way, as an act of duty rather than from affection or gratitude for what he and Karin had done for German music over the last six months.

The Karls now lived in some style and Emmerich appeared to be eager to assert his importance in the community. He told Jack that he had been invited to conduct a concert for the British Forces Radio and later to visit the Americans in Frankfurt, for a series of concerts.

"Good," said Jack, secretly rather put out that nobody had told him of this arrangement. That he was losing control of the musical organization was obvious. Perhaps it was just as well that his job would end soon.

Hoping to appear nonchalant and unimpressed, he asked casually "Is Hildegarde to go with you?"

"*Ach, ja*," said Karl, "she will drive the car and act as my secretary; will you not, my dear?"

Frau Karl had just come to join them; elegant, wearing an expensive scent and very attractive at forty-six. Jack saw the Karls as perfect examples of survivors. The sort of people who pop up like india-rubber dolls if they are pushed down, however unpromising their predicament.

Furthermore, the Karls' life-style was symbolic of the change that was now taking place everywhere in Occupied Germany. The fighting troops of the victorious Allies were being superseded by armies of civil servants belonging to the so-called Military Government, most of whom had never heard a shot fired in the war. They were arriving in droves, wrapping everything in Whitehall-type red-tape, and issuing endless regulations and instructions, it seemed with the express purpose of confusing and bewildering the German population; and alongside this new form of occupation, Germany herself, with incredible resilience and determination, was recovering, slowly pulling herself out of the wreckage of war; rebuilding, reconstructing, and beginning to stand on her own feet again.

On the drive back from Brühl, Jack pointed out to Karin the

various signs of recovery to be seen *en route*: here and there brand new road signs had appeared to replace the hastily-improvised ones set up along the shell-pocked roads by the Allied forces; where a block of shops had been demolished in the bombing a large site had already been cleared and rebuilding had begun; a damaged bridge over the River Sieg was under repair; at a level crossing just outside Bonn gangs of German labourers were repairing a length of railway line under the supervision of a British Army RE unit.

Commenting on all this, Jack began to talk of a new chapter beginning for Germany, and for everyone; how things would never be quite the same again; how life has to move on. What he was trying to do was to prepare Karin for the shock, if a shock it was to be, of the news that he would soon be on his way back to England, which meant that the idyllic spell they had shared for a little less than a year was inescapably nearing its end.

It was not until the Jeep stopped at the door of Karin's lodgings that Jack actually found the words to tell her.

"Karin, darling. Listen to me. We've got to start getting used to the idea that – all this has to end – quite soon."

Karin stared at him anxiously, her eyebrows raised.

Jack went on, keeping his voice low and grave, "I'm afraid I've had orders for my demobilization, darling. It had to come, sooner or later. Now it has. I leave here on the sixth of February for good. And you and I will have to say goodbye to each other."

"For ever?" Karin's eyes were wider and bluer than he'd ever seen them, filled as they now were with pain and fear.

"I hope not. – We'll have to see."

"You don't know?" Karin gave Jack a searching look, and when he did not reply she got quickly out of the Jeep and went to her door. She had her back to him now, as she inserted her key in the lock, hurriedly and clumsily, as though it was desperately important to get indoors quickly. Jack, who had followed her, put his arm round her to open the door. But Karin didn't turn round.

"Aren't you going to let me in?" he asked. Still with her back to him, she shook her head vigorously and dashed indoors, slamming the door behind her.

Jack stood there for a moment, a bit stunned. He'd known Karin would be upset, until she could get used to and accept the inevitability of his departure, but in the meanwhile he had hoped he could console her. Did this mean they were to have no more fun together, no more walks in the mountains or evenings in her room with *glühwein* and love?

He found himself wondering how Ingrid Pauels would react to the news. Perhaps his departure would cause her and Julius a moment of gentle sorrow and regret, but it would not disturb them greatly. Ingrid was not in love with him, and she and Julius had each other for company. But poor Karin would be all alone. The thought sent a pang of conscience through Jack's heart. He remembered all the hours she'd spent with him and the evenings she'd passed alone in her room, when they were not together, writing poetry and love notes to him. The poor girl hadn't had time to make friends with anyone else. None of the officers knew her, except young Peter Franks. He might help.

Jack resolved to speak to Peter in confidence, asking him to keep an eye on Karin, to be nice to her after his departure; to invite her to a concert occasionally and, if possible, introduce her to some of the other officers in the Mess, the younger ones.

Then, as he drove back to the Mess for a belated Sunday lunch, the conceit and presumption of this line of thought struck him and he smiled wryly to himself.

'Who do you think you are, Jack Hamilton? Casanova? Byron? By what right do you presume that Karin, or any woman for that matter, is so madly in love with you that your departure is going to cause misery and pain? Are you so irresistible that a bright, beautiful and sexy German fraülein like Karin Freidl is going to pine away in your absence, go into a decline with a broken heart or retire to a nunnery?

'Hell, no. – You're a shit, Jack Hamilton. A ruthless, randy shit to lead the girl on like that, all but make love to her, allow her to write passionate poetry and love letters to you and then bugger off back to England without a thought for her. You're worse than that bloody American naval officer in *Madame Butterfly* . . . except that Lieutenant Pinkerton left the little Jap girl in the family way, pregnant. – At least there was no danger of that . . .

Jack reached the Mess and parked the Jeep outside, before going in for lunch.

KARIN came to work as usual the following day but she was very subdued and not her normal, cheerful self.

Corporal Bridges sensed her mood and might even have guessed its cause, for he fell over backwards to be nice to her. "Don't you worry about that copy, dear; I'll see to it. You run along, if you want to," or "Anything I can do to help you; just you let me know, eh?"

SOMEHOW Jack and Karin managed to get through a whole week without either of them once mentioning his imminent departure. More and more of Jack's colleagues were now leaving the Rhine Army for home, and the evenings were rammed full of farewell parties, some at the Officers' Club, some at the Bergischerhof Hotel, so he saw very little of Karin, outside the office.

Soon it would be his turn and as the implications sank in more fully, the farewell parties began to seem just a trifle alarming. Somehow they forced him to think about his future, the new chapter of homecoming and resumed studies for the law.

On Christmas Eve, Jack closed down the Entertainments Office at lunchtime. Bridges left for a beano in the Corporals' Mess, while Jack was due at a farewell lunch for the Field Security Officer.

It was a particularly amusing party with plenty of witty speeches and Jack drank a good deal of wine, so he decided to go to his billet and sleep it off. Thus it was not until late in the evening that he went round to see Karin. He found her on the floor playing her records, so they spent most of the evening holding hands listening to a recording of Verdi's Requiem. When it was over Karin said she would like to go to Midnight Mass at Cologne Cathedral, so around eleven-thirty they set off, well wrapped up against the cold.

It was a clear, frosty night and the sky was peppered with stars. A full moon shone down on the snow, making the countryside seem almost as bright as in daylight.

Arriving in Cologne, Jack made for the Cathedral, steering the Jeep through bumpy, cratered streets, between wrecked buildings and over mountains of rubble. Bricks and plaster had been piled up on the roads and beaten down by the passage of countless lorries and army vehicles that plied their way through the devastated city. Some of the streets were so bumpy that Karin had to cling on to Jack, for fear of being hurled out of the vehicle.

When they finally bounced round a corner into the Domplatz, they were met by an amazing sight. The tall Cathedral with its famous twin towers stood like a vast tree in a huge forest that had been cleared for miles around.

It appeared that the Cathedral was already filled to overflowing, for a vast crowd of people who could not get in were standing all round the outside on piles of rubble. It was a great sea of faces, ghostly pale in the moonlight, all looking up into the clear starlit sky, as the Wise Men must have looked up almost two thousand years before, searching for a sign of peace and hope. The service was relayed by loudspeakers to the massive gathering outside. At one point the choir and the congregation inside began to sing 'Stille Nacht, Heilige Nacht'. Almost at once the evocatively simple Christmas hymn was taken up by the huge gathering outside the cathedral, and the sound of those thousands of voices singing in the open on that icy, clear moonlit night beside the Rhine hit Jack with an emotional sledgehammer.

He and Karin stood together, quite close to the West Door in a crush of people, holding hands to ensure they didn't lose each other in the throng. As they both joined in the singing, Karin looked up at Jack. She noticed a tear on his cheek, glistening in the moonlight, and knew that it was not caused by the cold air. They were both weeping unashamedly.

When the service was over and the cold, ragged people of Cologne began to disperse, wishing each other a Happy Christmas, Jack spotted Klaus and Lili Spiegel, some way off, their arms around each other, making their way across the rubble. It was touching to see them there, but he forebore to mention the fact to Karin, as they found the Jeep and drove back to Godesberg.

Outside Karin's lodgings they kissed and wished each other a Happy Christmas, Jack saying he would fetch her around midday on the morrow to go and spend the day at Ingrid's.

As he drove away from Frankengraben, Jack felt a strong urge to see if anyone was still up and about in the Mess. He could do with a stiff whisky after the cold outside the Cathedral. Also, he felt a need to talk to some of his own kind, his brother officers. He wanted to shake off the disturbing effect of that moonlit scene outside Cologne Cathedral, with its ghostly throng of hungry, defeated Germans lifting their voices to God, and come down to earth again; to mingle in a British Mess with some of the types he'd been to war with, the types he would soon be living among once again.

"Might have known I'd find you up and about," Jack said, as he entered the ante-room to find Peter Franks perched on the fender in front of the fire with David Levy and the Senior Chaplain, all three enjoying a nightcap.

Jack chose not to mention the Midnight Mass in Cologne, for a variety of reasons. First, he felt incapable of doing justice in any words that he could find to the deeply moving spectacle he had just witnessed; second, they would probably see his emotional response to the Mass as a sign that he'd gone soft on the German masses in their plight. And third, he was damned if he was prepared to share an experience like that with anyone but Karin.

So the conversation focused mainly on the big farewell party for Geoffrey Wynn-Davies, which was to take place the evening after Boxing Day.

"You going to it?" Peter asked Jack, taking a generous swig of scotch.

"Yes, I am. Definitely."

Jack had been invited, and had decided he would certainly go, for it was thanks to the DAQMG that he'd been allowed to employ Karin in the first place. But he kept his reasons to himself.

"By the way," Peter Franks said, "what do you think about your successor?"

Jack looked puzzled. "I've no idea who's taking over from me. Have you?"

"I have. Yes," said Peter. "Happens to be a chap in my regiment. He told me himself, when I dined over there on Tuesday night."

"Anyone I know?"

"Bobbie Kirkwood. Tall chap with a slight stammer. Commands No. 2 Company."

"What's he like?"

"Bit of a drip but friendly and keen to do well."

"Oh God!"

Peter laughed and swallowed another draft of whisky. "Does it matter any more? I'd have thought things could take care of themselves now. You've got all the music going, you and your German friends. Three opera companies and three orchestras plus a ballet, all going flat out."

"Four opera companies and four orchestras," Jack corrected him. "You forgot Aachen."

The Senior Chaplain beamed at him through his thick pebble-lens glasses. "You've done a good job, Jack."

"Thanks, Padre."

"When's your demob.?"

"February the sixth."

"Lucky bastard," said David Levy who, like Peter, still had some months to go.

Chapter 13

JACK woke up late the next morning and lay in bed, thinking of the Christmas mornings of his childhood. He remembered the excitement of opening a stocking stuffed with small toys, a box of dates, a torch and finally, a tangerine wrapped in silver paper. It occurred to him how delicious it would be right now to be snuggled up to Karin in bed to watch her open her presents from him. She would be wide-eyed and excited, like a child, and she would kiss him as each successive parcel was opened.

This led him to ponder yet again the idea of marrying and having children with Karin. It would be a gamble and there would be a real possibility of disaster. 'Anyway,' he consoled himself, 'how do I know she would accept me, even if I did propose?' He pushed aside the immediate retort that the answer was fairly certain, making the excuse to himself that it was only a combination of vanity and guilt that made him think she would say yes.

By midday, when Jack arrived at the Mess, he found the ante-room and dining-room were decorated with paper bells and coloured bunting, and the table was laid with a quantity

holly in the middle and three crackers beside each plate.
ck joined two officers in the ante-room, who were already
dering whisky macs and cigars from Otto. Jack asked for a
ass of dry sherry.

When the short, stocky mess waiter went off for the order,
e of the two officers, a captain in the RASC, commented on
e excellent German in which Jack normally addressed Otto.

"Only thing is," said the other, a balding gunner, "if you
lk German to him all the time, the fellow'll never learn
nglish. Look what happened last week."

It appeared that Otto had slipped up a few evenings before,
hen the officers of B Mess had decided to entertain the GOC
eneral Tom Harrington to dinner. Everything had been
refully laid on and Otto, much of whose English was culled
om a small dictionary, had been briefed to enter, at a suitable
terval after cocktails had been served, to announce dinner.

"I wasn't dining in that night," Jack said. In truth, he'd
ent the evening with Karin. "What happened?"

"Pre-dinner drinks were in full swing, you see, and the
eneral was in a corner grasping a Dry Martini and chatting
a circle of officers. Suddenly the sliding-doors into the
ning-room were flung open and Otto appeared in his white
cket and announced in a loud voice, 'Gentlemen, dinner is
ished.'"

Jack laughed. "Poor Otto must have looked up the word
rtig in his dictionary and chosen the literal translation instead
'ready'.

The RASC captain added "There was a moment's horrid
lence, until someone said 'let's go in, then,' – but nobody
ughed. Not so much as a flicker of a smile. Least of all the
eneral."

"I'm glad to hear it," said Jack, who did not like the idea of
tto being embarrassed. He was a sterling chap and a reliable
ly.

Jack had decided only to show his face in the place for half

an hour so, as soon as Otto came back with the drinks, h
swallowed his sherry, got up, wished the two officers a Happ
Christmas and left for Ingrid's house.

By signing out for lunch, he would avoid the hearty laughte
the blowing of squeakers and the wearing of absurd paper ha
that would continue until everyone quietened down to listen t
the King's radio broadcast.

THE atmosphere was festive enough at Ingrid's.

Jack and Karin arrived just after one-thirty, to find quite
little gathering already there. Julius was in the window reces:
stirring hot punch in a silver bowl; Ingrid herself in a flowere
apron was popping in and out of the small kitchen in order t
deal with the roast goose at the same time as entertaining he
guests; while Willy Pohl, Otto Maier, the two Grün brother
and a couple of girl singers from the Bonn Opera were i
animated conversation. Notably absent were the Emmeric
Karls, who were spending Christmas in Frankfurt as guests o
an American general.

The lunch was simple but good: the goose, with potatoe
and red cabbage, and sugar-iced gingerbread to eat with th
coffee. A NAAFI Christmas pudding and other necessary in
gredients had been acquired by Jack from the Officers' Mess b
arrangement with Otto.

Ingrid had protested against Jack's contribution, saying sh
could manage to feed all her guests adequately from her ration
and what she could find in her store cupboard. But Jack tol
her he would feel grievously insulted if she refused th
provisions and so Ingrid had, in the end, accepted them.

When her guests had finished eating the main part o
the meal and Karin had cleared the table, Julius called fo
silence and got to his feet, saying he had an announcement t
make.

"My friends, I have the pleasure to announce today an ever
that will shortly take place in Bad Godesberg. Can you guess?

"I can," Jack piped up from down the table, slightly flushed after several glasses of *rotwein*. Thinking of the character of the young poet, he called out "You are going to sing Rudolpho in my favourite opera, *La Bohème*!"

This was greeted by hearty laughter. Then Ingrid's voice said huskily "No, no. He is much too young for the part."

Willy Pohl said "I know: Dr Heuss will be the next German Ambassador to London."

More laughter. "He would be most welcome, I assure you," said Jack.

Karin now spoke up, just a bit shy and hesitant: "Please tell us, Herr Doctor Julius, what will happen shortly? We are all dying to know."

"Very well, my dear friends. I am so glad to tell you all that I have asked Ingrid that she will be my wife and she has agreed. We will be married in February, *so*."

Julius Heuss sat down to prolonged cheers and applause.

At once Karin ran round to Julius' chair and flung her arms round his neck. Everyone kissed Ingrid, whose eyes were soon running with tears of joy and emotion through happy laughter.

When Jack embraced her, she took his hand in hers and said "I think you will say it is very soon after I lose my Werner but he always say, you know, if either of us will be left alone, we should marry again, if we get the chance. He understands that." She glanced quickly up at an oil painting over the sideboard of Werner as a young man.

"Of course he does," said Jack tactfully. "Werner would be very pleased. He loved you and he would want you to be happy."

Ingrid just said "Darling boy," and clasped Jack to her ample bosom for a moment, then with a sniff she broke away from him, saying "I shall make now some coffee."

After a while Julius drew Karin into a corner and sat her down on a chair. Jack heard him say, "Come, *Karinchen*, and sit with me for a moment. I have a plan to discuss with you – *etwas geheim* – something secret . . . "

As she sat down, Jack noticed that Julius darted a quick look in his direction. Clearly, they were going to discuss him, and to his uneasy state of mind it seemed obvious that they would talk about his relationship with Karin, probably in view of his imminent departure from Godesberg. All sorts of odd thoughts flashed through his mind. Would they put pressure on him to marry Karin? Was it conceivable that Ingrid and Julius would go to see the General, complain about his behaviour, accuse him of acting in a manner unbecoming an officer and a gentleman? Or even mention a breach of promise? Rubbish, he'd never asked Karin to marry him, never even suggested it! The fact that she had said in one of her love notes to him that she often dreamed of having his child – well, that was just – her extravagant way of expressing herself, not to be taken literally. What, then, could Karin and old Heuss be plotting?

The answer to that question became clear, when, a few days later, Jack walked into the Entertainments Office and found a poster pinned to the wall, announcing an event of which he had no previous knowledge.

The poster read 'January 12 1946, at 8 p.m. at the Park Theatre, Bad Godesberg DADAWS. Guards Division, presents a Farewell Performance of *La Bohème* by Giacomo Puccini. Tickets from the Entertainments Office, Bad Godesberg' – etc. etc. . . .

So that was it. Julius, hearing that *Bohème* was his favourite opera, had arranged with Ingrid, Karin and probably Corporal Bridges, without his knowledge, to set up the production as a parting present from the musical community.

Jack was staring, almost unbelieving, at the poster, when Karin and Bridges came in together with some costumes they had collected from the Cologne Opera wardrobe.

"You are pleased?" said Karin.

"What do you think?"

"Julius will produce and conduct."

"I am so very, very touched. It is a wonderful surprise."

Karin sat down at her desk. "Good," was all she said.

Corporal Bridges asked "Poster all right, Sir?"

"Perfect."

"Sir."

Bridges went on with his work and Jack, too, settled himself to business. But he let out a sigh, for in spite of the surprise about the opera, he felt at a loose end, as if he had already left the army and should be by now on his way home to the UK. The feeling gave him a strong sense of anti-climax, of no longer belonging.

THE farewell performance of *La Bohème* in Jack's honour was a bitter-sweet affair. Karin was very quiet and hardly spoke a word all evening. Old Julius was quite nervous, having not conducted an orchestra for at least seven years. But he had dug out his slightly moth-eaten tail coat and white waistcoat and managed to cut quite a dash. His ovation on each entrance into the pit obviously pleased and moved him; it showed him, in no uncertain terms, how much the population of Bonn and Godesberg, as well as the Allied service people in the area, appreciated what he had done for music beside the Rhine.

Otto Maier sang Rodolpho beautifully and the Mimi, a young soprano called Irma Gerhardt, whom Ingrid had unearthed from a music academy in Düsseldorf, was so touching that Jack had to swallow several times to keep back the tears. He told himself he was tired, a bit overwrought, and suffering from anxiety about his future.

At a small party afterwards at Ingrid's house, the elderly Grün brothers, Joachim and Heinrich, who had designed and built the sets for the opera, made a formal presentation to Jack of a model theatre, made in their workshop from old bits of timber.

It was a labour of love and a little work of art. The miniature stage inside displayed a model of their set for Act II of *Bohème*, depicting the street corner and Café Momus, and it was perfect in every detail. There was the small street corner, the café, a baker's shop and a milliner's opposite. Minute tables and chairs, made of cardboard and painted in bright colours, as you would find in an old-fashioned doll's house, were glued to the pavement outside the café. There was a tiny street lamp, made from a matchstick, and somehow the Grün brothers had found room to insert a miniature Paris *fiacre*, which might have brought Musetta to her assignation with the wealthy Alcindoro at the Café Momus.

As the little miniature theatre was placed in his hands, Jack was completely overwhelmed and, for the third time in a week, almost burst into tears. As soon as he could risk speaking, he thanked them warmly. Then, when he put his gift down on a table, Joachim Grün switched on the little coloured lights, and Otto Maier started to sing one of his arias from the piece. Everyone laughed and applauded.

After that, Julius and Ingrid gave Jack a beautifully bound and illustrated book on Wagner, inscribed 'Herrn Major Hamilton, *zur Erinnerung an die ersten Aufführungen der Bonner Stadtoper. In Dankbarkeit stets Ihre Ingrid und Julius*'.

Jack knew he would be able to get the book back safely to the UK but he had grave doubts about the model theatre, which was awkwardly large, bulky and heavy. There was a strict baggage allowance for officers returning to the UK. When he finally left the party with Karin, he put the model into the back of the Jeep, thinking that he would have to think about what to do with it another day.

Jack took Karin home, and as he drew up outside her house, a light came on in an upstairs window. Evidently the Inners were waiting for her to come in, so he could not easily go upstairs with her. He kissed her goodnight at the front door. A pang of guilt went through him when Karin whispered "I wish that we were married, so that you could come in without fear of the Inners. – When you are kissing me, I feel that my dream will never end. We shall be always together, joined like this for the rest of time and nobody will ever take you from me."

Jack said rather feebly "I'm afraid the British Army is about to take you from me, or rather me from you."

As soon as the words were out he wished he hadn't said it. It sounded flippant and bitter; and weak, too. If he really wanted to go on seeing her for the rest of his life, all he had to do was tell her they'd keep in touch by letter and that, as soon as it could be arranged, he would somehow get her over to England and marry her. Or come back as a civilian to Germany and ask Herr Freidl for her hand. He compromised by saying "If you wanted to, you could write to me, you know." Gently, Jack disengaged himself from her and walked back to the Jeep.

The next morning he rose early and collected the model theatre from his Jeep outside, bringing it into his room. Here, he put it on the floor and dismantled the little cardboard cut-outs from the model stage and put them into his valise. These, at least, he could take home as a souvenir of his stay by the Rhine. He also removed the small bulbs of the stage lights and the battery. The model theatre itself, Jack decided with sorrow, must be secretly disposed of, so he took it in the Jeep to an open space at the end of the Hugelstrasse, together with a box of matches and some old newspapers, and prepared to set fire to it. As he lit the match, Jack noticed a small inscription of his name on one panel. Quickly, he blew out the match, prised the small inscribed panel away from the rest of the model theatre, and stuffed it into his pocket. Then, with one last sigh of regret, he lit another match and put it to a corner of the *Rheinische Tageblatt* newspaper that was protruding from under the wooden frame.

'They'll never know,' Jack told himself with more than a tinge of guilt. 'At least, the Grün brothers made the gesture and expressed their feelings. And I have the bulbs and fittings to remind me of them and their work.'

Mercifully, it was all over quickly, for the wood was dry and there was a slight breeze to fan the flames. Jack returned to his billet, feeling strangely unhappy. The little wooden theatre was somehow a symbol of his nine months stay in Godesberg and, in a way, of his relationship with Karin. And he'd destroyed it. When he reached the Mess in time for breakfast, he found he couldn't eat anything, so he drank a cup of coffee and then went to the office.

The next week went by very quickly and, two days before his departure from Godesberg, Jack decided to say goodbye to Karin on the following day and not let her see him off on the Tuesday. They discussed this and reluctantly she agreed.

"I don't wish to seem morbid, darling," he said, "but I'd like just to go for a long walk tomorrow by the river and up into the hills so we can talk and be together, all day. Then, at dusk, I shall walk away from you and you won't see me again."

Karin had nodded without a word, and turned to start typing out a memo. on the Olivetti.

Before he went into his own office Jack paused, and said "By the way, I've spoken to the new DAQMG and he says you can stay on the payroll and work for my successor, if you want to. I mean, your job here is secure."

"Thank you, Jack," Karin said. "I'll see what I will wish to do."

THE following morning found Jack and Karin strolling together on the far bank of the Rhine, looking for the rock on which they'd first sat and talked, nine months earlier. The spot where their rock protruded from the water looked very bleak and unromantic that grey February day, and an icy East wind forced Karin to hold tightly to Jack's arm as they trudged on.

Soon they were opposite the spot where Jack had hidden his uniform the previous summer, before mingling illegally with the German population splashing in the river.

"How about a swim now?" Jack shouted against the strong wind.

But Karin was in no mood for jokes. She stopped, let go of Jack's arm and turned to face him. Her pale blue eyes, framed in a fur hat, were gazing up into his; tragic, despairing and without hope.

"Don't go, Jack. Please stay with me."

"I can't, darling. You know I can't. Not unless I stay on in the army. And it's too late for that now; besides, I'm going to study Law. I want to be a barrister, I don't want to go on being a soldier. I've had enough of that."

"Will you not come back, then, as soon as you can? I will die without you. I will die . . . "

"Oh, come on, Karin! I'm only an ordinary Englishman, nothing special. You won't die without me."

"You are special to me."

Jack turned away from her and stared out across the wide river. "Don't make it difficult and sad for us to say – "

"To say goodbye? How can it not be sad?"

"I know. – But can't we *try* to be happy together while we still can?"

"You are not reasonable, Jack, to ask for what is not possible," she replied vehemently.

Jack pondered for a moment, then he took Karin's gloved hands in his and squeezed them. "Don't you see that the longer we put off parting; I mean the longer we hang about here together, getting sadder and sadder, the worse it will be, when the moment comes?"

In a quiet voice Karin said "Yes, I think so."

As it appeared that nothing was going to console Karin, Jack suggested that they should part there and then, for ever, at the exact spot where they'd first met, and he proposed that she should leave him there, sitting on the bank, and walk away.

But Karin wanted it the other way round. "You are an Englishman, a foreign person, and you are leaving my country. I should stay here, by my river, and watch you go."

"You'll be cold. Let me stay."

"No, I will prefer to remain here. Please."

"Very well."

Jack took Karin in his arms and kissed her long and tenderly. Then he took her hand to help her sit down at the river's edge. The current was strong and the deep, dark water of the Rhine washed furiously against the bank, so that Karin had to sit well clear of the stream to avoid getting her feet wet. She sat there with her knees up to her chin, a small, sad figure covered from head to foot in fur, reminding him of a baby seal that had lost its mother.

Jack turned his back and strode away purposefully across the meadow, over a fence, down a path and behind some bushes, until he was lost to view. Not once did he turn to look back or hesitate, until he reached the Officers' Mess. There, he flopped into a deep leather armchair in the ante-room and closed his eyes, feigning sleep. At that moment, he could not have borne a conversation with a brother officer, on any subject whatsoever. He only wanted to lie still and focus his mind on the future, to try to empty his head of Karin and all she had meant to him, and come to terms with the new, rather alarming phase of his life that was about to begin.

THE following morning, the soldier servant Jack shared with two others in the billet called him early, so as to have some time to pack his valise and suitcase before the truck came to pick him up for the journey to the railhead at Aachen.

Shortly before nine o'clock, the 15-cwt truck was at the door with eight cheerful guardsmen, a sergeant and two corporals packed into the back, laughing and cracking jokes. 'They'll start singing once we get started!' thought Jack, with slight misgivings, for he was in no mood for cheerful songs. Then he thought, 'Why shouldn't they, poor buggers? They're being demobbed, released from the army, going home, after a boring spell away from their wives and sweethearts and mothers.' was different for him . . .

He climbed in beside the driver and the truck set off on its way to catch the train for Ostend, the Channel steamer and home. They hadn't been bumping along over the cratered roads for more than five minutes before the men in the back started to sing 'Ghost Riders in the Sky' with a lot of shrill and tuneless 'Yippee-I-Ay's.

Wondering whether they would all find new jobs back home or be able to carry on with their old trades, it occurred to Jack that quite a few of the younger men would never have had jobs in peacetime – those who had joined up at eighteen or nineteen.

He knew that one of his fellow-passengers had been a bricklayer in Nottingham before the war. Surely, Jack reflected, they'd need bricklayers now for all the rebuilding of bomb-damaged houses. That fellow would get a job all right.

Then his mind turned to his own future. He was twenty-five and starting a career from scratch. Pre-war barristers had a direct, uninterrupted line of training from school to university to law degree to 'eating dinners' to starting off in chambers. But Jack and all the other would-be barristers of his generation had to overcome the great gap caused by the war between university and being called to the Bar. 'At least,' he thought, 'we're all in the same boat.' He would just have to work very hard and hope for the best.

Hours later, when the white cliffs of Dover loomed up through the mist, Jack was still deep in thought about his future. The sight of land caused a good deal of excitement on deck. A party of gunners from Hamburg started cheering, and one of them produced a mouth organ, on which he attempted to render, or tear apart, a relevant popular song of the day, while another gave a passable imitation of Vera Lynn, screeching out in a falsetto voice "There'll be blue birds over the white cliffs of Dover . . . " until the ship's siren drowned him.

ON arrival in London Jack and his draft of fellow demobbed soldiers were taken straight to the barracks in Albany Street, alongside Regent's Park, where a storeman handed him a dreadful light tweed suit, a mac, a pair of shoes and a soft hat

It was a bit like being discharged from prison but one had to be grateful to HM Government for small mercies and there were plenty of men who would be more than grateful for a suit of clothes, a hat and a mac, ready for that first, tentative walk down the road from the 'bus stop to their homes.

Jack had a week's leave on full pay, all of which he intended to spend relaxing at home, playing golf and, no doubt discussing his future with his parents.

"HOW did you fill in your time out there?" Mr Hamilton was pouring some wine into his son's glass at dinner on his fourth night back from Germany.

Jack knew that he really ought to be a dutiful son and describe to his parents in detail all his recent activities as DADAWS. He should tell them of his collaboration with the German musical folk around Bonn and Godesberg, the concerts, the opera perform- ances, the parties at the Officers' Club, the ENSA shows and, above all, the state of Germany itself, and the devastation he had seen, including the nightmarish spec- tacle of Cologne, like a desert waste with its acres of rubble and jagged remains of buildings that surrounded the solitary Cathedral.

Just now, he couldn't bring himself to think back to Germany, let alone describe it to his mother and father. Whether it was something to do with Karin, he couldn't be quite sure, but her name had not been mentioned and his parents were quite unaware of her existence.

He was home now and facing the next stage of his life. Nothing that had happened in the last nine months: the misty almost unreal figure of Karin, his life beside the Rhine, the music, the mulled wine, the passion and excitement of those dream-like months; none of it must be allowed to invade his mind and distract him from his purpose, which was to become a Barrister-at-law.

Jack knew deep down that allowing Karin to fall in love with him and then walking away from the situation, as from an awkward encounter with a beggar in the street, was shabby. By using his position to employ a German girl in his office out of sheer, physical desire-at-first-sight, he had landed himself with a responsibility that he had not discharged. It was not the duty of officers in the British Army of the Rhine to go about the zone of occupation breaking the hearts of young German girls. 'Nevertheless,' Jack thought, 'our attraction was mutual. She didn't have to engage in conversation that afternoon beside the Rhine. She was not ordered in the name of the British Army to speak to me. She could have dived into the river and swum away . . .'

"I mean what did you do with yourselves all day?"

With a jolt, Jack realized his father's question was still unanswered. "Oh, nothing really. – Just dishing out sports equipment to the various units in our area and organizing an occasional concert. . . .

"I say, would you mind if I went to bed a bit early tonight? I'm frightfully tired, for some reason."

"It's those thick, heavy law books you've been reading, I expect," said Mrs Hamilton.

"Probably," her son agreed, and escaped to his bedroom.

Then, in spite of his resolution not to think of Germany, Karin came to mind again. One of the reasons why he didn't want to talk to his parents, he supposed, was that he was missing her. For a moment he wished with an intense longing that they were curled up together on the rug in her room. But it was no good. His conduct had been 'unbecoming an officer and gentleman,' and the realization caused him to turn his thoughts to a fresh, unsullied track; that of his career.

IN the early weeks of his return to civilian life, Jack thought several times of writing to Karin, but he found it surprisingly difficult to know what to say to her. Each time he remembered that he had suggested to her that she might write to him, and knowing her fondness for putting pen to paper, he felt sure that she would, if she wanted to get in touch. So each time he left her letter unwritten, thinking that he would wait until there was one from her that needed to be answered. But no letter from Karin arrived.

The idle days of the spring sped by surprisingly fast, and as the weeks passed, so Jack's intentions of writing to Karin faded. When he did think of her, several times he found his thoughts leading on to Audrey Cornish. Audrey had been so much more patently seductive and sophisticated than Karin, and she was English, so perhaps she would have been a better fit in Sunningdale; besides, where she was concerned, he had no feelings of guilt. By the summer, Jack's life as a gentleman of leisure had become well filled, for he was determined to make the most of his freedom while he had it, and his busy routine left him few opportunities for thinking of Karin.

IN the autumn of 1946 Jack joined the Middle Temple and embarked on his three- year student period, 'eating dinners' as it was quaintly called. After a lecture, from time to time Jack dined in the Great Hall of the Middle Temple, when he would look up in awe at the fine oak beams, the elaborate, gilt-encrusted cornice, the painted ceilings, the coats-of-arms, and the portraits of distinguished judges who had been benchers of the Inn. Above all, he would savour the strange, musty smell of antiquity and tradition that pervaded the place, not unlike the atmosphere of his College dining hall at Oxford.

He sensed a feeling of belonging to a great British institution, the legal profession, with centuries of justice behind it, and the thought produced in him a glow of pride.

On the other side there was the book work. Heavy volumes to be read and understood, definitive works on libel, property, divorce, probate and other forms of litigation, which quoted cases and laws going back over hundreds of years; Burnard v.

Haggis, scutage and estoppel, Regina v. Northern Coal and Gas Company. The work was hard and demanded great concentration. Jack's mind had become a bit lazy and slow and the effort of absorbing massive tomes on the Law made him, at times, wonder what he was doing reading for the Bar. There were certainly easier ways of making a living. But the fascination of the English legal system gripped him, and he persevered.

Anxious to avoid the distractions inevitable when living in his parents' home, he took a small basement flat in Belgravia, and limited his visits to Sunningdale to occasional weekends.

He was there one Saturday morning when a letter came for him from Peter Franks. He wrote to say that his Battalion had been posted home to Chelsea Barracks where it was to undertake a spell of 'public duties'. He would be back in London in a couple of weeks' time and wondered if Jack would like to come and dine with him 'on guard' one evening at the Bank of England. 'Or, if you think that sounds a bit stuffy and too far to travel,' Peter went on, 'we could fix an evening when I'm not on duty, and dine at the Guards Club or, better still, at Pruniers.'

At first Jack was not at all sure he wanted to see Peter. He was a nice enough chap but the memory of his help in extricating him from the awkward Spiegel affair was more of an embarrassment than anything, and reminiscences and news from Bad Godesberg that might distract him from his exacting law studies were just what Jack did not want now.

Mostly out of courtesy but with a faint glimmer of curiosity, Jack replied to Peter to tell him his own news, and arranged a meeting.

Three weeks later Jack and Peter settled down to an excellent dinner at Pruniers, where Madame Prunier herself, chic, charming and attentive as ever, offered them a liqueur 'on the house'. Peter's father was a regular customer of that delightful Parisian fish restaurant in St James's Street and

Madame P. knew that both young men had recently fought in the war to liberate her native France.

Jack and Peter talked of their futures and compared notes. Peter had decided to stay on in the army. "Can't think of anything else to do, really. Not sure I want to be a regimental officer for ever; rather get seconded to something pleasant – ADC to the governor-general of somewhere; get plenty of ski-ing and fishing and that sort of thing."

Jack told Peter of the long slog he was in for, before he would hear the Senior Bencher of his Inn pronounce the magic words 'John Francis Hamilton, I hereby call you to the Bar and publish you barrister'.

"That'll be terrific, Jack. Then we shall start reading about you in the *News of the World* defending murderers and sex maniacs."

"I'm afraid not," Jack said, sipping his free glass of Grand Marnier. "I'm sorry to disillusion you, but I'm going in for Civil Law."

"What, you mean people suing each other and all that stuff?"

"That's right. When you decide to sue Harrods for slipping on their marble floors and breaking your leg, you can instruct me through your solicitors and I'll get you $25,000 worth of damages."

"It's a deal," said Peter, raising his free glass of brandy with a smile.

They talked for a couple of hours and were on the verge of getting up to leave before Jack said, in as casual a voice as he could manage, "See anything of Karin before you left?"

Jack thought that Peter hesitated for a fraction of a second, though it might have been his imagination, due to his guilty conscience, that made him dread the answer and which made the gap between question and answer seem long.

"Oh, she left, soon after you went."

"How soon?"

"A couple of weeks. Told Corporal Bridges her mother

236

needed her at home, so he fixed with the new DAQMG for her to be released from her duties. There's another girl there now, interpreting and helping Corporal Bridges. Rather a plump, friendly creature called Heidi something."

"So Karin's gone home to Coblenz?"

"Presumably."

"What about Ingrid and Julius?"

"Hardly seen them. I did bump into her in Bonn a few weeks back and she told me the old Prof. wasn't too fit. Got a bronchial chest, apparently."

"Did she know about Karin going?"

"Yes. She said Karin hadn't been too well either. A bit under the weather. Probably missing you, Jack, you rotten old heart-breaker."

They were now outside in St James's Street so Jack was spared from replying to Peter's last remark. Instead he asked the doorman to whistle up a taxi. He offered to drop Peter off but Peter had a car and was driving back to Chelsea Barracks, so Jack said goodnight to his old colleague and asked the cabby to take him back to his flat in Belgravia.

But a wave of loneliness, tinged with stirrings of lust brought on by Madame Prunier's free cognac on top of an excellent claret, caused him to change his mind quite suddenly. He leant forward and slid open the glass partition.

"As you were," Jack called through to the driver, not yet able to shake off his army phraseology. "Take me to the Coconut Grove, please. Regent Street. Do you know it, half way up on the left?"

The driver made no reply but executed a skilful U-turn and headed north. Jack settled back in the cab, resolved to look into the old 'Grove', order a bottle and see what the form was in one of his favourite pre-war night haunts.

THE form was as it had been for at least the last seven years. Edmundo Ros, in his usual frilly Caribbean costume, was leading his famous Rumba band in a haunting number called 'Sand in my Shoes'.

The dance floor was crowded and Jack was on the look-out for some shapely dance hostess to share his table, the price for which he knew was the purchase of champagne for her to sip and waste, a woolly rabbit and a box of chocolates.

There were only two hostesses in sight, both uninteresting to look at. They were sitting huddled together at a table just inside the door drinking coffee, chatting and awaiting a summons from a customer.

The only promising looking girl in the place was to be seen across the dance floor, but only from behind. She was wearing a dress with a back that was slashed right down to her pelvis and she was obviously very drunk for she kept throwing back her head and screaming with loud laughter as she gyrated to the music.

The girl's behaviour was causing several people on the dance floor and at the tables around to stare at her with disapproval, for she was making an exhibition and a nuisance of herself, but she was also of note to Jack because for some reason she looked familiar.

Jack caught an occasional glimpse of her partner, a greasy-looking, balding individual in his fifties, wearing a crumpled city suit and a bow tie. He was every bit as drunk as the girl, and as she whirled and wriggled her hips round the floor, he appeared to be getting hotter and more excited. They came nearer Jack's table, and he could see large beads of perspiration standing out on the man's forehead and running down to stain his bow tie.

Suddenly the girl spun round only a few feet from where Jack was sitting – and he saw that it was Audrey Cornish. Instantly he ducked his head and covered the lower part of his face with a napkin, pretending to wipe his mouth, and fortunately she didn't see him. That fleeting glimpse of her had shown Jack an over-painted, puffy, creased face with dark ircles under her eyes, betraying the unmistakeable signs of drink. The sight made Jack determined to get as far as possible away from her and his memory of her.

Keeping his head averted, he beckoned to the head waiter whom he knew of old, to tell him he'd changed his mind and wouldn't be staying. Then he made his way up the stairs again, out into Regent Street and into a taxi for home, feeling strangely depressed.

The following morning, despite a mild hangover, he took the District Line from Sloane Square to Temple, ready to tackle another day of preparation for his all-important Bar Finals.

A couple of Sundays later, after a round of golf at Wentworth with his father and the pro., during which Jack found his concentration lacking so that he missed a couple of four-foot putts, he realized that Karin was still very much in his mind and on his conscience. That evening, back in his London flat, he sat down and wrote to her.

He pondered for a couple of minutes whether to put 'My Darling' and finally decided that it would be hypocrisy – for she was in no way his property – and the possessive pronoun was capable of being misconstrued:

Darling Karin,

I dined in London the other week with Peter Franks, who told me you had left Godesberg and gone home to Coblenz. How sad! What will Corporal Bridges do without you? I hope Heidi is efficient but doubt if she can replace you; nobody could! I also heard that you were not well. I do hope it's nothing serious. I don't quite know how to say this, Karin, but I must try to convey to you honestly and truthfully my feelings about us.

I loved you very deeply during our wonderful nine months together and still do. But to 'be in love' with someone is not the same as to love someone for life. I'm sure you can understand what I mean. Of course, I did think seriously many times about the possibility of marriage and of our being together for the rest of our lives. But I had to be absolutely certain that it wasn't just a romantic dream, an idyllic fantasy due to the Rhine, the music, and the aftermath of war, which would have burst like a bubble once we both had to face reality. I feel this would have been the case.

I just couldn't see you in my rather dull, respectable world of the golf club and stuffy retired colonels (many of whom, I am afraid, would turn their backs on you, because you are German) and I *know* you would not have been happy in England. Besides, there is another aspect of it and that is that I am just not good enough for you, as a man. I am well aware of my shortcomings and weaknesses and, after all, you had an example of me at my worst over the Spiegel affair. I'm sure I would have let you down sooner or later. You deserve someone with a greater sense of honour and integrity than I could ever have.

Of course I am deeply touched and flattered by your beautiful poems and love letters, which are so romantic and totally undeserved.

All I want, dear Karin, is for you – like me – to see our friendship as something to remember and treasure always and, that done, to go on with our respective lives with a warm glow, whenever we remember each other.

Noel Coward wrote a rather touching song in a revue I saw before the war, called *Words and Music*. The song went 'Let our affair be a gay thing and when these hours have flown, there'll be no forgetting happiness that has passed, there'll be no regretting fun that didn't quite last; let's look on love as a plaything, all these sweet moments we've known, mustn't be degraded, when the thrill of them has faded, let's say goodbye and leave it alone'.

Please write to me, when you have a spare moment, and tell me that you understand and agree. I feel sure that, when a little time has passed, you will get things into perspective and look back to our time together at B.G. as a happy chapter of your life but nothing more.

My love and gratitude for everything you gave me, Jack.

A year passed and, although Jack had addressed the letter correctly to Karin's home at Coblenz, no reply ever came.

IN March, 1948, while on holiday at Bembridge in the Isle of Wight, Jack collided in his sailing dinghy with another that contained a tall and rather beautiful girl with long legs and healthy suntan. Both had to be pulled out of the sea and aboard a rescue launch, in the cabin of which they introduced themselves. When dried out and revived with Oxo, they made a date to meet at the yacht club dance the following evening.

Thus in the course of time the slightly ageing law student, Jack Hamilton, became engaged to Christine, only daughter of Admiral Sir William and Lady Bartlett of Alton, Hants. They were married six months after Jack was called to the Bar and settled down to married life in a small house in Chelsea.

In 1955 their first and only child, Giles, was born.

Nine years later, while Giles was at a preparatory school in Oxford, a proud and gowned Jack heard the long-awaited words addressed to him by the Lord Chancellor: "Her Majesty having been pleased to appoint you one of her Counsel, learned in the Law, you will take your seat in the Bar accordingly!"

And in 1979, the year that Giles was commissioned as a subaltern in the Kings Dragoon Guards, Jack was appointed to the Bench as a Circuit Judge.

Chapter 14

"SHE is my aunt, Karin Brander."

"Is?"

"Yes. I am the son of her brother, Dieter. He was also a doctor, you know. He died two years ago."

"I'm sorry to hear that." The Judge tactfully counted two respectful beats before going on to ask "How is she?"

"I do not often see my aunt. There are reasons."

"What reasons?"

"She will explain."

At this point the surgery bell rang and Dr Hans Freidl had to cut short the interview. A mother had arrived for an appointment with her diabetic child and Hans only had time to scribble the name Brander and a 'phone number on a piece of paper and hand it to Jack.

"Baden-Baden is not so far. You can get an Intercity train from Coblenz and change at Karlsruhe, or maybe, some trains will go direct."

The Judge thanked him and left, clutching the magic note, the key to his reunion with the past.

IT was impossible to tell from Karin's voice over a bad line what she would look like. Jack could not envisage her face. In his mind he could only see the fresh smile of the young Karin while hearing over the telephone a mature, elderly voice that belonged to someone else.

His call was not wholly unexpected, for Hans had previously warned his aunt that an old friend from London would soon be in contact with her. All the same, she expressed surprise.

"Jack – I don't believe it – after so long . . . "

"I would like to come and see you – is it possible?"

"But of course! It is amazing – you are here, in Germany; it is good."

She sounded astonished and pleased to hear from him, but became instantly practical. "I am busy always during the week," she explained, "but for the weekend I will be free and we can talk."

It was arranged that Jack would take the train down to the Black Forest on Friday and arrive at Baden-Baden in the late afternoon. She would book him into a hotel. 'Odd,' Jack thought. 'Hasn't she a spare room?' – and would meet him at the station. Then she would take him to a good restaurant for dinner and a long talk.

Before Jack had time to ask any questions about herself and her present situation, she had hung up, leaving him with no clue as to whether she was a wife, a divorcee or a widow. He would have to wait and see.

The magic of that train journey on a railway line winding and bending along the edge of the Rhine, in a smooth, quiet Intercity train that overtook slow barges heading south and offered fleeting glimpses of castles perched high upon rocks and of lush vineyards rising uphill from the river valley, all helped Jack to relax. While he enjoyed the view with his eyes, in his mind he pondered the wisdom of meeting a woman who, as a girl, had apparently loved him nearly half a century ago and whom he, frankly, had used badly.

When the train began to slow down for Baden-Baden Sir John got up to collect his belongings and made his way along to the exit. He had reached that age at which men become afraid of failing to open doors and get out of trains in time and anxious about being carried on to the next station. 'Oh, Mister Porter, what have I done? I should have got out at Rotterdam but they carried me on to Cologne . . .'

The smile on Jack's face at this mis-remembrance of Marie Lloyd was wiped out by a sudden jolt which threw him violently forward, so that he was forced to clutch at a young girl passenger to prevent himself from crashing to the floor. 'Not a good start!' he thought to himself. 'I *must* not look to her like a frail, ageing and clumsy old man. However decrepit she may be, I must look young for my age.' So as the train came to a halt, he gripped his case firmly, and stepped out just as the tannoy announced "Baden-Baden. *Abfahrt des Zuges auf Gleis Drei nach Wiesbaden und Basel in zwei minuten.*"

Head high, but on the look-out for an elderly woman who would be looking for someone, Jack strode towards the steps that lead down to the *Ausgang*. No doubt Karin would be waiting for him with a taxi down by the station exit.

But halfway down the steps he heard a voice calling out, just above his head: "Jack!"

He looked up to see a tall, slim woman with blonde hair waving to him from the top of the steps. She was dressed in neat, well-cut slacks, a medium length belted trench-coat with epaulettes and, perched at a jaunty angle on her head, a man's tweed country hat. She was smiling radiantly, as she hurried down the steps to greet him. Then she stopped, and for a second the couple stood frozen, like statues, just staring at each other, as other passengers flowed past them down the steps.

"I don't believe it; this is not real!" was all Jack could say, astonished that at last they had really come face to face – and that in spite of all his dark forebodings, after forty-three years Karin was looking like a million dollars.

With both hands full, Jack leant forward in an awkward attempt to plant a kiss on her cheek. But Karin, ever practical, forestalled any public exhibition of emotion by taking his heavy case from him. "I take this – come; the car is outside . . . "

Mildly hurt by the presumption that he was too old to carry his own suitcase, Jack murmured "No, let me," but she would have none of it.

"I am strong," she said and went on "We will go first to the hotel, so you can see your room and maybe you will like to wash and *so* – then I shall send the car back for you . . . "

They had reached the station exit now, where Jack saw a large navy blue Mercedes drawn up with a young uniformed chauffeur at the wheel. At Karin's approach the youth jumped out and opened the door, taking Jack's case from her.

"*Zum Hotel, Klaus, bitte.*"

The chauffeur stowed Sir John's case in the boot and took his seat at the wheel. Karin and Jack settled formally in the back. Although the glass partition was closed Karin seemed mildly inhibited by the chauffeur's presence, and she embarked on a discourse on the history and beauty of Baden-Baden, pointing out the marvellous baroque spa buildings, the architect Weinbrenner's Temple, the world-famous casino, the theatre on the Goetheplatz and the blue-domed Russian church among the trees at Lichtental.

Jack thought impatiently 'I didn't come all this way for a conducted tour of Baden-Baden, beautiful and historic as it may be.' In an effort to steer the conversation round to their mutual past, he interrupted "I found Bonn and Godesberg very changed since our . . . time."

There was quite a long pause until Karin said "I have not been there for many years."

"I suppose not," Jack replied, wondering if the whole encounter was going to be conducted in small talk, with trite irrelevant remarks concealing deeply buried emotion that must not be allowed to surface . . .

The Mercedes began to slow down and Jack saw that it was approaching the grand entrance of a large, extremely modern luxury hotel. As the car pulled up, two hall porters appeared at once, one to open the car door, the other to get the Judge's luggage out and carry it in.

"*So*," said Karin getting out, "we are here. *Guten Tag*, Herr Kessler." She nodded to the black-suited manager, who had appeared from nowhere and Jack, suitably impressed, wondered whether Karin had laid on this VIP treatment for him because Dieter had told her that her English friend was now a retired High Court Judge, to impress him with her obvious wealth, or simply because this was the way she lived now. The question was quickly settled when Jack spotted the name of the hotel in gold letters over the entrance: Branderhotel.

They followed the luggage porter across the vast foyer to the lift and a girl receptionist greeted Karin with a respectful smile. Then a stout bar-tender on his way to open the American Bar stood aside for them and as they passed, bowed his head, as if to royalty.

Karin insisted on seeing Jack up to his room, they stepped into the lift, and the porter pressed the second floor button.

"I must make sure you are comfortable, Jack, in my hotel," she said.

"You own it?"

"Yes. Also one in Freiburg, two in Wiesbaden and a new one in Strasbourg. It was my husband's business, you see."

"That's a big responsibility."

"It is my life."

They got out at the second floor and Karin showed Jack into a large, luxurious suite with a balcony overlooking the pine forests surrounding Baden-Baden. It had every modern facility including an electric trouser-press, a TV set, a small fridge stocked with every kind of liquor and a marbled bathroom stocked with toothpaste, after shave, toilet water and shampoo.

"I will send Klaus back at seven and we shall have first a drink at my house; then I will take you up to our famous Bocksbeutel for dinner. OK?"

"OK," Jack agreed, and Karin left.

He stood for a while looking round the suite and out at the view from the balcony. Then he sat down heavily on the bed with a sigh. Of relief? Of amazement? Even of envy?

'So much,' Jack thought, 'for our pathetic, hungry, impoverished little German girl from Coblenz, who cried in her digs at the dentist's house in Godesberg when I left, who wrote me all those passionate love letters and poems and whose life I thought I had ruined, destroyed by my callousness, my failure to realise the depth of her love for me.' He helped himself to a drink from the fridge and then dropped into a chair and began to laugh. He laughed at his own arrogance, presumption and conceit with a long, ironic, bitter laugh. Then he laughed with pleasure, at having discovered Karin again, and found that she was all right; more than all right, that she had survived with triumph, and that she was as attractive now, if not more so, than she had been as a young girl in 1945 and 1946.

After a few moments he got up to unpack his things and run himself a bath, for he felt sweaty and stiff after the train journey. He would enjoy the facilities of this first-class hotel, he thought. Then he wondered who would pay the hotel bill. He couldn't allow her to put him up free. Yet it was her hotel. She owned it. There might be an argument over the bill. Well, at least he could pay for the dinner tonight.

As he lowered himself stiffly into the warm, refreshing bath he marvelled once more at Karin's looks, her elegance, her style. It must have come from being married to a rich man for most of her life. It had given her confidence, chic, all that goes with a combination of wealth and intelligence. Good for her!

At seven o'clock sharp Jack went downstairs to the foyer, changed and refreshed, ready, he suddenly realised, for his first evening with Karin since that last sad and gloomy farewell beside the Rhine in February, 1946. The thought made him a little apprehensive.

As he stepped out of the lift he saw the Mercedes sweep up to the entrance. He went out, nodded to Klaus who was holding the door open for him, and got in. The car wound its way up into the wooded hills round curves and bends and finally passed through some wrought iron gates, which Klaus opened by remote control. Then the car pulled up in the courtyard of a fine old mediaeval *Schloss*. As Klaus jumped out to open the car door, a manservant in a white jacket appeared, nodded politely to Jack and led him up some curved stone steps into the great hall. There Karin was standing with an elk hound curled up at her feet by an ornate mantelpiece. She had changed into a simple short evening dress with a dazzling diamond necklace at her throat, and there was a divine smile on her face.

"Welcome to my home, Jack."

Sir John looked round the great hall, which was hung with the antlers of Black Forest deer, fine oil paintings and tapestries.

Karin said "This castle belonged to Baron Kurt von Brander in the time of Friederich *der Grosse*. He was an ancestor of Rudolph."

"Your – ?"

"Husband. *Ja*. It was sold when the family lost their money in 1912 and became for a while a – *Kloster*. – What is that?"

"A monastery."

"*So*. But Rudolph always had dreamed of returning it to the von Brander family, so . . . when he has made very much money from the hotel business, we have bought it in 1968 from the *Kreisverwaltung*. It has been restored, as you can see, like it had been in old times."

At this point the white-coated servant appeared with a bottle of champagne in an ice bucket and two glasses on a silver salver. Karin opened the bottle herself with the ease and skill of one who is accustomed to opening champagne bottles.

Feeling oddly subdued, the Judge raised his glass and said "There is so much I want to hear later on, Karin my dear, but for now, may I just drink to your health and happiness and my delight, after so many long years, at finding you in such wonderful good looks and so unchanged."

"You too, Jack," Karin replied, with just the suspicion of moisture in her eyes.

They sipped the Krug '69 and Jack risked the first of two vital questions he knew he had to ask. "How long ago did your husband – ?"

"Rudi died in 1973."

"I'm so sorry."

"He worked too hard and his heart failed." Karin took her glass of champagne over to glance out of a vast window across the surrounding countryside. "It was a lovely warm summer day, just before we were due to leave for Rome. I was waiting at home with my cases packed, all ready to go, when they telephoned me from his office. The secretary had come to him with a letter to sign and found him collapsed over his desk. He died in the ambulance. He was sixty-seven."

Sir John only needed confirmation of her widowhood. It had been plain enough from the outset that she hadn't been divorced. Not even in California could a divorcee expect to receive a large hotel chain and a mediaeval *Schloss* in the Black Forest as alimony.

"You've been alone for a long time."

"I am used to it. I have my business and my freedom. I can go to see beautiful things, listen to music, travel abroad, live my life as I choose."

"Absolutely."

After a while Karin rang for the manservant and gave orders for Klaus to bring round her smaller car, the BMW. The chauffeur would not be needed again that evening.

Jack finished most of the champagne himself while Karin confined herself to one glass.

Forty minutes later they were sitting together at a quiet corner table at the famous Bocksbeutel Restaurant, perched high up in the hills amid the vineyards overlooking Baden-Baden. The view from the glassed-in terrace was magnificent. Karin told Jack that on a clear day you could see as far as Strasbourg.

When they had ordered dinner and, at Karin's recommendation, a bottle of the local Steinbach wine, Jack outlined the course of his life from his departure from Godesberg in February 1946 right up to the present time. He showed Karin a photograph of Christine beside a friend's swimming pool in Portugal, taken three or four years back, and another of their son Giles as a cadet at Sandhurst.

With Karin's sixteen years of widowhood in mind, Jack said he'd been exceptionally lucky all his life, both with his career and with his marriage, which, apart from the usual small ups and downs, had been very happy. Forty years of happy marriage.

Karin listened with her eyes fixed on Jack, taking in every detail.

As he rambled on through his life, it began to sound to Jack like a man giving his CV to an examiner, or an entry in *Who's Who*. Biographical facts. 'What else is there?' he thought. 'This is all far too formal. When are we going to get down to our feelings for each other? – Perhaps she's never given me a thought all these years. Come to that, why should she? And why did I ever feel so guilty? Guilt for what? Here is a girl who has grown up, married an immensely rich and successful German baron, lived happily with him for twenty-three years and is now enjoying a comfortable, fulfilled and busy widowhood.' As he thought this, he felt a vague feeling of oppression lifting. It was a feeling that had been with him whenever he thought about Karin – for how long? – For about the whole of his adult life, since the time when he knew her forty years earlier. He smiled at her across the table, and she said "Go on, Jack, tell me more about yourself."

"There's not much more to tell," he said, but he went on with his potted life-story until he came to the end. Then he observed "It seems we've both been pretty happy in our marriages. But you have been on your own for much longer than I have. I'm a beginner, not sure how I shall cope. And I suspect you've got more to do than I have, which must make it easier."

Karin said "You will find it gets easier after a few years. But you must have an occupation, something to make sure you are never lonely."

"I agree."

There was a pause, as the waiter brought their first course. Intense conversation must always be suspended, while dishes are served. At last the waiter departed and Jack took a good drink of Steinbach before saying to Karin "What I really needed to know, the reason I wanted so much to come over here from England to find you again, was to . . . make sure I had not behaved badly to you; I allowed you to love me, as I believe you did, and then I walked away, as though our six months together had meant nothing to me."

Karin smiled sadly and shook her head. "I loved you, Jack, with a great passion. You remember the poems I wrote for you?"

"I have them still, at home. They are precious to me, just to me. Nobody else has ever seen them." There was no need to say that Christine had never known of their existence.

"It is strange," Karin said, "that this evening, sitting here with you, it's like it was; nothing seems so very different. Yes, I cried for you when you left but I knew I could not expect for us to marry. It was a romantic time and we were both young."

"I thought you might write to me," Jack said, "soon after I returned to England. But you didn't. In the end I wrote to you – a long, very deeply felt letter, but you never replied. Why was that?"

Karin looked down at her plate. "At that time, I was friends with a young Dutch boy at Medical School. We were students together and he wanted to go and study in America and take me with him. I did not want to open up an old wound by writing back to you."

"Why did you not go to America?"

"I did not love him enough to leave my home and my family and my country - at such a time. But I was very sad for a year or so after this."

"I didn't realise you studied medicine."

"For a time, yes. Then, on a holiday with my parents in Greece, I met Rudi. He was ten years older than me and his first marriage had been unhappy. We sailed together and I came to love him. When I married him, I was thirty-six already."

Jack's second vital, unanswered question now loomed up and demanded an answer. "So – there were no children?"

Karin shook her head again with a suspicion of a sigh but it was quickly covered by a little laugh. "That is another difference between us. You have your son. I have my hotels."

The Judge refilled Karin's glass and replaced the bottle in the ice-bucket. "I was sorry to hear about your brother, Dieter. I remember how you worried about him when he was a prisoner-of-war."

"He was released very soon after you left and went back to my parents' home at Coblenz."

"Your nephew Hans who gave me your telephone number said he'd not seen much of you over the years."

"It's true. We are almost strangers." Karin hesitated, seeming uncertain whether to reveal an intimate family secret to an outsider. But she continued "I can tell you, as an old friend."

"Please do."

"Dieter married a girl he had known during the war. Her father was an official of the NSDAP in Hanover. My father was very opposed to the Nazis, as you know. Many times were the Gestapo at our home when I was a small girl, asking questions. My father was a *Landrat* but he must always be very careful

252

ot to speak too much politics. I can remember my mother was
o afraid that they would one day take him."

"So your father was not happy about Dieter's marriage?"

"Not at all. Else, that is the wife of my brother, was a
voman of strong character. She influenced Dieter very much
nd they brought up Hans to believe that Hitler was betrayed
y his generals. Hans spoke little of politics because of his
raxis but he was . . . "

"What we now tend to call a neo-Nazi?" Jack asked.

Karin nodded. "*So*. It was sad for me, but I could not agree
vith Dieter and Else and when they left our house in Coblenz
nd went to live in Andernach, I lost touch with them. At
)ieter's funeral, Else would not speak with me. I was not
ivited to go back after the church service, so I returned very
ad to Freiburg, where I was a student, and – I never saw Else
r Hans any more."

"That explains it," said Jack, wondering where the late
aron Rudolph von Brander had stood vis-à-vis the Nazi
egime. 'Better give him the benefit of the doubt,' he thought.
He's dead now, anyway, and Karin was happy with him for
wenty-three years. He must have been OK.'

Jack and Karin went on to reminisce, and soon they were
aughing and sighing nostalgically about Ingrid and Julius
Heuss, Willy Pohl, Emmerich Karl, Peter Franks and the other
eople they had both known. They exchanged anecdotes about
heir concerts and opera performances and compared mem-
ries of incidents they had experienced and places they had
isited together, of which one would remember one detail, the
ther another.

At last they became aware that they were the only diners left
a the restaurant, and it was well after midnight.

Karin drove Jack back down the winding road to Baden-
aden, both in a thoroughly sentimental mood, mellowed by
he wine and as close to each other, Jack thought, as they had
een on *glühwein* in the old days.

"If you had been as charming as a young captain as you are now, I would have wasted away for love of you and never looked at another man again," Karin told Jack.

They laughed and Jack leant over her, as she drove, and kissed her cheek.

Back at the hotel they agreed to say their goodbyes, for Jack was to catch an early flight that morning from Stuttgart to Hanover to join his son, Giles.

Jack said "Strange to think that my son is a captain in the British Army in Germany, aged twenty-eight, almost exactly the age I was the night you and I and Ingrid and old Julius Heuss put on Act I of *The Valkyries*.

Karin took Jack's hand and they strolled a little way along the road outside the hotel away from the parked car, simply to be alone – like young lovers – and away from the inquisitive eyes of any of Karin's hotel employees who might be about.

"It is different now," Karin said, as they walked slowly along the road. "When you came to Godesberg straight from the war and the fighting, your people did everything they could to forgive us and feed us and help us to rebuild our broken lives and our ruined cities, and *you* did it through rebuilding our music. Like Germany itself, I was able to hold up my head a little with your help and your love to encourage me; and knowing you, *mein lieber* Jack, gave me the hope and strength to – how will I say it – to stand up against sadness and grief first when I would not go with Adrian to America and later when Rudi died and I was left alone."

Sir John felt a distinct lump in his throat at this declaration and at the same time a sense of relief that Karin felt no kind of resentment about his behaviour to her in the past or for the circumstances of their original parting, or indeed for the way her life had turned out – which, after all, had not gone badly for her as the *Baronin* von Brander, he reflected.

Karin broke into his thoughts. "We must go back now and

ust leave you," she said. 'At our last separation,' he thought,
he could not have borne to say those words, and it was I who
ad to say them, or something similar. This time it is indeed
fferent.'

Practical as ever, Karin turned Jack round so they could
alk slowly back to the hotel entrance, where she got into her
Aw and wound down the window to kiss him goodbye.

"Must it be the end between us, Jack, as it was in 1946, or
ill we meet again?"

"We will meet again, Karin my dear. After I've spent a week
ith Giles, when I get back to London, I shall write to you. We
·e both free people, able to visit each other, and there is still
ɔ much we have to say."

"That is what I was thinking, Jack," Karin said.

Jack watched her drive away into the darkness.

The next morning he found his bill had been paid by the
aronin, and instead of being embarrassed, he was pleased, for
gave him the excuse he needed to insist on returning the
ɔmpliment as soon as she was free to come to London or to
Ieet him in Paris or Rome or Venice. . .

His life was by no means over. And nor was hers.

OTHER FICTION FROM TABB HOUSE

KANDY KRAK *by* Howard Abbott

'The book focuses on a multinational corporation and its candy-making division in Europe. A first-rate management team discovers a soft spot in their operations and then swings into action – cutting costs, payrolls; beefing up sales, making their decisions with a swiftness that in many cases is designed as much to impress each other as to get the desired results. The hero is a new arrival to the team – a young Englishman who blows the whistle on them all when they decide to proceed with marketing candy that they know to be contaminated with salmonella. *Kandy Krak* is fun to read.'

Dorothy Crouch

Hardback £9.95

WHEELSTOCKS AND PLOUGHSHARES *by* Thomas Hudson

'Fortunately there are a few writers today who can capture the essence of country life as it used to be. Thomas Hudson has done just that, in this story of an apprentice wheelright in Oxfordshire in the years before the First World War. Hudson tells this story with humour and detail that could only come from complete familiarity with the life he descibes. The scent of freshly wood wafts from every page.'

The Countryman

Hardback £10.95

A YEAR AT POLVERRAS *by* Sylvia Ouston

Set in Cornwall in the 1920s, *A Year at Polverras* records the life of the village of Polverras and in particular the poignant story of the Treloweth family and their daughter Winnie, who after disgrace and exile, is eventually reconciled again to village life and her old sweetheart.

'Rarely have I come upon a book which in its small way, captivated me so totally . . . I found it to contain something of the directness and charm, together with the presentation of human drama and tragedy, and tremedous emotion, of a novel by Thomas Hardy . . .'

Susan Hill, *Good Housekeeping*

'Marvellously funny and original. Deserves the widest audience'.

Sunday Telegraph

Hardback £9.95. Paperback £3.95

OTHER FICTION FROM TABB HOUSE

THE DARTMOOR YANKEE *by* Malcolm Lynch

Sally, a resourceful Cornish girl making her living on Dartmoor, gives refuge to an escaped prisoner-of-war from Dartmoor Prison during the Napoleonic Wars, and by doing so she fuels an adventure that ends only when British, French and Americans are once more at peace together.

'The quality of the dialogue in this book is brilliant and it helps the story to move with pace and colour.'

Plymouth Sunday Independent

'Combines historical romance with gritty realism that will appeal to most tastes.' *Herald Express*

'This attractive novel is one of Malcolm Lynch's best. It is full of lively narrative and vivid characterisation.' *Contemporary Review*

Hardback £12.95. Sewn paperback £6.95